NELSON'S WAKE

NELSON'S WAKE

Under Admiralty Orders
The Oliver Quintrell Series – Book 6

M. C. MUIR

ISBN: 9798631825413

Horatio Nelson – *"...the hero who, in the moment of victory, fell covered with immortal glory. Let us now humbly trust he is raised to bliss ineffable, and to a glorious immortality."* Proclaimed by Sir Isaac Heard, Garter King at Arms, at the conclusion of funeral service.

Acknowledgements
With sincere thanks to H.M. Mills and Jacqui Smart

With recognition of the author's primary source: Fairburn's second edition of the funeral of Admiral Lord Nelson 1806. Other references used in the writing of this book appear at the end of the text.

Cover image
Scene of the Battle of Trafalgar – scanned from original (1807) by Louis-Philippe Crépin (1772-1851). Public domain work of art.

Chapter 1

Isle of Wight - 5 November 1805

The fire in the hearth spluttered and the candle flames flickered, bowing to an unseen draught coming from beneath the door. Meanwhile, the casement clock delivered its monotonous beat, *tick-tock, tick-tock*.

For the present, those were the only sounds Oliver Quintrell was conscious of, despite the wittering conversation between his wife and her sister that had been on-going since before breakfast. For the sea captain, the subjects they broached were totally inconsequential and, as he was seated near the window away from the women, he was relieved they made no effort to draw him into their discussions.

Having sailed into Spithead only four days earlier and been home for only two nights, his thoughts were still with his previous command – the 32-gun frigate, *Perpetual*. Having been at sea for the previous six months, as part of the British fleet serving in the West Indies, he was pleased to be back in Portsmouth. Pleased, also, to welcome the chill of an English autumn, though not happy to recollect the manner in which his time in the Caribbean had ended. *Perpetual*, having suffered severe damage from a late tropical storm, and needing considerable repair work, was ordered to return to Portsmouth rather than refitting in Port Royal.

After limping across the Atlantic under a jury rig, *Perpetual* had been towed through Portsmouth harbour's narrow entrance and moored alongside the jetty at the Royal Navy Dockyard. Even prior to an examination in the yard, he knew the frigate's future was in the balance.

Subsequently, the crew had been paid off, leaving Captain Quintrell without a commission. His future, like that of many other post captains, would depend on the outcome of the navy's current mission, recently departed from Spithead, under the command of Vice-Admiral Viscount Lord Nelson.

In command of HMS *Victory*, Horatio Nelson had departed Portsmouth a few weeks earlier to meet with other British fighting ships from the Channel and Mediterranean fleets. His mission was to confront and defeat the combined forces of the Spanish and French navies. This encounter had long been mooted and at last was to become a reality.

Captain Oliver Quintrell would have relished being part of Lord Nelson's fleet but, as frigates only played a supportive role when men-of-war stood in line to face the enemy, it would not have been possible, even with a sound ship.

For the naval captain, it was hard to swallow his frustrations yet not difficult to visualize the magnificent sight on Spithead when the fleet had made preparations to sail; the colours of the flags and the glittering gold lace decorating the officers' uniforms; the sound of canvas crackling as it fell; lines screaming through wooden blocks, and braces straining against the weight of the mighty yards. Then the gun salutes reverberating across the water signalling the ships' departure and watching them swim gracefully down the Solent to where the pyramids of sails rose higher as the fleet entered the Channel and headed west.

Oliver closed his eyes and fixed his thoughts on the sea off Cadiz, one thousand miles to the south, where the British fleet was heading to meet the enemy. He wished them God speed.

Suddenly, a smouldering log dropped from the fire and rolled from the hearth spitting sparks over the floor rug and reigniting the dying embers in the grate. The chatter stopped abruptly, the women watching in slight alarm, as fragments of burning ash shot out and floated across to the carpet.

But at the very same moment the fire distracted them from their conversation, another sound alerted Oliver's attention. Sitting bolt upright, he turned his head and listened.

'Did you hear that?' he demanded.

'Hear what?' his wife replied quite vehemently. 'It's the fire. It needs to be attended to.'

Oliver Quintrell did not answer but pushed himself up from the wingback chair and moved to the window. Drawing back one of the heavy velvet drapes, he peered through the glass but was met with a totally black canvas. In daylight his outlook, from the drawing room, afforded a view across the Solent and southward to the English Channel. That busy waterway never failed to hold his attention, whether it carried ships of the line, merchant ships of the East India Company, or local fishing vessels heading out to the rich fishing grounds in the Celtic Sea.

'What on earth is the matter?' Victoria Quintrell bickered, but before she had time to turn around to face him, her husband had reached the door. Pulling it wide open, he shouted down the empty corridor, 'Casson!'

The maid's head popped out from the kitchen half way down the house. She immediately scuttled along to the end door which led to the servant's quarters and repeated the call. 'Mr Casson,' she bellowed.

It reminded the captain of orders being relayed aboard ship.

'Was that really necessary?' Victoria Quintrell asked, complaining both about her husband raising his voice and for allowing all the warm air to escape from the room.

The captain was unperturbed.

From his room in the servants' quarters, Michael Casson appeared in his stockinged feet with a blanket wrapped around his shoulders and a nightcap on his head. Oliver met him halfway down the passage.

'A lantern, if you please, Casson. And put on your shoes and coat and join me. I intend to head outdoors.'

The man, who had served for several years as the captain's steward when aboard ship, had always been happy to take up a post at his residence on the Isle of Wight and work in the household until the captain was granted his next commission. He neither looked surprised at the request nor questioned it.

After collecting his glass from the study, Oliver reached for his boat cloak from the hall stand, swung it around his shoulders and waited by the kitchen door that opened onto the cottage garden. Beyond was an area of lawn that ran on a slight decline and ended with a low whitewashed dry-stone wall. From the house's elevated

7

position on the top of the hill, the land beyond dropped off quite steeply. The township of Bembridge and the Bembridge estuary snaked below. The vantage point by the wall afforded a clear view directly north across St Helens Road to Spithead and to the port towns of Portsmouth and Gosport.

Though not distinguishable in the darkness, Oliver was familiar with the location of every cove, cliff, rocky headland and beach on the opposite coast. He knew exactly where the entrance to Portsmouth Harbour was, even when fog or sea-fret veiled his view. With no moon, Spithead was as black as soot, broken only by a few pinpricks from ships' running lights. But neither that body of water nor the Royal Navy dockyard was visible. All that appeared in the distance was an ink-black line against an even darker sky. Overhead, the few visible northern stars offered limited illumination. For a moment, however, a light flashed. It was followed by an unmistakable sound coming from the direction of the town. Oliver blew out the lantern.

'There it is again,' he announced. 'Did you hear it?'

Casson cupped his hand to his ear and waited. A minute later the sound was repeated. Muffled and unremarkable, but distinctive to any sailor. Cannon fire.

'The timing's regular,' Casson noted. 'Firing practice, maybe?'

'Unlikely at this hour of the evening.'

'Or could be a salute.'

'I think not,' Oliver replied. 'No ships have entered harbour in the last four hours and I saw none preparing to depart. So why is the cannon being fired every minute? What message is it conveying?'

It was a rhetorical question, not demanding an answer. With no semaphore or signal flags to assist the enquiry, the pair screwed their eyes as they gazed into the distance. For a split second, another burst of light blinked from across the water. It was little greater than a large pinprick on a black backcloth but it was tinged with an orange hue. Oliver opened his glass and directed the scope to where he saw the distinctive flash. The pair waited.

Less than three seconds later, the dull thud from a distant gun again carried across Spithead.

'It's from the saluting battery,' Oliver announced, passing the glass to his steward.

Without the telescope, the captain scanned the horizon, which in daylight provided a view of the Hampshire coast from the Haslar Hospital to the centuries old battlements; to the Spur Renown; and to the beaches to the east beyond.

'What do you make of it, Captain?' Casson said, returning the glass. 'Could it be news of the fleet?'

'Indeed, it could be. I see no other reason for it and, hopefully, it's a harbinger of good news.'

The seaman looked enquiringly at the captain.

The pair remained in the same position for several minutes waiting for each flash of light, nodding in acknowledgement when it appeared then counting the seconds and waiting for the muffled thud to follow.

'What are your intentions, Capt'n?'

'We can do nothing at this hour. It is too dark. In the morning, however, I will visit the port.'

A half smile curled the corners of Casson's lips.

'Speak with Jenks. Tell him I will require the carriage at first light to convey us to Ryde. From there we will take a boat across the water. Kindly inform him that we will return to Ryde before dark tomorrow evening and for him to wait in the town and meet us there.' He paused. 'You will accompany me,' he instructed.

'Aye, Capt'n.'

'And I will require my undress uniform.'

Confident Casson would attend to all those matters, Oliver returned to the drawing room but only after removing his cloak and dew-soaked shoes and exchanging them for a quilted dressing robe and a pair of slippers.

'Forgive my unseemly behaviour, ladies,' he said. 'It was as I expected. The sound that alerted me was that of cannon fire from across Spithead.'

'Are we under attack, Oliver?' his wife asked, smirking cynically at her sister. 'What made this event so demanding?' she asked. 'I hear gun salutes almost daily when you are away at sea. They fire every time a fighting ship enters or leaves the port.'

Oliver paused for a moment then delivered his response. 'I sense the repetitive gun fire is announcing news. It is possible the fleet is returning and has been sighted in the Channel.'

'And what is so urgent if that is so, pray may I ask?'

Oliver inhaled quickly. 'Much rests on the news it brings. If the British fleet has been successful in defeating the combined forces of France and Spain, England will be safe from any further invasion from that tyrant across the water. If, on the other hand, the fleet has been defeated, the coast of England, from Penzance to the Humber, will be vulnerable to attack from Napoleon's forces. I think you do not understand the significance of the ramifications.'

'And if we win this battle,' Victoria Quintrell asked, 'will I be at liberty to order French lace again and not have to wait more than a year for its arrival?'

Oliver chose not to answer. How different were the thoughts and concerns which occupied him and his spouse. He considered how far apart their lives had drifted during his years in the service – a void that had become broader and deeper with each mission he had undertaken, some taking up to two years to complete.

'I intend to travel to Portsmouth tomorrow,' he advised. 'I will learn what has transpired when I speak with the port admiral.' He bowed his head to the company before turning to the door. 'You will have to pardon me ladies but presently I have several important matters to attend to.'

'And when can I expect you back?' his wife asked bluntly.

'Tomorrow evening,' he said. 'Hopefully, I shall be bearing good news.'

The early morning air carried the chill of winter though it was only early November. Both passengers in the carriage were wrapped in woollen boat cloaks fastened at the neck and each had a woven plaid resting across his knees. The drive over the twisting potholed road was slow, uncomfortable but uneventful. The captain spoke little on the journey; his thoughts were still pondering over the likely news the cannon fire was heralding. He knew he would learn more when he reached the Navy dockyard.

But even before stepping down from the carriage in Ryde, the sound of singing and excited voices in the town offered an answer to his questions. The message from Portsmouth, carried across Spithead, the Motherbank and St Helens Road was being broadcast by the crews of every launch, wherry and fishing boat that crossed the Solent to the Isle of Wight.

'It's victory! A great victory has been won!' The cry was echoed along the wharf by the sailors who crowded into the tavern doorways. The calls were repeated by the townsfolk, including women and children who had come out of their houses to join the celebrations. 'Victory! Britannia rules the waves!' It was a non-stop cry.

But there were also tears, not of joy, but real heartfelt tears spawned by the other news being passed around – that of the loss of a national hero.

'Lord Nelson is dead!'

That announcement struck like a bolt to the captain's heart, as a newssheet was thrust into this hand.

Oliver's mind went blank. 'Dear God,' he said, on a hushed breath. Horatio Nelson dead – the man many believed was invincible – the man sent to lead Britain to a great victory. *How could that be?* He must verify the news that was creating the hubbub.

With barely a breath of wind over the water, the captain was dependant on the boat's crew to row him the six miles over Spithead and come up on the Hard adjacent to the Royal Dockyard. Fortunately, the sea was calm.

Stepping into the launch, Oliver took a seat in the stern sheets and waited until the coxswain had pushed off before enquiring from the boatman as to how the news has arrived in the port while no war ships had entered Spithead.

'News came up from Falmouth by road,' he said. 'It was heading to the Admiralty in London. It seems that at every stop the coach made, the message was relayed. I heard that at Salisbury the driver changed his horses for the fifteenth time and, from the staging post there, the news was carried by courier to Southampton. It arrived in Portsmouth several hours ago and spread like wildfire when it reached the town.'

Oliver wanted more. 'Which of the fighting ships carried the news home? Was it *Victory*?' he asked.

'I can't tell you, Capt'n. I don't know. I've told you what I heard. All I can say is the folk in Portsmouth went crazy. I doubt anyone slept in his bed last night. They were dancing in the streets. The taverns never closed their doors, and every window was ablaze with light, due to the celebrating that went on.'

Though Britain's victory against the combined fleet of France and Spain was certainly worth celebrating and would be celebrated throughout the length and breadth of Britain, the loss of Vice-Admiral Horatio Nelson – a great naval hero – would be felt throughout the land even by those who knew little of him.

As the boat neared the Hard, the crew shipped their oars and allowed it to nose up onto the gravel. Before it came to a halt, two of the boat's crew stepped into the water and heaved it further up the beach.

Casson disembarked first and waited for Captain Quintrell, offering his arm. But the captain was quite capable of stepping out unassisted. Having settled the fare, he turned to his steward. 'Meet me outside the porter's office at the main gate at three o'clock.'

Casson heard the order and nodded, but was distracted by the shouts coming from a knot of sailors gathered on the pavement opposite. They were not the only group to be congregated outside the tavern door with tankards swaying in their hands.

Captain Quintrell recognised several faces of seamen who had sailed on *Perpetual*, members of the crew he had farewelled only four days earlier.

Standing out from the crowd was the West Indian sailor, born a slave, Ekundayo, who had sailed with him aboard both *Elusive* and *Perpetual*. Standing head and shoulder above the majority that only reached around five and a half feet tall, his shiny black pate glowed in the lantern light.

'Captain, I think you are being hailed,' Casson dared to say.

Oliver turned his head and politely acknowledged the group. In response, a few sailors raised their pots or knuckled their forelocks respectfully.

Aside from the sailors – boatmen, townsfolk, artisans and fishermen were loitering around the tavern's entrance, while children played on the short stretch of beach oblivious to the celebrations going on.

From his purse, Olive took two silver coins and handed them to Casson. 'Pass on my regards to the men and share an ale with them. I would like to celebrate Britain's great victory with them, or join their wake lamenting the loss of a great sea captain, whichever it may be, but I have business to conduct. The main gate at three o'clock,' he reminded. 'And engage a boatman to ferry us back to Ryde.'

'Aye, aye, Capt'n, leave it to me. And thank 'e, Captain,' he said, clinking the coins in his hand. 'I'll pass on your well-wishes to the men.'

With the cries echoing in his head, Oliver strode across the cobbles to the Dockyard's entrance. Though he had several matters on his mind, his first priority was to hear the true facts behind the stories being bandied about on the street, to discover details of the recent conflict and its outcome, and learn the fate that had befallen Lord Nelson. For the present, the information he had received was scanty and only second-hand hearsay.

The gatekeeper at the main entrance to Portsmouth's Naval Dockyard, acknowledged the captain who, though not a frequent visitor, was familiar to him. He touched his hat as Oliver Quintrell entered.

Passing under the broad archway, the captain was confronted with a scene similar to that he had just witnessed on the street. Several groups had congregated in the yard and were all deeply engaged in conversation. The striking difference to those lingering outside the taverns was their appearance. Here the knots comprised of officers or gentlemen, who, even at this hour of the morning, were neatly apparelled, many in naval uniform displaying gold braid and epaulettes on one or both shoulders, with swords hanging from their belts. Another striking difference was their posture and demeanour and the sombre tone emanating from their discourse. There were no boisterous outbursts or any loud drunken cheering. Here, some of the faces were drawn and pale and racked with worry, quite different to the expressions on the faces of the common seamen.

Striding through the yard parallel to the ropewalk, Oliver spied several officers who he had encountered during his years of service – plus captains, post captains and even an admiral or two. In some cases their meetings had been brief though the consequences of those encounters had been highly significant. John Gore, the captain who had burdened him with several chests of Spanish treasure – a burden that had left a sour taste in his throat but half a fortune in his pocket. And there were several others he recognised but, being unsure if they would remember him, he strode on.

Ahead, standing alone was a man who had intrigued him, Captain Boris Crabthorne, the man dubbed *Boris the Florist* by his men because of his keen interest in all things botanical, and for the array of flowering plants that always accompanied him on his voyages.

Oliver had thought of this officer on several occasions recently and was pleased to see he was still active and, for that matter, still alive. He was also relieved to see Captain Liversedge who appeared to be in good health. From the trauma he had suffered, the last time their paths crossed, Oliver was worried that his long-time friend would still be carrying the mental scars from that mission.

'Captain Quintrell,' the post captain called, immediately taking his leave from the group he had been talking with. 'It is good to see you, Oliver. I read in the Gazette that you were in the Caribbean and doubted I would find you here today. I trust you are well.'

'Thank you,' Oliver replied, accepting his hand and the warm greeting. 'And you?'

William Liversedge merely nodded. 'You have heard, no doubt, that the fleet won a great victory but at a dear cost.'

'I have heard little more that those brief facts. I was hoping to learn more. Has the fleet returned?

'I'm afraid it will be some time before it does.'

'How, then, did the news reach us here?'

'It came overland from Falmouth. The armed schooner *Pickle* was designated to convey the news to the Admiralty in London. After Nelson's death, Lord Collingwood took command of the fleet and ordered the captain of the schooner to proceed with all haste to England and deliver the news personally to Lord Marsden and the Lords Commissioners in London.

'Being a schooner and not a line of battle ship, while being present at the battle off Cape Trafalgar, *Pickle* had not come under fire and was able to make all speed to reach the English coast. On disembarking, the lieutenant hired a coach and four, and headed for London. On the journey, he shared his news at all the coaching stops; hence the news arrived in Portsmouth possibly before it reached Whitehall.'

'But what of Admiral Nelson and the flag ship?' Oliver begged. 'I heard some disturbing news.'

'His Lordship was hit by a bullet fired from the rigging of one of the French ships. He died shortly after he fell. The doctor was unable to save him.'

Oliver was at a loss for words. 'And what of HMS *Victory*?' he asked.

'Word is that *Victory* is still afloat, though sorely wounded. Lord Nelson's body is still aboard her.'

Oliver shook his head, as he tried to absorb the devastating news. 'And the rest of the fleet? If Britain vanquished the enemy, why has the fleet not yet returned?'

'The details are not yet to hand.' William Liversedge paused. 'Are you anchored at Spithead?'

'No. I am without a ship. I returned from the Americas only a few days ago and was hoping for a new commission. However, I presume with the loss of ships and men their Lordships will be fully occupied for some time.'

'And a state funeral is to be arranged,' William added. 'While you are here you must apply for a ticket to attend. Three thousand tickets will be available but on request only. Speak with the secretary to the port admiral. The list is filling rapidly and that is only here in Portsmouth. Imagine what the demand will be in London.' He paused for a breath. 'I presume you will be attending.'

Oliver confirmed his intention, thanked his friend for the information, but with little more information to be gleaned, bid him farewell. He was certain they would meet again in the coming weeks.

As he returned to the gate, Oliver encountered three naval lieutenants who were well known to him. Having seen all three stepped up from the rank of midshipmen to lieutenant, he held them in high regard.

'Captain!' Three voices rang out in unison.

'Gentlemen,' Oliver replied.

'Begging your pardon, sir, but is *Perpetual* due to sail again soon?'

'I fear not, Mr Hazzlewood.' His voice conveyed his disappointment. 'I am not yet aware what fate awaits her. That is for the Navy Board to determine.'

'She's a good ship, sir, and not ready for the breaker's yard,' Mr Tully said. Mr Nightingale agreed.

'Perhaps repair and refit,' Oliver said. 'Time will tell. However, if and when I receive my orders and a new commission, word of it will be posted around town. I would welcome you to sail with me if the Admiralty should allocate you.' He paused and considered the three men, so different in their ages, their backgrounds and their talents, but he did not doubt their courage and ability. 'In the meantime, perhaps one of you can assist me with a minor matter.' The three men nodded.

'You all remember Dr Whipple, I am sure. I wish to locate him. The last time we spoke was nine months ago when we disembarked here. His intention was to settle in Portsmouth and establish himself in private premises to pursue his calling in the medical profession. Failing that, he said he would offer his services to the Haslar Hospital. At the time he had no desire to apply for another warrant.'

'I can help you there, Captain,' Mr Tully said. 'You'll find Dr Whipple's rooms on High Street. He occupies a two storey house about half a mile on the town side of the George Hotel. There's a brass plaque on the door with his name on it. I've walked past it several times. As he's established his business there, I doubt he will be wanting to sail again.'

Oliver agreed.

'Thank you, gentlemen. Kindly excuse me. I have pressing business and my time is limited. Good day to you all.'

Chapter 2

Dr Whipple - 6 November 1805

With three hours remaining before the time he had nominated to meet Casson at the entrance to the dockyard, Oliver Quintrell determined he had sufficient time to address a delicate matter that was currently clouding his thoughts. It was imperative he dealt with it as early as possible and certainly before he took up his next commission.

Having only been made aware of the unusual situation since he arrived back from the West Indies, he had found it impossible to broach the matter with anyone, not least Victoria, his wife. It was a burden he was destined to carry in silence. The only person he felt he could talk to, and seek advice from, was Doctor Whipple.

Despite allowing ample time to walk across the town, he decided to go by cab in order to avoid the noisy rabble celebrating in the streets. It appeared the town's people had held their combined breaths since the day the fleet had sailed, and now, with news of a great victory, they had emerged from their homes and hovels to share that news. But many of the womenfolk had mixed emotions. To await the return of husbands, fathers and sons, with the possibility of prize money to boost their pockets or save them from the workhouse, was their greatest wish, but with no ships yet returned from the battle, their more fervent hopes were that their husbands had survived and would come home in one piece.

As yet, Captain Quintrell had no idea what to expect when he visited the address on High Street. He knew the location well. It was close to the place, outside the George Hotel where the coaches to London arrived and departed daily. He had used that service on more than one occasion. However, the doctor's residence, set somewhere close by, was new to him.

As the carriage rumbled along, several minor questions ran through his head, first and foremost – would the doctor be at home? Not having sailed with *Perpetual* on its last cruise, it was possible that Dr Whipple had taken up a warrant on another ship and was away at sea. It was even possible he had been aboard one of the line of fighting ships in the recent encounter off the coast of Spain. In so, he definitely would not be home. He also wondered if Doctor Whipple was living alone. Being a younger man than himself, it was possible he had taken a wife. Or, being practical, it was reasonable to imagine Dr Whipple could be attending a patient and would not be available to receive visitors. There were many unanswered questions on Oliver's mind. But it was imperative he speak with the doctor – and the sooner the better.

After fifteen minutes enduring an uncomfortable, cold and exceedingly draughty ride, the cab drew up outside the location indicated by Mr Tully. From the cab's window, Oliver could see the polished brass plaque on the wall bearing the name: *Jonathon Whipple*, and beneath it the word – *Physician*. The tarnished metal reflected a watery sun now at its lowest point in the sky. The shortest day of the year was not far away.

The driver leaned down, twisted his torso and stuck his head into the cab's window. 'This is it, Captain,' he called, not bothering to climb down from his seat.

Oliver reached through the window, opened the door and stepped down.

The house before him consisted of three floors with a loft. It was a relatively new Georgian style building with Gothic columns supporting a small portico at the front door with three marble steps leading up to it. An eminently suitable residence for a doctor to conduct his trade.

While making the short journey, he had pondered over the pressing matters he wanted to speak with the doctor about, these being the sole purpose of his visit. But how to broach one delicate subject, he had not yet resolved. He held Dr Whipple in high esteem and trusted his integrity. Besides being a skilled surgeon, he was a reputable gentleman who would hold any shared confidences and reveal them to no one.

Stepping away from the cab, the captain removed his boat cloak, folded it neatly and draped it over his arm before climbing the three stone steps and approaching the door. When he tugged on the bell-pull, he felt slightly inadequate having no calling card on his person. Taking one step back, he removed his bicorn hat and slotted it under his arm.

Within moments of the bell tinkling in the hallway, footsteps approached the door. It was opened by a robust matronly lady with an apron wrapped about her and a kindly expression on her face. Oliver was surprised. It was neither Mrs Pilkington, as he had half expected, nor Mrs Crosby.

'Pardon me, for arriving unannounced,' he said. 'I do not have an appointment, but if the doctor is at home, would you kindly inform him that Captain Quintrell begs to speak with him. I promise I will not take up much of his time.'

The woman bobbed slightly at the knees. 'If you would care to step inside, Captain, I will see if the doctor is free.'

After only a few moments, Oliver heard footsteps on the stairs before Jonathon Whipple stepped down and strode down the corridor, his hand extended in a greeting. 'Oliver!' he announced. 'What a pleasant surprise to see you.'

'Likewise, Jonathon.' The pair shook hands in a very cordial greeting. 'I apologise for this unannounced intrusion.'

'Do come in. I am delighted to see you. But first, I am sure you will want to warm yourself by the fire. I have ordered some refreshments for us. They will arrive shortly.'

Oliver acknowledged the welcome and after dispensing with his cloak and hat to the care of the housekeeper, he unbuckled his sword and deposited it against the hall stand beside several umbrellas. Following the doctor up the stairs, he was invited into a pleasant drawing room with a log fire burning brightly in the hearth. It was obvious that the room also served as a library. While the number of items on the shelves was limited, from a cursory glance it was evident that most of the leather bound volumes were of a medical nature including some prodigious tomes. An interesting display of glass bottles and specimen jars occupied a bank of shelves in one corner. The containers ranged in size from miniatures of only a few ounces in volume, to those large enough to hold a man's intestines or lungs. They reminded Oliver of the collection the doctor had held in *Perpetual*'s cockpit.

It was apparent that apart from the staff there was no one else at home, though the doctor made no mention of it. Having been invited to sit close to the fire, polite conversation ensued until the housekeeper re-appeared with a tray of refreshments, which she placed on a small table between the two men. Dr Whipple thanked her and, on leaving the room, she closed the door.

Oliver was about to speak but Dr Whipple interrupted him. 'Before you say anything, Oliver, let me first express my thanks to you for your very generous sponsorship of young Charles Goodridge. The funds you provided are above and beyond the boy's present requirements – namely tuition fees, books and some items of clothing – that were indeed necessary after coming ashore with virtually nothing.'

Oliver was taken aback. This was one matter that had not entered his mind. 'I prefer not to discuss this,' he said, attempting to hide a hint of slight irritation. 'I find myself somewhat embarrassed regarding this situation because, as you are aware, in the past I have spoken out vehemently against sponsorship in the service. Yet now find myself becoming a partner in this form of patronage.' He paused for a moment. 'How is the boy?'

'Very well, I am pleased to say. As you know, Charles has a sharp mind, is intelligent and enjoys learning. His tutors speak highly of the progress he has made in a very short period of time.'

'And is he still of a mind to go to sea?'

'That desire has not wavered. And I doubt it will, although,' he hesitated, 'with the number of questions he puts to me about medicine and my profession, I sometimes wonder. However, he often mentions your name and greatly enjoys recounting some of the experiences he had aboard *Perpetual*, especially if given the opportunity to do so when I am entertaining guests.'

'What age is he now?'

'Almost thirteen.'

'Interesting,' Oliver observed. 'Kindly pass on my regards.' Oliver considered his next statement for a few moments before delivering it. 'There is a post captain, I have known for some years, and encountered him after a lengthy absence only an hour ago. While I have not put the question to him, I feel, if asked, he may be prepared to enter Charles as a ship's boy or captain's servant on his next cruise. If that is so, and if Charles agrees, it will open the way to him entering the service as a midshipman at a later date. Any study he is currently doing will stand him in good stead.' Seeing no dissent in the doctor's expression, Oliver continued. 'If you have no objections, I will make an enquiry with Captain Crabthorne. In the meantime, I will continue to sponsor the lad's endeavours while ever he is here or at sea.'

'That will be put to good use,' the doctor said.

'However, if I am ordered to sea before any arrangements are made, I would have to call on you to attend to his personal requirements for a life aboard ship. And, of course, once he is at sea, he will be out of your hands and also split from Mrs Pilkington who, if I remember rightly, took him under her wing and was very attached to him.'

Jonathon Whipple smiled warmly, 'Indeed. Consuela – Mrs Pilkington, will miss him and worry about him as all mothers do when a son leaves home for the first time. Though she is not his mother, he is as close as any son would be. As you will remember, she lost two young infants of her own to the malignant fever in Gibraltar, at the same time Charles lost his parents.'

Oliver's heavy sigh did not go unobserved by the doctor. He continued. 'Might I take the liberty to enquire after Mrs Pilkington, and Mr Crosby and his wife who sailed with us when we departed the colony? Is the carpenter at sea or did he find work here in Portsmouth?'

'Mr Crosby was engaged as a wright at the Naval Yard and has no wish to ship out. He and his wife have taken rooms near the dockyard. Mrs Pilkington is no longer my housekeeper. As you will have noticed I have engaged another woman in that role. Connie – Consuela assists me with patients on a regular basis. She and Charles reside under this roof.'

Oliver was surprised. *Was there something more to the relationship between the doctor and the widow?* he wondered. An awkward lull in the conversation followed while Oliver cleared his thoughts. 'There is another item I wish to speak with you about, Jonathon. It is of a personal nature and a cause of great embarrassment to me. Of all the people I know, you are the only one I can approach for an honest opinion.'

The doctor leaned his head to one side. 'Captain, I may be a few years your junior and lack your worldly experience gained through travel to foreign parts, but as a member of the medical profession, having worked with the dregs of society in the London Borough Hospitals, having witnessed sights and sounds even a sea captain would find hard to tolerate, having had dealings with resurrectionists – body snatchers, and having personally suffered fever in the tropics, and treated hundreds of dying soldiers in Gibraltar during the time of the epidemic, I can assure you there is little I have not seen and, can honestly say, there is nothing that disturbs me. I invite you to share your problem with me. Whether I can be of help is yet to be determined. However, I can assure you it will go no further than these walls.'

The mention of Gibraltar provided Oliver with the opening he needed. It reminded him it was Dr Whipple who had attended his friend, Susanna, before her death and that the doctor had been aware of a relationship that existed between them.

'You treated a young Portuguese lady in Gibraltar on my behalf,' Oliver said.

'A tragedy,' Jonathon Whipple replied. 'I was sorry for your loss. I know you had a great affection for her and she for you.'

Oliver reached for his cup, swallowed the contents, and began. 'I find myself confronted by a situation I did not know existed until a few days ago. When I returned home from sea, there was a private letter awaiting me. Fortunately, it had been addressed to the care of the port admiral in Portsmouth.' He touched his hand to his waistcoat pocket. 'I wish to share the contents of that letter with you.'

The doctor leaned back in his chair as Oliver retrieved the envelope and placed on the table.

'Several years ago, during a brief visit to Cornwall, I was introduced to a young widow, Senora Vargas. She was accompanying the wife of a Portuguese diplomat who was paying a visit to the West Country. They were all from Funchal, in Madeira – the place where she lived. On meeting Susanna, we immediately found we were attracted to each other and very quickly a brief but intimate friendship developed.'

'Forgive me for asking an imprudent question, but were you not married at the time?'

'Indeed, I was and had been for several years. So I knew nothing could ever come of the relationship. After that, for months, perhaps years, we saw nothing of each other and never corresponded. Subsequently, however, whenever my ship touched those islands, I could not resist the desire to call on her. As you will realize, our meetings were very few and far between. The last time I saw her was when she visited me in Gibraltar during the epidemic. And it was there you treated her and she succumbed to the malignant fever.'

'Those terrible days and weeks are imprinted on my memory. I will never forget them.'

Oliver took a deep breath. Nor could he. 'When I returned home last week, this letter was waiting for me. It was from a solicitor in Lisbon, advising me that some years prior to her death, Susanna Vargas had borne a daughter and that the child was mine. He requested my instructions.'

The doctor's expression changed, first to one of surprise and then to grave concern. He leaned forward.

'Were you previously aware of this situation?'

Oliver shook his head. 'It was the first I had heard of it. It came as a total shock.'

'Why do you think she withheld this fact from you for so long?'

'Because she knew I had a wife.'

The doctor's brow furrowed. 'And until this recent revelation, you had no inclination of a situation that had existed for quite some time?'

Oliver shook his head again.

'No pressure or claim was put on you regarding your paternity?'

'Knowing Susanna, she would not have done that. Besides, she was in a comfortable financial position and would have been able to meet any expense without calling on my help.' He sighed again. 'In fact, I think the child would have filled a void in her life.'

The doctor's brow furrowed again. 'I find it hard to believe that there was no evidence of the child during, at least, one of your visits.'

Oliver paused. 'I saw nothing to indicate a child was present in the house and have cast my mind back, over and over again, as I tried to recollect the words we shared together. As you can imagine, the time I spent in the Portuguese port was fleeting and my time with Susanna was brief in the extreme.' He inhaled deeply. 'I admit I indulged myself in brief interludes of exquisite pleasure cut short by the demands of my office.' He sighed. 'Only once when I was holding her, I remember hearing an infant cry. I was always on the alert for the sound of a cannon shot coming from the harbour, telling me to return to the ship, so the infant's cry was unusual but I thought nothing more of it. Rather, I drew the conclusion that the child belonged to her maid, Isabella.'

'And how long ago was that?'

'It was October in 1803. A little over two years ago.'

'So the child is now perhaps three years of age?'

'That would be correct.'

'And where is the infant presently?'

Retrieving the letter from the envelope, Oliver offered it to the doctor. 'Since Susanna's death, she has been in the care of a family member in Lisbon – an ageing aunt. However, ill-health has meant that this relative can no longer continue her guardianship. I am advised the child is mine and that she was named Olivia –

appropriately. The solicitor asks that I take responsibility for her as I am her rightful father.'

'Do you believe this claim to be true?'

'I have no reason to doubt it, though I wish I could,' Oliver said.

'And what is stopping you from exercising that right? How can the paternity be proved?'

'I shall not contest the fact.'

'Has your wife raised an objection?' the doctor asked.

'I have not told her and could not.' Oliver sighed deeply. 'Regrettably, my wife and I are no longer close and extended periods of time spent at sea do not aid in reversing that situation. While Mrs Quintrell continues to enjoy the luxuries afforded by my position and the considerable amounts of prize money I have accrued over the years, there are much more than sea miles between us.'

'Perhaps you could persuade her,' the doctor quizzed.

'I know my wife and her views,' he said. 'She has been outspoken about Lord Nelson's relationship with Lady Hamilton and the ongoing hurt caused to Lady Nelson over the years. She expresses her feelings with bitterness and disgust bordering on rage. Sadly, I feel if my wife was called upon to accept the infant under our roof, she would reject it and the child would grow up in an atmosphere totally devoid of affection. That is not what Susanna would have wished.'

'Forgive my boldness, but have you considered ending the relationship.'

'With Victoria? No, I would not do that,' Oliver said. 'That is the dilemma that confronts me and the reason I am approaching you for your advice, direction and assistance. You are the only friend I can speak candidly to on this matter.'

The doctor leaned forward, rested his elbows on his knees and intertwined his fingers. He lowered his voice. 'I appreciate you sharing this news with me but, as you know, I am not a married man, nor am I well-practiced in relationships, therefore I am at a loss as to how I can help you.'

Oliver took a deep breath before continuing. 'The person I had in mind, but who I am in no position to approach about a solution to this problem, is Mrs Pilkington.'

The doctor's eyebrows rose.

'Do you think she would consider raising a child that is not her own. The reason I arrived at this proposition, is her acceptance and obvious devotion to the orphaned boy, Charles Goodridge who she cared for when his parents died.'

The doctor leaned back. 'Are you asking me if this good lady would take on the responsibility of another child?'

'I am. As the child's legal guardian, there would be ample funds for both her and the child, not only now, but in the years to come. I would make sure of that.'

'And what if Mrs Pilkington were to remarry?'

'The funding would continue until the girl came of an appropriate age – let us say twenty-five. And I would hope that any adoption that took place would be accepted by Mrs Pilkington's future husband.' He paused; his features expressed the weight bearing down on him. 'I beg your advice, Jonathon. I do not wish to see my daughter raised in an orphanage, either in England or Portugal, and, at my age, I do not wish to retire from the service to care for an infant.'

'Leave it with me, Oliver, I will speak with Consuela on your behalf but I think I know what her immediate response will be. She is a good-hearted woman.'

Oliver looked hard at Doctor Whipple. He had seen that look in his eyes before. Firstly, when Mrs Pilkington was carried aboard after being brutally attacked on the streets of Punta Arenas and, later, at sea off South America when she was sent aboard the 74-gun ship and he had to remain on the frigate. At the time, he had noted how the doctor's heart had ached when he was parted from her. It was obvious an affection existed between them.

'I realize this is a lot to ask, Jonathon. You have already accepted the boy, Charles and allowed him to reside under your roof. Now I am asking another enormous favour.'

A light knock on the door interrupted them.

27

'Come,' the doctor called.

'Beg pardon, sir. May I take the tray?' the housekeeper asked. 'Is there anything I can get you?'

'Thank you, no.'

The china cups rattled on the saucers as the housekeeper removed them.

'Let me interject,' Jonathon Whipple said. 'Sailing with you aboard *Perpetual* was one of the most notable experiences of my life. While my memories stretch back to my time serving the London Borough Hospitals and my days of study in Edinburgh, you alone allowed me to broaden my knowledge, and experience both adversity and adventure, be it for good or bad. For the present, I have all I wish for. Subsequently, having learned only this morning of the victory of our fleet at Cape Trafalgar, in the days and weeks to come, with the return of damaged ships and wounded men, I believe my services will be called on both here in Portsmouth and at the Haslar Hospital. For that reason, I do not see me leaving Portsmouth in the foreseeable future.'

Oliver was obliged to agree.

'Regarding your situation, I can assure you your confidence is safe with me and I thank you for holding me in high esteem. Leave it with me, Oliver. I will speak with Mrs Pilkington on your behalf and, though I cannot answer for her, I believe she will willingly consider your proposal.' Sliding the letter across the table and returning it to the captain, he added, 'However, it will be necessary for you to put this request to her personally. I will be happy to facilitate a meeting, to act as witness, or to engage Mrs Crosby to attend as a chaperone, if you think that would be appropriate. I can guarantee she will also hold your proposal in confidence. If you prefer, I can refer to the child as your *ward* and not your *daughter*.'

'Please speak honestly with Mrs Pilkington and explain the situation as it exists. And put the idea to her. I shall be here or in London for the coming weeks, at least until arrangements are made for Lord Nelson's funeral, or I receive new sailing orders, though I think the latter is unlikely.'

The doctor nodded. 'If the child is presently in Lisbon, how will she arrive here? Do you intend to collect her?'

'I cannot offer to do that. However, pending the outcome of your conversation with Mrs P, I will write to the lawyer and make all the necessary arrangements for her travel to England. The packet boats take only a few weeks to sail from Lisbon to Portsmouth. However, an exchange of correspondence with the Portuguese capital and her subsequent arrival may take months.'

'I gather you have not met your daughter,' Jonathon asked. 'Do you know what language she speaks?'

Although Oliver had given the matter considerable thought, this question was not something he had considered. He shook his head.

The doctor answered his own question. 'Having lived many years in Gibraltar, I think you will find both Mrs Pilkington and young Charles speak Spanish and some Portuguese, so the language should not be a problem.'

Oliver sighed once more. This time the relief was obvious on his face. 'I shall visit with you again in a few days' time to learn the outcome. I am in your debt, Jonathon. Thank you.'

Chapter 3

Bembridge – Tuesday, 4 Dec 1805

It was now almost a month since news of Britain's victory at Cape Trafalgar and Lord Nelson's death had arrived at Falmouth on the Cornish coast. From that port, only 30 miles from Land's End, word had been conveyed to London and on receiving the long awaited news, presses were quickly turning. Newssheets were printed and distributed to the counting houses, coffee shops and taverns, some carrying a full transcript of Lord Collingwood's message.

Since that time, however, very little additional information had filtered back to England. Rumours were rife that following the battle, a storm had struck the Spanish coast damaging ships of all three fleets and washing wreckage and bodies ashore. But this, as yet, was unconfirmed.

What was strange was that after this lengthy period of time, since the fleet of fighting ships had sailed from Spithead, not a single ship had returned. On the docksides and in the naval yards, even in the fishing villages along the coast, the initial elation had turned to concern. Cheers had been replaced with tears and in the towns up and down the Channel, wives and families were becoming impatient for the safe return of their menfolk. Their voices were being heard on the streets. Was the news of Nelson's victory fact, or a ploy to placate those left at home? And at what cost? Many other questions followed. How many ships had been lost? How many lives lost? How many men had survived? How many would return? And, more importantly, where were they now?

The only news, relayed from London, confirmed that there was to be a state funeral for Admiral Lord Nelson and all naval officers who wished to receive an invitation to attend the service must apply. After members of the royal household, ministers and members of parliament, high ranking naval and military officers, ministers of religion and masters of the various Guilds and other notables were accounted for; a limited number of tickets would also be available to members of the public. The news was formal and impersonal and did nothing to allay fears, nor answer any of the questions, nor reduce the rumours that were spreading.

Standing on the sandy beach close to where the muddy Bembridge River oozed into the Solent, Oliver Quintrell gazed across Spithead. Both the sky and water were dull grey with a dark distant smudge indicating the horizon and the port towns of Gosport and Portsmouth.

A breeze of chill wind, blowing off the Isle of Wight, ruffled the Solent. The water looked uninviting. Even the gulls balanced one-legged on the sand in preference to bobbing on the troubled surface. Although, in past times, the captain had swum regularly in the river's mouth – much to the chagrin of his wife – it now being mid-winter, he had no inclination even to remove his cloak. Having served for the past six months in the warmth of the Jamaica station further enforced his resolve. A brisk walk along the surrounding hills and the beach nearest to his home was currently his preferred alternative form of exercise.

During what seemed like a long interlude, though it only amounted to four days, Oliver had paid another visit to Dr Whipple. While his first meeting had been embarrassingly uncomfortable, his second filled him with much relief. While it was not ideal that his daughter would be raised under another man's roof, the doctor assured him the child would receive the love and attention Susanna would have showered on her from the young widow, Mrs Pilkington.

Subsequent to his meeting in the doctor's premises, Oliver had despatched a letter to the legal firm in Lisbon explaining the proposed arrangements. He had no idea how long it would take for a reply to be forthcoming. Prior to the conflict, the packet mail boats had taken only two weeks to sail to England and, as Portugal had remained neutral during the fighting, he hoped the mail deliveries would be unaffected. If he was ashore when a letter arrived, arrangements would be made for the child to travel to Portsmouth and be delivered into the care of Mrs Pilkington, care of Dr Whipple's house on High Street. Oliver hoped he would have the opportunity to meet his daughter before he took up his next commission. But if the mail was as slow as the returning war ships, it was likely he would sail before any arrangements could be completed.

On reaching the mouth of the small tidal estuary, the grey silt and muddy banks were replaced by firm yellow sand dotted with pebbles and seashells. Stopping for a moment, Oliver leaned down and, despite the cold and his previous convictions, removed his shoes and stockings and stretched his toes in the cold damp sand before picking up a pebble and tossing it into the sea. Looking beyond the line of foam curling from the small breaking wavelets, he turned his gaze down the Solent towards the English Channel.

For a moment, he screwed his eyes and blinked in an attempt to focus on what he saw. If only he had his telescope with him.

Several miles to the south, entering the Solent, was what appeared to be a hulk, not dissimilar in size and shape to some of the aged and damaged ships chained together in Portsmouth Harbour – the repositories for prisoners both French and Spanish, and for convicts sentenced to transportation over the seas. But this vessel was neither anchored nor was it under tow. With a huge bulbous hull it was proceeding under jury rig and swimming, albeit very slowly, towards Spithead.

It can only be—! Oliver thought. Turning on his heels and sprinting from the beach, he hurried up the inclined track to his house on the hilltop. Arriving at the kitchen door quite out of breath, he quickly rubbed the sand from his feet on the course winter grass, pulled on his stockings and shoes and entered the house through the back door, almost knocking the kitchen maid off her feet. After grabbing his glass from the study he returned to the kitchen garden.

'Dear God!' he sighed, after focusing on the ship in the distance. It was as he had thought – His Majesty's Ship, *Victory*, the 104-gun flag ship – Lord Nelson's command at Trafalgar. Oliver shook his head in disbelief. *Victory* had been the pride of the British fleet. But look at it now!

If this is the condition of the victor, God help the enemy, Oliver thought.

His immediate inclination was to rush to Portsmouth. If only he had a ship on the water in order that he could see *Victory* at close quarters as it drifted in. But he knew the fighting ship would anchor on Spithead for powder and shot to be taken off before entering the harbour. Then he smiled at this thought, doubting there would be an ounce of powder left in her magazine, or shot of any size remaining on the ship. The victory she had won at Trafalgar would have exhausted all of that. He wondered if she would stay at Spithead or be towed through to the dockyard when the tide permitted. If so, he would visit her there. If she remained anchored on the waters of the Solent, by morning, the port authority's barges would be in attendance with carpenters and shipwrights from the dockyard eager to make the necessary repairs to ensure she stayed afloat.

With word of *Victory*'s arrival, the waterfront would soon be abuzz with crowds. There were so many questions to be posed, and news about the battle would filter from the ship quicker than sand through the half-hour glass. Broad sheets would be printed and posted in shop windows, on lamp posts and on street corners, and special editions of the local newspaper sold on the streets. Undeterred, Oliver intended to join the throng in Portsmouth on the morrow.

Having discovered the captain standing by the wall in the cottage garden, Michael Casson walked down the grassy incline to join him, coughing into his hand to inform the captain of his presence.

'Take a look,' Oliver said, handing his steward the telescope without turning around. 'Tell me what you see.'

Michael Casson quickly found the ship, steadied his view and studied it. 'It's *Victory*, ain't it, Capt'n?'

'Indeed,' I believe it is,' Oliver said.

'Goodness! Look at the state of her,' Casson exclaimed. And, as *Victory* swam further up the Solent, he could see the extent of much of the damage. 'Almost everything shot away down to the weather deck. Bowsprit's gone. Head and stern rails gone. Gunports shattered and pock marks all along her beam.' He heaved a deep breath and adjusted his focus. 'Chain plates shot through and mizzen mast gone with only a stump remaining. The main mast looks like it's been shot through too. The main yard's gone, and the main tops'l yard's been shot away. The foremast is full of shot holes and it's lost its mainyard. Spritsail and spritsail topsail yards gone too.'

'Enough,' Oliver called, he'd seen it for himself and he didn't need to hear more.

'See her main – looks like she's sailing with French lace bent to the jury rig. What of her hull, I wonder? She's riding low in the water. I'm surprised she's made it home.'

Oliver nodded, accepted the glass and looked again confirming that everything Casson had said was true. As they watched, an undeniable gun salute was fired from the Portsmouth battlements where dozens of eyes, gazing through telescopes or squinting towards the returning warship, could hardly believe what they were seeing.

Bravely, the wounded ship replied with an explosive thunderous round from one of its massive 32-pound guns. At close range a shot from a 32- could penetrate two feet of solid oak.

Without taking his eyes from the shocking spectacle, Oliver Quintrell instructed his steward to again advise the stable to be ready to convey the pair of them to Ryde in the morning.

Wednesday, December 5th, 1805.
To the raucous cheers from the crowd of dockyard workers, three navy cutters, bearing the name of *Victory* on their transoms, moored at the King's Stairs at the Royal Dockyard. Apart from the twelve oarsmen, the first boat carried several officers and midshipmen, their uniforms showing various states of battle weariness, their faces reflecting the same, plus several injured sailors.

On the jetty, marines stood ready to control the crowd but, as the public was not permitted to enter the dockyard, numbers were kept to a minimum. However, they were unable to stop the interest shown by the rope makers, sail makers, coopers, block-makers and every other mechanic employed within the yard.

After the senior officers had disembarked the first boat, three stretchers were carefully lifted from the thwarts and handed to the workers waiting on the stairs. With the tide being low, the bottom five stone steps were covered in fresh green weed. The badly injured men, barely protected from the cold by holed blankets, closed their eyes to the noise and confusion. There were more sick and wounded in the second boat – some plastered and bandaged, four supported by crutches but all with expressions that they were thankful to be back on English soil. They all needed help to mount the slippery staircase to the naval yard. Sitting in the third boat was a group of mechanics from the first rate. They were not identified by any uniform, though some carried the tools of their trade.

One of those men was a young shipwright. His grubby hands were empty and his face bore a wearied expression, but Captain Quintrell recognised him immediately.

'Will. William Ethridge,' he called, as the wright climbed up the Kings Stairs. The young man turned and scanned the crowd of onlookers to see who had hailed him. His face lit up when he recognised the captain.

'Can you spare a few moments?' Oliver called from the jetty.

'Captain Quintrell, it would be my pleasure.' Pushing his hair behind his ears, Will Etheridge climbed carefully, while assisting an injured seaman up and into the arms of a waiting porter. Then he headed to where the captain was waiting.

'I was surprised to see you come ashore from *Victory*,' Oliver said. 'How is that so?'

The lad grinned, 'I sailed back from Gibraltar with her after helping fix her up after the battle. You'd not believe the sorry state she was in when she was towed into Gibraltar Bay. Believe me, sir, she's in a far better state now.'

Oliver found that hard to believe. 'Walk with me for a moment. Let us find a less congested area to talk. There is much I need to hear.'

The pair walked across the yard, leaving the gathering crowds behind them.

'And what of Lord Nelson?' Oliver asked, as he slowed his pace.

'His body is still aboard,' Will said, lowering his eyes and his voice and glancing over his shoulder.

'Are you leaving the ship here, Will?' Oliver asked.

'No, Captain, I've come ashore to deliver an order from the master shipwright for urgent materials needed on board. There is so much work still to be done.' He sighed. 'Because both the government and private stores in Gibraltar had been stripped clean there were insufficient supplies even to start some of the repair jobs. At the moment, *Victory* is barely seaworthy. Everyone was surprised we didn't lose her on the Bay of Biscay.'

'But you made it successfully.'

'Only with the help of *Belleisle*. The 74-gunner towed us part of the way home, though that ship had suffered a worse mischief than *Victory*. She lost all three masts and her anchors too.'

'Where is *Belleisle* now?' Oliver asked.

She parted company with us off Plymouth. Her captain decided she could not make it any further and took her into the naval yard to undergo the work there.'

Oliver shook his head. 'How long before *Victory* is fit to sail again?'

The young shipwright was unsure. '*Victory* will likely be at Spithead for five days or more. If we can manage to keep her afloat, her yards can be hoisted and new canvas bent on, then she will head up the Channel to Chatham for major repairs. That's where she was built, I heard.'

'What are your intentions, Will?' the Captain asked. 'Do you plan to stay in Portsmouth and work here in the yard?'

'No, sir, I intend to sail with *Victory*,' he said. 'I hope to get work in the Chatham Yard. I think they will need all the help they can get for many months to come.'

'Let us find a quiet corner to sit,' Oliver said. 'I doubt the local taverns are an option. 'I would like to hear more, if you have the time.'

The lad nodded cautiously, conscious of the errand he was on. But he welcomed the chance to speak with his previous captain, yet finding a suitable place to converse was not easy. The dockyard was milling with people from admirals in full dress uniforms to grubby salts pushing barrows of gravel or loading timber. Flat topped wagons loaded with rope, barrels of nails and tar trundled noisily across the cobbles. Crowds were flocking to the jetty around the Kings Stairs. Voices were growing louder by the minute. Inquisitive yard workers were eager for more news of HMS *Victory* since her arrival at Spithead. Across the courtyard, a regimental band was playing the national anthem, *Britannia Rules the Waves*. Cries of '*Immortal Nelson,*' were heard.

Oliver indicated to an old 32-pound barrel that had lost its cascabel – no doubt blown clean off in a recent fight. The pair sat down on it.

'First,' Oliver began, 'tell me about yourself, Will. It's over six months since you left *Perpetual.*'

'Aye, Captain. I wanted to see my mother in Hampshire. But she no longer lives at Buckler's Hard. So I took work in the dockyard here. But after only a few weeks, an urgent call went out for carpenters and wrights to work in Gibraltar, so I volunteered to go back. As you know, I'd worked on the Rock before the epidemic. That was the time me and Mr Crosby and several other wrights sailed with you aboard *Perpetual*. When we left the colony, only a couple of skilled artisans remained there to attend to the Mediterranean Fleet.'

'You were not concerned about the malignant fever, when you decide to return?'

Will shrugged his shoulders. 'What was there to be afraid of?' he asked. 'The epidemic had been declared over, and besides, I had suffered from the fever and was told by both Dr Whipple and the government surgeon that I would not catch it again. Apart from that, I always liked the town and the people who made up the population. A real mixed bag. I was happy at the chance to go back and rekindle old friendships with some of the acquaintances I'd known there. Of course, at that time, no one could foresee the major battle that was going to blow the greatest ships of the British fleet apart.' He paused for a second.

Although that opinion was not entirely correct and a confrontation had been mooted for a long time, Oliver did not interrupt, allowing the lad to continue at his own pace.

'A week before the action took place, word reached the carpenter's shop that the fleets were massing off Cadiz and a battle was looming. We were warned to make ready to repair damaged ships, the same as we had done for the Mediterranean Fleet. We were also warned that the damage could be more than usual, but nothing on the lines of what we were confronted with.'

'Pray continue.'

''Twas on the morning of October 22nd, the semaphore tower on the Rock announced that the British fleet had won a victory over the combined French and Spanish navies.

'We watched the arms on the signal tower flailing about as it dipped and rose continually. Of course we didn't know what it was saying but the message was soon translated and the news of a great victory was quickly passed around. Everyone in the town was jubilant. You should have heard the cheers that rang out along Gibraltar's waterfront and the sound of the bells ringing from all the colony's churches. There was dancing on the streets and on the mole, and free ale was served in the taverns. There was no better feeling.'

Oliver's thoughts jumped back to the time, more than a year earlier, when anchored in Gibraltar Bay, he too had watched the semaphore arms dancing and spinning and contemplated what crucial information those wooden slats were conveying.

While Will Ethridge's expression was filled with enthusiasm, Oliver Quintrell remained unmoved. Once again, he allowed the boy to continue.

'After that, we expected the ships to arrive in harbour later that day or, at least, on the following morning. Everyone waited. There was great excitement. They built bonfires on the mole and some kept vigils throughout the night. But no ships arrived and no one in Gibraltar could understand why.'

'Was the fleet perhaps gathering off Cadiz to sail home?' Oliver suggested.

'Not so. We later learned it was due to a mighty storm that blew up the day after the battle. They said it was the type of storm that only blows once in every 50 years. The story goes that Admiral Nelson, knowing that a storm was imminent, ordered all ships, including the captured prizes, to drop anchor off Trafalgar, but when he fell, Admiral Collingwood ignored or didn't fulfil that order.'

'Be careful, young man,' Oliver warned. 'Those are libellous words.'

'I am only relating what I heard, Captain.' He paused a moment, then continued. 'They said it was because of that changed order that many fighting ships failed to drop anchor before the storm arrived and drifted onto the rocks. Eight of the French and Spanish prizes ran aground or sank after the conflict.' He sighed. 'That was felt as a huge loss by almost every sailor aboard the British fleet who had risked his life for prize money – money he felt entitled to, but now would never receive a penny of.'

'*Hmm.*' *The ill fortunes of war*, Oliver thought.

'The tragedy got worse,' William said. 'One of the Spanish war ships had picked up the survivors from another victim of the battle but it went down in the storm with one thousand men on board.'

Oliver had no response to that.

'When did the fleet come in?' he asked quietly.

'As you know, Captain, it's only forty miles from Cape Trafalgar to the Gates of Hercules then into Gibraltar Bay. Everyone waited anxiously for the victors to arrive, to sail into the harbour and drop anchor and for the real celebrations to begin. But after two days of waiting and wondering still nothing appeared – not a single vessel of any description.' He shook his head. 'We expected at least a few ships to have suffered some damage in the battle and be in need of repair. It was thought unlikely the fleet had won a glorious victory and headed home not having received a single scratch.'

Oliver watched a troubled expression cloud Will's face. 'At that time, we weren't aware of the storm that had struck the Spanish Coast. We only got news of it when the first few ships were towed in.'

'When did they arrive?' Oliver enquired.

'It was a full five days after the battle, the first ships limped into the Bay.' He shook his head again. 'The damage was shocking. And with their catheads blown away many ships were unable to drop anchor when they arrived. Masts, yards and rigging had been shot to shreds. As a result, several ships were towed in on the end of a cable. Once in the Bay, those that had lost their anchors were tied to another's hull to prevent them from drifting onto the rocks, or to the mole or across to Algeciras.'

Oliver heaved a deep sigh. 'Unimaginable. But what of Lord Nelson's, *Victory*? Was she the first to come in?'

'No, *Belleisle* had come in before her. She was first to enter Gibraltar Bay. We stood on the mole and watched her arrive. She was a shattered wreck – completely dismasted and her anchors gone. It was hard to image how she had made it back. The next day – six days after the victory was announced, other ships came in. Within a few days, we had six dismasted ships tied up against the mole, plus the few remaining prizes. Gibraltar Bay looked like a breaker's yard.

'And the flag ship? What of her?'

'*Victory* was little better than the others. She was unable to sail and was towed in by *Neptune* an 80-gun ship. What a sorry state she was in.'

'My goodness.'

'And what of the Spanish ships from Algeciras, across the water?' Oliver asked.

'Word was they'd returned to Cadiz along with some of the French ships. It was far closer to Cape Trafalgar, and Cadiz has an excellent naval dockyard, as I am sure you know.'

'But what of the men? So many killed and wounded.'

The lad looked grave. 'The news was terrible and just got worse. I heard it said that more men died from drowning than from the battle itself. I don't know how many were brought to Gibraltar. Sadly, the settlement did not have enough medical help to provide for their needs. The epidemic had deprived the town not only of medicines but of surgeons to treat the wounded. Most of the injured had to remain on the ships they'd served on, but with the hammocks shot to ribbons in the netting, there was nowhere for them to rest but on the decks. The bodies of those who died on the ships were thrown into the Bay. The few who died in Gibraltar were buried in the local cemetery.'

Mention of the awful place rekindled memories Oliver would have preferred to forget.

'There was one good luck story,' Will Ethridge related with renewed verve. 'It came from the cockpit of one of the ships. Seems a sailor aboard *Belleisle* had been struck in the head by a bullet and was thought to be dead. He was almost tossed overboard with the others who'd died, when one of his mates noted he was still breathing. Though, for several days, he showed no signs of life, he made a sudden recovery when the bullet emerged from his mouth.'

'Lucky fellow,' Oliver said, forcing a weak smile, though there was little to smile about in the story. He quickly changed the subject. 'So how is it you sailed with the flag ship when she returned to England?'

Will Ethridge's expression changed again, his face filling with pride. Looking around, he explained: 'At the start, when Gibraltar Bay began filling with damaged ships, most of the dockyard workers were spread around the fleet. Then one morning, several chippies and shipwrights were ordered to gather their tools and report to HMS *Victory*. I was one of those to be ordered to go aboard. The priority was to patch her up to make sure she didn't sink in Gibraltar Bay then to make the necessary repairs so the ship, carrying the Admiral's body, was able to sail to England. It was thought imperative to allow the country to share in the triumph. It was only then I learned that the Admiral's body was still aboard. I'd noticed a huge water barrel – a leaguer, sitting on the quarterdeck. I was told Lord Nelson's body was inside it.'

'You saw the barrel on board?'

'Aye, Captain. 'It was sitting proud on the deck draped in Victory's flag, you couldn't miss it.' As the tears welled in the young man's eyes, Oliver looked away.

'Indeed, it was a great victory but hardly a triumph with the Admiral dead.' Oliver shook his head. 'When news arrived in England, it was celebrated as glorious, marking the end to the sea war against Napoleon. But at such a terrible cost.' He paused and looked towards Spithead and the damaged 104-gun warship that had been the pride of the British navy. It was currently surrounded by a flotilla of smaller craft.

'Tell me, Will, having been aboard her, how do you rate the ship's condition now?'

Will Ethridge's eyes were wide as he described the first rate ship of the line. 'Even with the loss of much of her top hamper, she truly is a huge ship,' he said. 'Bigger that any of the sheer hulks used as prison ships in Portsmouth harbour that I have seen. Though the destruction was not as devastating as in some of the other vessels, her condition was pitiful. Fifty shot holes were counted betwixt wind and water. It was only the thickness of Victory's oaken hull that saved her from filling and being lost.

'But it wasn't until I went below that I saw the full extent of her injuries. Beams, knees and riders had been shot through. But, as I said, the Gibraltar dockyard did not have the timbers suitable for the shipwrights to replace those members. The starboard cathead had been completely shot away and the best bower anchor gone with it. Below deck, the bulkheads had either been shot through or tossed overboard when the ship was cleared for action. The stern windows of the great cabin had been raked which put paid to all the frames and glass, and the fine furnishing from the great cabin were smashed to matchwood. The same applied to the officers' quarters on the deck below – they were unrecognisable.

When the mizzen mast fell, it created its own damage crushing part of the deck and rails, and bringing down its rigging with it.'

Oliver listened intently.

'She had swallowed a lot of water and, though the pumps had been manned since the time of the battle, there were men still working on them both day and night when we went aboard. The pumping never stopped when we departed Gibraltar and I think it will go on until we are in the Chatham yard.'

'What repairs were you engaged on?' Oliver asked politely.

'Our first job was to patch the leaks in the hull. We worked in the hold for most of the time – almost a full week, standing knee-deep in water. We even worked through the night by the light of lanterns. We caught a little sleep on the deck when we could. Then, when it was decided that sufficient had been done to make her seaworthy enough to sail home, the call went out for volunteers to sail with her back to England and continue the repair work on the voyage. I volunteered and was proud to be one of those chosen. So, here I am.'

'Tell me about Lord Nelson, Will. What did you hear of the Admiral after he fell?' the captain asked. 'Was his death spoken of when you were aboard?'

'The talk was non-stop,' the carpenter replied. 'Although it was spoken in whispers, when it passed around the mess. I was told that, while at sea off Trafalgar, immediately after the battle, the Admiral's body was placed in the leaguer. Dr Beatty, *Victory*'s surgeon, attended to his Lordship and he ordered it to be filled with brandy. But before Nelson's body was placed in it, his hair was cut off and his clothing removed. I am told he was dressed in only his shirt when he was submerged and the barrel sealed.'

Oliver's brow furrowed.

'Some time later the brandy was drawn off and replaced with spirits of wine – pure alcohol – that was to preserve the body for the homeward voyage. I also heard that one of the marines, who was posted to stand guard through the night, was scared half out of his wits, when the top of the leaguer popped off.'

The captain frowned.

'The doctor said it was due to the gasses escaping the body as it decomposed.'

'Continue,' Oliver said, choosing to ignore the previous description.

Before we sailed, an argument on Victory spilled over onto the mole about which ship should carry Lord Nelson's body home. After the battle, Lord Collingwood had transferred his flag to the frigate, *Euryalus* and, as that ship was in sound condition, he ordered that Nelson's remains should be carried home aboard the frigate and not on HMS *Victory* because of its sorry state.'

'Perhaps a wise decision, if *Victory* was in danger of sinking.'

'Not for the sailors who served Lord Nelson. There was an immediate outcry. It was led by *Victory*'s boatswain who argued that if their captain could not sail home with them: "They would go to the bottom with their sacred charge." Those were the very words.'

'Obviously Lord Collingwood conceded,' Oliver noted, 'and Lord Nelson's body remained aboard *Victory*.'

'I think his lordship had little alternative.'

For a moment, the pair watched, as a group of women was allowed to enter the yard. They were met by two midshipmen who conducted them to the area on the dock, close to the King's Steps, where some of the injured men were sitting. Their bandages indicated cracked skulls, broken arms and legs, and blinded eyes. The women's wails and cries were a mixture of pain and joy on being reunited with their menfolk.

'What was the scene when you departed Gibraltar to sail home?'

Will Ethridge thought for a moment. 'There were crowds gathered around the bay, along the mole, on the beaches and around the battlements. But despite the peal of church bells and shots being fired from the fort and the decks of the other damaged ships, the tone was sombre. There was no cheering. Every hat had been removed and most people stood in silence. Everyone was still shocked about what they had seen.

'Once out of the Bay, our progress along the Strait was exceedingly slow as we headed towards Tarifa. Off Cape Trafalgar, just a few miles short of Cadiz, I saw things I found hard to believe.'

Oliver listened intently.

'Although two weeks has passed since the battle, wreckage was still piled up along the sandy beaches. And much tangled flotsam was still floating on the water – spars, masts, canvas, lockers – and bloated bodies, both inshore and far out to sea. Some of the dead had suffered dreadful injuries with loss of arms and legs, and worse. Some of the bodies had been ripped to shreds by the circling sharks. One poor soul had lost his head. It must have been blown clean off, but he was still wearing the full dress uniform of a French officer, yet there was not another mark on him. I heard the same fate befell Captain George Duff, of the *Mars*. His head was severed by a cannon ball. He was buried at sea with twenty-eight of his men who died with him on the same day.'

The revelations were astounding.

Will paused again in his recounting.

'A time many will never forget,' Oliver Quintrell said.

'Never.'

'Are you able to continue?'

The shipwright nodded. 'So, we sailed west and then north along the coast of Portugal to the Bay of Biscay. But despite a breeze of wind, we were unable to make any progress and *Victory* was put under tow for several days. *Belleisle*, though she was also in a poor state, was able to raise some canvas and proceed slowly, hauling *Victory* in her wake.

'With *Bellerophon* and *Belleisle* for company, *Victory* proceeded under part sail and part tow to the Channel. The two seventy-fours parted company with her near Plymouth as both ships were taking water and also in grave danger of sinking.

'The voyage from Gibraltar took two weeks and never was the crew happier than when we sighted the Needles and entered the Solent, and to hear the guns firing from the Portsmouth ramparts.'

'Indeed.'

'As we neared the port, the welcome was unbelievable. The cheers, of course, for Britain's glorious victory against France and Spain, but also the tears, both for the Admiral, and for the hundreds of sailors and officers who had not come back.'

'And never would,' Oliver added. Having witnessed the spectacle from his house on the island, Oliver nodded. 'And what will happen to *Victory* now?' he asked. 'Will she remain in Portsmouth to undergo the repairs she needs?'

Will Ethridge shook his head. 'The artisans have all been ordered to continue their work while she remains at Spithead – those include the chippies, shipwrights, riggers, coopers and sail makers – until the ship is deemed in a fit condition to sail to the Medway and the Chatham yard. That is where she will undergo major repairs.'

'Is it your intention to sail with her?' Oliver asked.

'Indeed, it is,' the young shipwright replied adamantly.

'And what will happen to Lord Nelson's remains once you arrive in the Medway? It has been announced, from London, that urgent preparations are afoot to honour the Viscount with a state funeral. It being over four weeks since Lord Nelson fell; I imagine time is of the essence.'

'I know nothing of that,' the young man said. 'All I can tell you is what I heard, that the body will remain aboard *Victory* until we make the Nore.'

'And once there?'

'An Admiralty barge will meet the ship and take the barrel up river to Greenwich. Before that, Lord Nelson's body will be transferred to a real coffin. When it arrives at Greenwich, it will remain lying in state for three days for the public to pay their respects.'

'A traditional wake.' Oliver said.

Will Ethridge nodded. 'I don't know what will happen from there,' he said.

'Thank you, William,' Oliver Quintrell said. 'I appreciate the knowledge you have shared with me. Now you must attend to your duty, I have delayed you too long.' The captain replaced his hat.

'From my home on the Isle of Wight, I shall be watching the progress made while you are here, then when *Victory* departs Portsmouth, I intend to travel up to London by coach and pay my respects while the Admiral's body is lying in state. I believe that the opportunity to mourn will attract quite a crowd. Good luck to you, young man. I would be pleased to receive you aboard my next command, should you choose to apply for a warrant.'

'Thank you, Captain. Do you know what ship that will be?'

'Not as yet. Until the fleet returns home, no commissions are being granted.'

With that, Will Ethridge nodded, touched his blonde locks, turned and hurried across the cobbled courtyard to the Royal Dockyard's workshops.

Watching him depart, Oliver could not help but think back to the weeks and months he had spent, at the Greenwich Hospital, recovering from an injury that had deprived him of most of the fingers of his right hand. But one thing he remembered was the way the patients celebrated the death of one of their own kind – particularly the Irish sailors.

A three day wake was necessary as an appropriate sign of respect. Three days was the time deemed sufficient to ensure the deceased was truly dead and not merely sleeping.

Chapter 4

HMS *Victory* at Spithead
December 10th, 1805

From the convenient observation post in his garden on the Isle of Wight, Oliver Quintrell checked frequently. He watched, as *Victory*'s masts were being stepped and the standing and running rigging attended to. Frayed lines were spliced and new ones rigged. Blocks were replaced, and new canvas bent to the yards that had withstood the battle. But the captain was particularly looking for any indication the ship was preparing to sail from Spithead.

He had already forewarned his wife that he intended to travel to London for the state funeral. He had also written to his sister advising her of this and requesting he stay with her, for several nights, at her house on Grosvenor Square.

Victoria was anxious to know if invitations to the funeral service at St Pauls included wives, but as seating in the cathedral would be very limited, Oliver greatly doubted it. In turn, he questioned whether she would have been prepared to make the long and uncomfortable coach journey to London and to contend with the huge crowds that were expected to attend.

The newssheets and local papers reporting the event had already attracted folk from around the country, not only from naval towns but from Ireland and across the Scottish border. For over a week, seats on the daily coach service, departing from outside the George Hotel on Portsmouth's High Street, had been completely booked, including the open space on the coach's roof that offered no shelter from either wind or rain. Because of this, Oliver arranged to hire a post chaise for the journey.

Every day, while *Victory* swung from her anchor, dozens of small craft visited the triple decker, circling its hull and appearing to bob respectful curtsies on the chop, much to the annoyance of the tradesmen working on the decks. Tempers flared as the coxswains of the flag ship's own boats, and local barges had difficulty getting close to the hull to make deliveries of much needed materials – timber, nails, pitch, paint, tar, turpentine, even oakum; plus sufficient victuals to supply the vessel and crew for the passage along the Channel to the Medway.

Undeterred, pilgrimages of endless visitors continued from first light until dusk, the boatmen making a tidy penny ferrying passengers out from the beaches and the Hard. Men, women and children were all anxious to get a close look at the much respected, battle-scarred warship. With eyes and mouths opened in awe, they gazed up at the gigantean 104-gun ship, though from water-level, dwarfed beneath its bulbous hull, they were likely to see less than from the shore. In particular, the leaguer containing Lord Nelson's body, draped in *Victory*'s colours and placed aft on the quarterdeck, was best seen through a telescope from the port's battlements. But for the hundreds who made the short return trip and were able to claim they had seen first-hand evidence of the now famous sea battle, they had a tale to tell when they returned home.

As the crowds and the number of pleasure boats increased over the days, *Victory*'s cutter was launched and a dozen marines balanced themselves between the thwarts, with their muskets levelled at anyone approaching to within pistol shot. The sight of a pair of swivel guns fixed on the port and starboard gunwales and angled down towards the water, was sufficient to ward off many of the over ambitious.

During the following days, work progressed, not only on *Victory* but on several other fighting ships anchored in Spithead and on others that had made it recently into the Royal Navy Dockyard. With nothing new to observe, Oliver accepted an invitation to take morning tea at the house of Dr Whipple.

Returning to the residence on High Street, Oliver was again welcomed by Jonathon Whipple. Mr Crosby, the carpenter was unable to be present and had sent his apologies. Like all the mechanics in the dockyard, his work was continuing unabated despite some outcry from the public that this entailed working on the Sabbath.

Talk of ships and injured sailors dominated the early conversation. However, after only half an hour, despite it being Sunday, the doctor was obliged to excuse himself to attend to a patient.

Only when Dr Whipple left did Oliver have the opportunity to speak directly with the young woman who had said she was prepared to raise his daughter. Mrs Consuela Pilkington was initially embarrassed to speak directly with the captain about the arrangements, but with the more matronly carpenter's wife alongside her for support, she quickly relaxed and quietly expressed her thanks and joy that the captain had put faith in her to take on the care of his ward.

Had the Doctor not revealed to her that the child was, in fact, his daughter, and not his ward, he wondered.

'Miss Olivia will be a sister for Charles,' Connie Pilkington said.

That was something Oliver had not considered but the idea pleased him.

'And where is young Charles at this moment?' he asked.

'Dr Whipple enrolled him at the Naval Academy. During the week he remains there as a boarder. I miss him, but believe it is for the best.'

'Indeed,' Oliver said, but his tone was not convincing.

Perhaps Dr Whipple's choice of education for a future naval officer was better than a private tutor or local school. Yet the lad was only twelve years of age. If he entered the service now, he would enter as a young gentleman or Captain's servant – third class. If however, he completed two years at the Naval Academy, studying geometry, trigonometry, geography, etcetera, he could be accepted into the service as a midshipman. This would give him an advantage over other boys of the same age.

Oliver tried to convince himself that this was the best course to follow, but, since returning to Portsmouth, Oliver had heard conflicting reports about the situation at the Academy including the fact it was facing imminent closure. With a lack of discipline and a surfeit of money to squander, the young aristocrats enrolled at the

Academy were gaining little benefit from their time there, while endowing the institution with a bad name. It was something he intended to further investigate and would ask Charles Goodridge for his opinion.

The only other alternative course was for the lad to enter the service directly under the supervision of a senior officer. This was perhaps the preferred alternative in Oliver's mind.

Not having encountered Captain Boris Crabthorne since they exchanged pleasantries in the courtyard of the naval dockyard, Oliver had been unable to arrange anything positive for the boy. But, now that the threat to Britain's coast had almost been obliterated, the urgency for the Royal Navy to prepare the next fleet was minimal and new commissions would be few and far between. Ships would still patrol the Channel, Ushant and Brest, the French coasts, and the Mediterranean but there was little likelihood of Britain embarking on another major sea battle with France, so both he and Boris Crabthorne could be on the beach for quite some time.

He hoped to have the opportunity to meet young Charles soon and speak with him. If not before, he intended to make a point of it when he returned from London.

'He's grown two inches since you last saw him, Captain,' Mrs Crosby said. 'He's still as inquisitive as he always was, but, with a little prompting, he's learned to curb his tongue, to ask his question politely and to be patient while waiting for an answer.'

'And with the doctor's tutelage, his manners have improved,' Connie added. 'A real young gentleman in the making, if you ask me.'

'That is good to hear,' the captain said, pondering on those thoughts. Despite being the son of a Yorkshire shipwright and Spanish mother and growing up on the streets of Gibraltar, twelve year old Charles Goodridge's background had endowed him with certain advantages. He could speak Spanish fluently and also had some French and Portuguese. And, having dogged his father's footsteps in the dockyard, he knew more about the structure and workings of a fighting ship than many a common sailor. At the tender age of eleven he had sailed aboard a warship, albeit with his mother, and had witnessed and played an active and very commendable part in a sea battle. No one could deprive him of those experiences.

Horatio Nelson, on the other hand, had gone to sea at age twelve and been stepped up to the rank of captain at seventeen. But Horatio had been born into a prosperous Norfolk family and joined the navy under the patronage of his uncle, Maurice Suckling. Suckling was a high-ranking naval officer, grandnephew of the first British Prime Minister, Robert Walpole, and Comptroller of the Navy, with a seat in the House of Commons. As such, Nelson had the advantage of breeding, while Charles Goodridge had none and could never be classed as a gentleman.

With his sponsorship, however, Oliver was confident Charles would have access to all the necessities of life befitting a gentleman, if not the privilege of birthright, title or lands.

'Is the war now over?' Connie asked timidly, interrupting his thoughts.

'I fear not,' Oliver said. 'Though the immediate dangers have been averted. And while the Emperor is busy fighting his battles over borders and territories in Europe, England will be left in relative peace. But for how long that will last, no one knows.'

Dr Whipple returned from his patient around noon, apologised for his absence and joined the company for a light meal. With a lull in the conversation, Dr Whipple excused himself from the table for a moment then returned with his walking cane.

'Do you remember this?' he said to the Captain.

'Indeed I do. How can I forget it?'

'You will be interested, I am sure, to learn that I have been giving young Charles lessons in stick fighting. When he is home he forever presses me to have a bout with him. He is surprisingly agile and quick and I fancy he will transfer those skills to an épéé in years to come.'

'I am pleased you maintained your expertise, Doctor. That stick is a lethal weapon in your hands.'

Having enjoyed a pleasant afternoon with Dr Whipple and his companions, Oliver farewelled the ladies and thanked the doctor for his hospitality. Before returning to the waterfront, he visited his bank and the rooms of his lawyer to ensure adequate measures were in place regarding the financial arrangements surrounding the future arrival of his daughter. But, to date, there was no word from Lisbon. However, despite the recent sea war, packet ships were still sailing to and from the Portuguese capital, the journey taking a little over two weeks. Like young Charles, Oliver accepted that he must learn to be patient.

Repair work continued throughout the time *Victory* was anchored on Spithead until it was agreed she was ready to face the vagaries of the English Channel. On the morning of Tuesday, December 10, the first rate battleship prepared to set sail for Sheerness and the Royal Dockyard at Chatham.

Under an overcast sky, with the anchor dripping water over the new cathead, the yards were raised, stay sails run up and canvas unfurled, as hundreds of pairs of eyes around the waterway watched the departure.

On Spithead and the Mother Bank, naval, merchant and foreign ships, flew their flags at half-mast, including those of the Russian fleet who were visiting the port. Officers, sailors and lubbers alike raised their hats, while women waved their handkerchiefs to say farewell.

Tears streaked many faces, while cheers and cries were supplemented by the regular explosive gun salutes from both the saluting battery and the ships' decks; each sound preceded by a puff of smoke that curled into the grey sky. The cacophony of noise vibrating the air was in honour of a proud and victorious warship that had returned triumphant and was now departing. But the greatest homage was being paid to England's fallen Admiral, undoubtedly revered as Britain's finest seaman.

With a distance of almost 200 nautical miles of Channel ahead of her and making a speed of almost four knots, a sound ship would be expected to arrive at Sheerness in a little over two days. But

Victory was still far from sound and despite the orderly appearances on deck, work continued below, the pumps being manned constantly to prevent more water rising in the well.

But the day following her departure, contrary winds blew across the Channel and the smooth passage that had been hoped was not to be. Unable to round the South Headland, *Victory* had to turn back. This delay meant she did not arrive at the Nore in the Thames estuary until 17 December – one week later.

Having watched the smooth departure of the 104-gun ship from his vantage point in his garden on the Isle of Wight, Oliver Quintrell planned to board a post-chaise in Portsmouth the following day. Without incident or accident, he would arrive in London early the next morning and, as pre-arranged, spend some time with his sister at Grosvenor Square before heading up to Greenwich later in the week.

Michael Casson, his ship's steward-cum-valet would accompany him.

Chapter 5

The Nore

After a slow and tedious voyage from Portsmouth, HMS *Victory* entered the mouth of the River Thames – a full eight weeks after the Battle off Cape Trafalgar. At the Nore, she was met by an Admiralty yacht that piloted her along the Medway and into the Royal Dockyard at Chatham where the war-weary ship was to undergo major repairs.

Having been built in that naval yard over 45 years earlier, a few of the older wrights and chippies raised their hats to her when she swam by. Some had been young apprentices on the day her keel had been laid down. It was not the first time *Victory* had revisited the Chatham yard. She had returned for refits on several occasions, and every time she returned, she was given the welcome afforded to a long lost son.

But while at the Nore and, before any attention was given to the ship itself, the body of Lord Nelson, still contained within the leaguer, had to be attended to.

First, the liquid was decanted from the barrel yet again. Then the Admiral's body was lifted from the spirits, stripped and redressed in a shirt, a pair of silk stockings, and his lordship's uniform waistcoat and breeches. A white cambric handkerchief was tied around his neck and another around his forehead. Those in attendance noted that his lips and ankles were a little discoloured but, otherwise, the preservation was excellent.

The body was then placed in a leaden coffin which in turn was placed in a wooden coffin made from the mainmast of *L'Orient*. In 1798, Nelson had been presented with the coffin made from part of the French ship that had blown up and burned when the British fleet, commanded by Rear Admiral Horatio Nelson, had defeated the enemy at the Battle of the Nile. While *L'Orient* was destroyed, before it sank, Captain Hollwell salvaged part of the mainmast and had a coffin made from its timber. Shortly after, he presented this to his friend, Horatio Nelson, as a memento of his victory at sea.

The coffin measured six feet in length and was rather narrow. But as Horatio Nelson was only five feet and four inches tall in life, it easily accommodated his corpse. The inside of the coffin was padded with cotton wadding and lined with white silk.

On 23 December, 1805, the heavy coffin was removed to the deck of Commissioner Gray's yacht and with the colours suspended over it, was sailed up the Thames to Greenwich.

Ships on the river lowered their flags, while Tilbury and Gravesend forts did likewise. Minute guns were fired and Church bells tolled.

At 1.00 o'clock on the 24 December, the day before Christmas, the yacht arrived at Greenwich, and was moored off the hospital grounds. However, due to its weight and the tide being low, it could not be landed until evening. At about five o'clock, the boat touched against the stone steps and the casket was lowered from the yacht into a boat, and immediately conveyed to the hospital stairs.

Illuminated by the light of lanterns and flaming torches that reflected on the slow-moving river, the coffin, draped in *Victory*'s colours was lifted ashore by Nelson's own – the same loyal sailors who had served with the viscount at Trafalgar and sailed back from Gibraltar with his body aboard HMS *Victory*.

From the stairs it was carried to the Record-chamber of the Great Hall. While already encased in two coffins, the remains were placed into a magnificent exterior coffin, made of mahogany, in preparation for viewing by the public. Here, in the Record-chamber, several private viewings took place under the ever watchful eye of the Reverend Mr Scott who had served as Lord Nelson's chaplain aboard the flag ship.

On 4 January, at one o'clock in the afternoon, the Princess of Wales, attended by her retinue, arrived to pay her respects in a solemn and private manner. She was followed by several other dignitaries.

Neither Lady Nelson nor Emma Hamilton visited.

At no time, during the eleven days the coffin was at Greenwich was it left unattended. Reverend Scott and the undertaker remained with the body throughout the night. During the following days, the chaplain sat at the head of the coffin along with ten official mourners from the Lord Chamberlain's office; all were appropriately dressed in deep mourning.

Besides Mr Scott, two naval lieutenants were posted to stand guard. They wore full dress uniform coats, with black waistcoats, breeches, and stockings, with black crepe bands round their arms and hats. Also in attendance were two junior Officers of Arms wearing colourful tabards emblazoned with the coat of arms of the sovereign.

On Sunday, the fifth of January, and for the two following days, the Painted Hall, at Greenwich Hospital, was open from nine in the morning till four in the afternoon. However, when the doors were first thrown open, following the morning service, the throng of thousands waiting outside, pushed forward crushing several women and children. It quickly became apparent that the numbers entering the Hall had to be limited to avoid further injuries. Volunteers from the Greenwich and Deptford Associations were charged with keeping the crowds moving in a safe and orderly fashion.

*　*　*

Having arrived in London several days before the damaged warship reached Chatham, Oliver Quintrell had plenty of time to attend to several matters.

His first concern was to visit the Admiralty in Whitehall to remind the Lords Commissioners of his availability and his desire for another command. This time his request was listened to, but no assurances were given that they would be addressed. He was politely informed that not all ships had yet returned from Gibraltar and because of the mounting costs due to the loss of ships and the damage that had been suffered during the battle; the priority for the Admiralty was to see the British fleet rebuilt. A navy without its line of battle ships was not worth its salt. Apart from the loss of ships, several senior officers had perished along with almost 500 seamen and well over 1000 sailors who had been wounded.

He also learned that the defeat of the combined French and Spanish naval forces had depleted the enemy's reserves to an even greater extent. France had suffered 3370 dead with over a 1000 wounded. Spain had lost over 1000 men and registered 2545 wounded. An enormous butcher's bill for both countries.

Because of this, the Admiralty felt less urgency to put the fleet to sea again. This, in turn, was another reason for the delay in offering new appointments and granting promotions. While the figures were shocking, the news was as Oliver Quintrell had expected.

Having thanked their lordships, the captain returned to his sister's residence where he received two letters – one forwarded from his lawyer in Portsmouth and the other from Dr Whipple. Enclosed within the correspondence from his friend was a letter sent from Lisbon. It had been opened in Portsmouth and forwarded to him care of his sister's address in London. In it were more details regarding Miss Olivia stating that arrangements for her transportation to Portsmouth were being investigated. A nanny could be hired to escort her to the English port. On receiving the captain's agreement with these tentative arrangements, the party would sail on the packet boat from Lisbon at a date to be determined.

Suddenly the enormity of the responsibility he was taking on struck him. Oliver Quintrell was a father in name, if not yet in deed. The fact he had withheld the information from his wife did not sit well with him. But she despised Nelson's blatant affair with Emma Hamilton while he still remained married to Lady Nelson, and she was bitterly scornful of their daughter, Horatia.

Being unable to bear children herself, Victoria Quintrell had always blamed her husband for his inadequacy. Now, after learning

58

he had fathered a child of his own, Oliver was privy to the truth. Yet, in all conscience, he could not tell his wife without causing her more distress with the fear he would lose her completely. Perhaps time would offer an amicable solution, though he doubted it.

In the meantime, Dr Whipple confirmed that Mrs Pilkington had agreed to accept the role of fostering the little girl. Consuela Pilkington was a kindly young woman who had suffered much loss and hardship herself and, as such, Oliver hoped the love of a child would bring her joy. In anticipation of the new arrival, a room in the High Street house has been set aside for the new addition. She had taken great delight in showing it to the Captain during his last visit.

Dr Whipple also confirmed his support both to the child and Mrs P – *Connie* – as he called her, but he was unsure about the insistence on secrecy, however, he accepted the captain's stipulations.

If nothing else, Oliver would ensure that no financial burden would befall either of them. Though Oliver struggled with the conflicting arguments in his head, in his heart he was longing to see the little girl – his daughter – Olivia – Susanna's child. *Would she look like Susanna? Would she have Susanna's loving nature?* He wondered.

On the Sunday morning, prior to the funeral, when Oliver stepped outdoors, the breeze was bitter, the air chilled and the sun not yet risen. Very soon after leaving the house on Grosvenor Square, he was grateful his sister had insisted he wear a pair of gloves and a muffler wrapped around his neck and tucked beneath his boat cloak.

She had been worried about him and commented that he looked drawn. She was concerned that he was unwell.

'Just a little troubled,' Oliver had replied.

'Can I be of any help?' she had asked.

'Thank you, but no. It is a difficult time.'

Thinking her brother was alluding to Lord Nelson's funeral, his sister had remarked that it would soon all be over, to which Oliver merely nodded and bid her farewell.

Striding briskly from the house, in an effort to keep warm, he headed across the Royal parks to Westminster and the Thames where he planned to take a carriage or a wherry to Greenwich.

Even as the day tried to dawn, the grey light of morning persisted until almost ten o'clock. The atmosphere was damp but at least there was no rain. Even with the date of the state funeral still five days away, the number of visitors to the city was swelling daily.

As he walked through St James's Park he was reminded of the same walk he took during the Peace of Amiens back in 1802. It was the time the Sea Fencibles were gathering momentum – when thousands of commoners were rallying to the call to support King and country to defend the British coast from an impending invasion force from across the Channel. On the day he visited London that year, a crowd of 100,000 men, women and children had gathered to see the King in Hyde Park. He wondered how many would turn out to see a dead hero.

As he strode on, Oliver considered that the numbers streaming into the city for the funeral could be even greater this time, making him wonder where the masses would be accommodated. As the inns and hotels would have quickly filled, it was likely many folk would be sleeping in the parks and alleyways.

Winter in England was the worst time of the year for this type of event.

With his route taking him across the Horse Guards' parade ground he could see the roof of the Admiralty building ahead. As he crossed the courtyard a pair of mangy dogs ran across his path almost causing him to fall, but he quickly regained his balance and strode on heading to Whitehall. For a moment he considered hiring a cab but with none lined up in the usual place, he opted to take a boat to Greenwich. With the strong outflowing tide to carry it swiftly downstream, he should make the distance in a little over an hour. By road, it would be a far more uncomfortable journey and with the state of the roads and the number of pedestrians on them, it could take a great deal longer.

On nearing the Thames, Oliver's nose was alerted to the smell of London's greatest open sewer. The foul coloured water was tainted by blood and entrails from the slaughterhouses and tanneries situated along the riverbank, together with waste from every house and factory and open drain running down from the city. He longed for the clean fresh smell of the sea.

On the river at Westminster, boats, barges and wherries of all sizes were in great demand. As each new boat tied up, irrespective of its nature, condition, usual occupation or stench, after handing over their pennies to the boatman, the crowds clambered over the gunwales and dropped onto the thwarts. Mothers scolded grubby children. Dogs yapped. Old men grumbled. Each boat conveyed a motley group of passengers. Oliver was not the only person intent on paying his respect to England's greatest sea captain.

As the sights of London swam by, Oliver Quintrell was shocked at the size and number of new warehouses that had sprung up along the river since he last passed that way. Standing three and four storeys high, the brick buildings stretched along the river's banks on both sides. Swamp land was quickly being filled in to accommodate London's expanding girth.

Being fully occupied with the sights and sounds the Thames thoroughfare produced, he had managed to ignore the constant chatter going on around him, and the journey was over too quickly.

Disembarking at Greenwich to more bustling throngs, Oliver was again amazed. There were not hundreds, but thousands of people of all descriptions gathered on the grounds at the Royal Naval Hospital and particularly around the entrance to the Painted Hall where the Admiral's body was lying in state for the public to pay their respects.

With one third of the British fleet being Irishmen, the three day's period of wake, prior to the funeral, would provide the appropriate time to observe the traditional ritual of both celebrations and lamentations. Tears would be shed and copious amounts of ale and spirits would be consumed in memory of the dead Admiral.

The smells coming from the street traders' carts, hawking seafood, roast chestnuts, potatoes and pies attracted plenty of customers. Many folk had left their homes in the dead of night and travelled long distances in order to arrive early. Unfortunately, they were then made to wait in the near freezing air until nine o'clock when the doors to the hall opened. The crowds were impatient. The mood was tense and irritable.

Oliver was loath to join the throng where ministers of the Government were obliged to mingle with washerwomen and waifs, all being jostled along together. But he had no alternative. Everyone was of the same intent. They were there to show their respect.

With the entrance to the Great Hall in sight, the crowd was ushered into the semblance of an orderly queue by armed soldiers, Sea Fencibles, volunteers and Naval Pensioners. Their task was to control the flow and prevent further injuries by ushering only fifty people into the hall at any one time. Yet, almost by the minute, more mourners were arriving at the Hospital's ground by boat and carriage, and on foot from London. They would continue pouring in for the next two days.

While standing in line with hundreds of others, Oliver thought back to the time he was a patient in the hospital. The smells exuding from the building were the same as back then – scented salves and pomanders, unwashed old men, weeping wounds and wet bandages, urine and excrement. He also remembered the times he had spent dining under the magnificent painted roof where meals were basic and unappetising, though not dissimilar to the diet sailors suffered at sea when on long voyages. The quality of the century's old paintings and the surrounding walls had also amazed him and, at times, distracted him from his discomfort.

Forced along with the crowd, the group of fifty, of which Oliver Quintrell was one, climbed the marble steps and headed slowly along the hall. To absorb the noise of hobnailed boots and clogs, the chamber floor had been covered in matting and black cloth. As the mob moved forward, the babble of the waiting crowd was soon left behind.

Lighted sconces glimmered from the hall's roof while individual candles burned from tables along the length of the hall. Being over one hundred feet long and fifty-six feet wide, the Grand Hall was an impressive arena. The magnificent ceiling provided a company of angels to overlook the proceedings.

The head of the coffin was turned towards the main entrance. It was covered in a black velvet pall with white satin lining. Barriers had been erected, to allow the mourners to pass close to the coffin when paying their respects but with such slow progress hundreds, if not thousands of visitors would not gain entry before the doors closed at dark.

With his sword by his side, Oliver cupped his hand over the pommel to prevent it swinging when he was jostled. He would have done well to leave it in London but in this environment, where the eyes of every second man bore the shifting expression of a scallywag or scoundrel, he felt comforted to have it with him.

'Move along!' one of the attendants shouted.

The feet shuffled along at a snail's pace.

As he neared the coffin, Oliver removed his hat as did the others. Mothers gripped the wrists of their children to prevent them from running amok. Tears flowed unashamedly. The air of hallowed solemnity was palpable.

'Watch it!' a raucous voice bellowed from behind as his sword swung back from his hip when he was pushed forward. The man who had made the call was immediately made to hush by others nearby.

'I beg your pardon, sir,' Oliver said, turning to face the stranger. Then his face expanded into a grin. 'Well, if it ain't James Tinker.'

'Bungs, to you Captain,' the old cooper replied bluntly, allowing his lips to twitch slightly. 'You be an unexpected sight amongst this rabble.'

'Paying my respects just like you,' Oliver said.

'*Shhh!*' a woman hissed.

Oliver turned his head and whispered, 'Might I suggest we continue this conversation when we are finished here?'

The cooper touched his forehead and followed in line to where the coffin was situated.

Chapter 6

Greenwich to St Paul's

When he reached the coffin, Oliver Quintrell bowed his head reverently and paused momentarily, but the constant creep of the crowd behind him did not allow him to linger as long as he would have wished. Volunteers from the Greenwich and Deptford Association had been posted to prevent disruptions and keep the crowds in continual motion. Like those moving slowly beside him Oliver was touched by the spectacle. Around him there were spontaneous sighs, tears and whispered prayers. Of those around him, jaws dropped open and eyebrows rose involuntarily at the confronting sight. Within the Hall, feelings of grief and awe, exultation and regret were palpable.

For Oliver Quintrell, the need for real contemplation would have to be satisfied later, at a time and place where he could be alone with only his thoughts for company. But for the present, his eyes embraced the scene and absorbed all he saw.

The mahogany coffin, with eight gold handles and gilded corner plates secured with double gilt nails, gleamed in the light of the multiple candles. Placed on top were sixteen gilded items including an ornamental gold plaque engraved with the Admiral's name, along with a list of his many titles and offices; a portrait of the deceased hero, and an urn with a British lion at its base. One of the lion's paws was resting on the French Gallic cock.

A pedestal, placed in front of the coffin, bore a richly fringed black velvet cushion. On it sat the Viscount's coronet, decorated with sixteen large pearl-like ornaments.

From beyond the walls of the building, the murmur from the crowds expressed their frustrations, as they awaited their turn to enter, but from within, all was still and silent, save for the slow shuffling of the mourners. Otherwise, there was no movement in the air. No flutter of the black velvet bows hanging from the canopy surmounting the coffin. Even the ten mourners posted alongside it stood like statues and the group of designated overseers sitting with Lord Nelson's body, hardly appeared to breathe.

On the ceiling above and on the surrounding walls, legendary heroes and kings and queens of a bygone era floated with angels – the exquisite details captured a century earlier, by Sir James Thornhill – the artist.

Captain Quintrell considered how different the farewell for Horatio Nelson was to the other poor souls, both English and foreign who also had fallen at the Battle of Trafalgar. How many bodies had been tossed through open gunports or heaved over the gunwales without a second thought or prayer? In some cases, the torso was minus its head or one of its appendages. While appearing dead, some of the men had not yet breathed their last, but with no time for the surgeon to examine them, they followed their brothers to a watery grave.

Yet, with Viscount, Lord Nelson, here was a man revered by all and elevated in the public's eyes almost to the level of a god. A man whose earthly remains had been preserved in brandy and then pure alcohol in order to retain its features even weeks after his death.

Then the captain's thoughts drifted back to the burial of Percy Sparrow, a carpenter, whose remains he had regarded as the worst corruption he had ever seen. His body, also confined in a barrel, had been despatched to the bottom of a Crater Lake in the freezing waters of the Southern Ocean. At least the respect of the crew and the heartfelt grief they felt had been expressed without shame.

On leaving the stagnant atmosphere and stepping outside, Oliver inhaled deeply gulping in air like a fish out of water.

Several onlookers acknowledged him with a respectful gesture, touching their hats or knuckling their forelocks, as though they knew him. Perhaps they did. Perhaps they were seamen who had sailed with him. Or perhaps they thought, being in dress uniform, adorned with gold epaulettes, and carrying an ornate sword, he was an important dignitary. In this instance, Oliver Quintrell was just one of the populace.

Looking to the boats almost filling the breadth of the river, he headed towards the water. A few yards ahead of him, filling his clay pipe, was his old cooper. While there was nowhere to sit and barely any space on the grass even to stand for a private conversation, the pair stopped at the railings on the edge of the grounds.

'What are you occupying yourself with these days, Bungs?' the captain asked. 'I'd heard, some time ago, you had bought yourself a share in a tavern with the prize money you'd accumulated over the years.'

'I thought about it,' the cooper grunted, sucking hard on the narrow clay stem to encourage the tobacco to burn. 'But I tucked my money away somewhere safe for a later date.'

'Are you of a mind to sail again?' Oliver asked. 'Every ship needs a good cooper.'

Bungs didn't need to be told. 'Not right now, Capt'n. My plans are to go to the yard in Chatham and get me some work. I heard that *Victory* is in the dockyard there and they'll need men to refit her. That's where I am off to. I just called in here on the way to find out what was happening.'

'Did you not work on *Victory* many years ago?'

'Nowt wrong with your memory, Capt'n. Indeed, I did. 'Twas in '98 when she came into Chatham for her last refit. I helped load tons of pig iron into her hold for ballast?' His laugh was a guttural growl. 'Remember the blocks we pulled out of the stinking slime in the ballast of that Portuguese slave ship in South America. That silver paid everyone on board a pretty penny in prize money.'

'Indeed,' Oliver agreed, not venturing to admit to the substantial amount he had been allocated.

'Perhaps I can convey you to the dockyard,' the captain offered.

'Don't trouble yourself, Capt'n,' the old cooper replied. 'I'm off to join the lads in the tavern. The wake will go on for three days and I recon I can spare me a few hours before I take a ferry down river to Chatham.'

'Then I wish you well. Come sail with me again one day.'

'Aye, maybe, I will. God speed you, Capt'n.' And with those words the old salt touched his forehead, turned and shuffled away into the crowd.

Though there were perhaps 20,000 people in the grounds of the Naval Hospital and more along the river bank, Oliver had never felt so alone.

*   *   *

On Wednesday morning, following three days of the body lying in state, the coffin, covered in a black velvet pall, decorated with a colourful escutcheon, was carried from the Great Hall to the jetty stairs to be transferred by barge to the Admiralty in Whitehall. The body of Britain's finest seaman was to take its last journey on water before internment.

The official line of funeral barges and boats, making up the procession, was slow to assemble on the Thames. With an extraordinary number of spectator craft on the water vying for a view, they almost blocked the river, making access for the official barges very difficult. From the hospital's grounds and streets nearby, thousands of faces strained to see, not only the coffin, but members of the Royal Family and other dignitaries who had arrived in their carriages to take part in the funeral procession.

The first barge to draw up was the state barge flying the royal standard. The second in line was the King's barge. A Knight of the Bath sitting at its head. In it were the Officers bearing the sword, helmet, gauntlets and spurs of the deceased.

The coffin was carried on board the third barge by *Victory*'s men. Completely covered-in black velvet, the barge was adorned with large black ostrich feathers. Six trumpeters sat in the stern sheets along with six naval lieutenants. An Officer of Arms was at the head of the coffin bearing the Viscount's coronet on a black velvet cushion. The standard of the United Kingdom flew at the stem. The funeral barge was manned by 46 sailors from HMS *Victory*. All were neatly dressed in white shirts, blue jackets and trousers, their hats bearing the name of the flag ship with black silk crepe bands tied around their hats and arms.

The fourth barge in the procession carried the official mourners all with mourning cloaks over full uniforms. The banner of emblems was borne by Nelson's Flag Officer – Captain Hardy.

The numerous barges that followed transported an array of distinguished notables representing naval, civil and commercial elements of the country: the Lords Commissioners from the Admiralty, the Lord Mayor of London, the navigation committee and representatives of various guilds and lodges – drapers, fishmongers, goldsmiths, skinners, tanners, tailors, ironmongers, stationers and apothecaries – each guild in its own barge; each with its own flag hoisted to half-staff.

The line appeared unending and the time taken, for everyone to embark on his designated vessel, seemed endless. Only when the hundreds of mourners were finally seated aboard their respective boats was the journey to Westminster able to begin.

As the lead barges pushed away from the Hospital's jetty, the minute gun commenced firing and the procession began its mournful journey. Although the flood tide was in their favour, the wind, blowing downstream hindered the rowers.

As the procession slowly moved upstream and the barge bearing Lord Nelson's coffin drifted by, every man lining the river bank removed his hat and stood in silence. Sailors hanging from the rigging of visiting merchant vessels, spectators lining the decks of boats, passengers on wherries and clerks from the windows and roofs of warehouse offices all showed their respect. Of the ladies in the crowds, there were many tear-streaked faces. Yet not a word was spoken.

Apart from the dip of the oars and the creak of the rowlocks, the silence was overwhelming.

After half an hour, when the leading barges reached the Tower of London, the great guns high on the castle's ramparts exploded with violent noise, smoke and fire. They were fired every minute as the convoy swam by. Moored on the nearby wharf, six barges decked with rows of the City Volunteers' regiment stood to attention with arms reversed. From both sides of the Thames, church bells tolled while on the water, the River Fencibles ensured the procession was not blocked as the oarsmen pulled into the wind.

At two o'clock, the funeral barges glided under the central arch of the London Bridge, their oars held upright. Forty-five minutes later, the head of the procession reached the Palace Yard steps, near Westminster Abbey. Here the first few barges drew alongside with a long snaking line of boats pulling up behind them. The solemn air was broken by the sound of trumpets and another gunboat firing every minute. To the chords of Handel's *Dead March in Saul*, the coffin was unloaded, preceded by the colour party.

Being blessed by weak winter sunshine during the journey up the Thames, when the barge was secured to the wharf, the sky suddenly took on a grey spectre. As if preordained, at the moment the body was landed and carried up the steps from the river, a mantle of dark and heavy cloud blocked the late afternoon rays. The temperature suddenly dropped and hail unexpectedly poured from the heavens creating a thick veil of mist over the river. Despite the sudden hailstorm, the sailors remained bareheaded, water running down their faces, dripping from their noses and ears and saturating their shirts, neckerchiefs and jackets. As if oblivious to the storm, the stalwart spectators also stood in solemn silence.

From the short walk from the Palace Yard steps to the Admiralty building, the party travelled on foot, the coffin being carried on a bier by eight sailors of HMS *Victory*. A canopy was held over the casket supported by six admirals of the fleet. The chief mourner, Sir Peter Parker, walked behind to the doleful sound of drums and trumpets.

Within the Admiralty building, the Captain's Room had been prepared to house the coffin until the time for its final transfer to St Paul's Cathedral. The walls were hung with fine black cloth and the room lit with long black tapers.

The crowd, that had congregated at the Palace Yard Steps and had followed the procession, were unwilling to leave. Many remained outside the Admiralty throughout the night conducting their own vigil.

* * *

While the formal pomp and ceremony of the procession was taking place, work continued on the roads leading from the Admiralty to St Paul's. Like all busy thoroughfares in winter, the way was deeply furrowed from the constant passage of carriage wheels and pitted with potholes.

From early morning, wagon after wagon rolled along the main roads delivering gravel. This was spread along Whitehall, the Strand and Fleet Street in preparation for Nelson's final journey; hopefully to prevent the carriages' wheels becoming lodged in the ruts as they passed along the London streets. While the main route was repaired, along the way, all minor roads and alleyways were barricaded by overturned carts, chests and barrels allowing only pedestrians to get through.

To contend with the growing number of mourners, sightseers, vagabonds and pickpockets that had suddenly arrived in the city, an army of volunteers was placed on duty from Constitution Hill to the Admiralty and from there to St Paul's Cathedral. The regiment of volunteers included Sea Fencibles, Greenwich Pensioners and soldiers. Amongst them were several marksmen and riflemen.

While the roads were prepared to carry the traffic that would make up the procession, provisions had to be made to accommodate the thousands of spectators who were arriving to watch the spectacle.

On the day before the funeral, every shipwright, carpenter and joiner not otherwise occupied, plus his mates and any volunteer who could wield a hammer, use a saw or bang in a nail into a length of wood, was called on. They worked, throughout the long night, by lantern lights and flaming torches, erecting scaffolding to support tiers of seats along the route the funeral procession was to take. From Whitehall to St Paul's Cathedral on Ludgate Hill, there was much noise and bustle.

At six o'clock, the following morning with the streets still blanketed in the blackness of night, the newly erected tiers of seats were already occupied by visitors who had travelled to London especially for the event. They had secured their seats early to guarantee a good view of the procession.

For the next few hours, London held its breath and waited.

* * *

Thursday, 9 January, 1806, was the day of Nelson's Funeral.

From before light, some distance away in both Hyde Park and St James Park, carriages were lining up to convey members of the royal family, and other naval, military and civil dignitaries, to the Cathedral. The assembled mourners were marshalled according to rank.

Among those holding tickets to the event was Oliver Quintrell.

Dressed in accordance with the instructions he had received, like all other naval officers, he wore a mourning cloak over his uniform coat with black waistcoat and breeches and stockings. A black crepe band circled his arm and hat.

On presenting himself to one of the stewards, he was directed to a location where he would find his respective carriage. Wandering through St James Park towards Hyde Park, he checked the carriage numbers as he went, eventually finding the one he was designated to travel in. He had hoped to be placed with at least one officer he knew, but he was not in luck. He was aware that Captain Boris Crabthorne was to attend and was anxious to speak with him, but that opportunity did not arise.

Taking a seat in the coach with another post captain, two flag captains and a Rear Admiral of the Blue, the topic of conversation in the coach was naturally about Lord Nelson. While two of the officers had served aboard his ship at the Battle of the Nile and expounded their experiences in great detail, Oliver offered what he could about the apparent state of HMS *Victory* when she recently returned to Portsmouth, but his topic engendered little interest.

When, eventually, after much waiting and complaining, all the listed passengers were seated and the line of almost 200 conveyances rolled slowly from Hyde Park to St James Park. At eleven o'clock, the procession entered Horse Guards where their Royal Highnesses, the Dukes of Cambridge and Kent, mounted and dressed in full regimentals, were awaiting the arrival of the coaches. Riding at the head of the line, they were flanked by a regiment of light infantry and three highland regiments of the Scottish Fusiliers. The Duke of York headed the 14th Light Dragoons. The mounted officers of the 10th Dragoons wore black cloaks.

His Royal Highness, the Prince of Wales, was resplendent on horseback, wearing full regimentals plus the velvet cloak and insignia of the Order of the Garter. His presence excited the most marked attention. The royal party was followed by eleven cannon each pulled by six horses. Next was the ammunition wagon. It was followed by four regiments of horse artillery and the Grenadier Guards.

Immediately after the royal and military contingents, was the funeral car carrying the body of Horatio Nelson. Designed to resemble HMS *Victory*, the front of the car was built to imitate the shape of the ship's bow. Similarly, the rear of the car was built in the likeness of *Victory*'s stern. Hoisted to half-staff on the flag pole was the British ensign.

Drawn by six black horses, the coffin placed within the car was shaded by a grand canopy. Standing fifteen feet tall, the funeral car was mounted on a sprung platform and carried on a four-wheeled carriage decorated with black velvet drapery with black fringes.

The leaves and vines festooned on the sides of the car encircled the word – TRAFALGAR. The tall canopy, above the coffin, was also surmounted with black ostrich feathers and supported by four palm-trees made of carved wood – silvered and glazed with green. At the foot of the each tree, wreaths of live laurel and cypress were entwined around the stem.

Following the funeral car were six mourning coaches carrying the heralds and their trumpets and then the state carriages bearing junior members of the Royal family – the sons of barons, earls, and viscounts. Next came fifty-six mourning coaches carrying naval and military officers.

Travelling amongst them, Captain Oliver Quintrell was unable to witness the whole procession, but from the carriage window he observed the street scenes as they rolled by. Uniformed soldiers, marines and marshals were stationed two-deep along the route from the Admiralty to Temple-Bar, together with mounted members of the City light-horse and the Westminster cavalry. Behind the guards, taking up the newly erected tiers of seats, were men, women and children from all walks of life. The near destitute were thrown together with businessmen and members of more affluent society. For both rich and poor, this was a spectacle they would relate to their grandchildren in years to come.

The procession proceeded to the music of the band of the Buffs: the Royal East Kent Regiment, one of the oldest regiments in the British Army. With muffled drums, they played Handel's *Dead March* and *Rule Britannia*. East of Temple-Bar the London regiments stood guard to preserve order and keep the way clear.

Discounting the royal and military contingents, one hundred and twenty-six private carriages and sixty-three mourning coaches rolled through Horse Guards and ground along the gravel from Whitehall to the Strand and Ludgate Hill.

The King was not present.

With many visitors to the city and non-ticketed mourners heading to St Paul's on foot, by eleven o'clock, the area around St Paul's was packed. Even the flat roofs of nearby buildings were lined, as was every window and open ledge.

The inside of the church was also filling quickly. Then, at around 1.15, the sound of bagpipes announced the arrival of one of the Highland regiments setting off a buzz of expectation that the procession was drawing close. Within the Cathedral, the wooden seating, rising to fifteen tiers high, recently erected by a team of carpenters, creaked and rattled. The construction was similar to the smaller ones built along the procession route. Ushers strode back and forth escorting mourners to their allotted seats.

Shortly after, the Prince of Wales, astride a lavishly caped horse, rode to the Cathedral's great steps. He was preceded by the mace and state sword.

As the procession arrived at St Paul's, hats were removed and tears were again shed unashamedly. A cacophony of sounds accompanied the procession, the band in the van played the 104th Psalm, along with music from the fifes of the infantry, the trumpets of the cavalry and the bagpipes of the Scottish regiments.

It was three in the afternoon, when the funeral car slowed to a halt, but a full fifteen minutes was needed to lower the heavy coffin from the carriage ready for it to be carried into the church. During that time, the majority of the mourners were able to disembark from their carriages and pass quietly into the cathedral and be directed to their seats.

Oliver Quintrell was allotted a raised seat, a dozen levels high, amongst the main throng of naval officers who made up the greatest percentage of mourners. He was seated between two aged admirals and a host of other officers, recognising very few. As any conversation was frowned on, most sat silently or shared only a few words of whispered conversation.

Barely had he taken his seat, than the fifes of the infantry, alternating with the trumpets of the cavalry announced the opening of the Great Western Door. The breeze that blew into the church caused the enormous flags of France and Spain, captured at Trafalgar and now hanging from the cathedrals inner walls, to wave gently. That movement elicited a great roar of huzzas from the crowd.

Sailors, from Nelson's flag ship, lined a passage to the Door displaying *Victory*'s colours. When the Prince of Wales and the Duke of Clarence passed through, they stopped to examine the numerous holes shot through the canvas. Amazed, they stopped and spoke to some of the sailors about them. The eyes of both royals glistened with tears.

Throughout this time, the crowds outside waited patiently. Within the great Cathedral, silence was observed.

As soon as the coffin was received on the bier, a red pall was thrown over it and a black canopy hoisted above it, decorated, in gold, with the crests and coronet of the deceased. It was surmounted with black plumes and carried by six rear-admirals who bore it up the steps.

With the entry, the trumpets sounded and a band of flutes alternately playing *The Dead March* and the *104th Psalm*, accompanied at intervals by muffled kettle-drums. The procession moved towards the empty choir – that part of a cathedral between the high altar and the nave. The whole area was illuminated by large wax candles. Organ music announced the reception of the coffin within the church.

The 92nd Highland regiment formed a single line circle, under the huge dome and along the entrances and passage to the choir. They stood with their fire locks clubbed. When the organ music ceased, the voices of more than 100 chorus singers, dressed in surplices with black silk scarfs, sang the hymn: *I know that my Redeemer liveth*. The singing continued while the procession passed to the choir area, the singers forming a line on each side near the gates.

The heralds preceded the official party and there was a fanfare of trumpets when the Prince of Wales and his royal brothers entered the Cathedral. They were greeted by the Dean of St Paul's. Finally, the banner of emblems, borne before the canopy was carried by the flag officer of HMS *Victory* – Captain Hardy.

The company now entered the choir. Nelson's older brother, the Reverend Earl Nelson was accompanied by his eldest son, Lord Merton and the Nelson's chaplain, the Reverend Mr Scott. Following these gentlemen, was the chief mourner, Admiral Sir Peter Parker, supported by Admiral Lord Hood and other naval officers. The rear was brought up by the colours of *Victory*. Borne by a select group of seamen from Nelson's ship, they were flanked by an equal number of Greenwich pensioners

The Duchess of York, attended by Lady Fitzroy was received by the Dean and conducted to the choir. As it was not customary for women to attend funerals, neither Lady Nelson nor Emma Hamilton were present, nor was Horatia, the daughter of Lord Nelson and Lady Hamilton

The coffin, when taken from the bier, was lifted into place on a long stool, covered with black velvet and decorated with gold tassels. It was placed directly beneath the centre of St Paul's great dome.

When all who had formed the procession had taken their places, the Prince being seated on the right of the bishop's throne, the choir doors were closed and the funeral service commenced.

Prayers and lessons were read. Psalms and the *Magnificat* were sung, and a sublime anthem chanted. Throughout the service, the whole area was illuminated by an enormous light made up of 200 piteni lamps. It formed an immense octangular lanthorn suspended by a rope from the centre of the Cathedral's dome. With dusk rapidly advancing, the huge light lit the whole Cathedral.

Though overawed by all he saw, for Oliver Quintrell, the most inspiring features were the massive flags of Spain and France suspended from the walls. Despite being pock-marked with shot holes, they best represented Nelson's glorious victory at Trafalgar.

Then commenced the most impressive part of the spectacle. His Royal Highness, the Prince of Wales, with the Duke of Clarence on his right and the Duke of Kent on his left, took his place with the other mourners as the coffin was uncovered and the coronet placed on it. The moment had arrived to consign the mortal remains of the hero to his final resting place. The light afforded by the great lanthorn highlighted the awful splendour of the scene,

At thirty-three minutes after five, the coffin was lowered into the crypt to the calls of those that witnessed the scene. *Oh! Immortal Nelson!*

The white staves that had been carried were then broken and tossed into the grave and the titles of the deceased peer were proclaimed and the ceremony was over.

During the closing moments, *Victory*'s colours were passed into the hands of the loyal tars. Having borne their captain on his final journey and followed him to the very end, they were determined to have a memento of their great and glorious commander. As such, they tore off a considerable part of *Victory*'s flag, of which they all obtained a small portion. Few other persons were allowed to get any of it.

The internment concluded just before six o'clock but it was not until nine o'clock that the Cathedral was finally emptied.

While thousands of mourners had been accommodated in the Cathedral, and thousands of spectators had gathered outside, leaving the great church was far more difficult than entering. Having been seated for many hours, as soon as the service was over, everyone was eager to depart. While the royals and senior officers of church, state and the military were afforded priority, those remaining had to be patient. But, on emerging from the entrance, the task of locating their transport in pitch darkness was near impossible.

Once outside, spontaneous outpourings of feelings, withheld for several hours, were expressed. Beside the noise of conversations, carriage wheels clattered on the cobbles, whips cracked, driver cursed and horses whinnied. Wheels rumbled across the gravel despite traffic blocking every road. The volunteers and soldiers, who had done such an efficient job in controlling the people on entering, had now gone, mingling with the mass of humanity filling the streets. Beside those on foot, coaches and carriages of all sizes and descriptions were lined up choking the roadway; many were completely hemmed in and unable to move in any direction.

Having instructed his manservant, Casson, not to meet him, Oliver Quintrell was content to walk the two miles to Grosvenor

Square and escape the crowds. Apart from needing the exercise, he wanted to be alone with his thoughts.

Although walking though the streets of London after dark was not normally recommended, on this occasion, every street was filled with mourners wending their way home. Gentlemen, officers and lubbers shared their feelings freely with their fellow travellers. All were tired. It had been a long day. But all were satisfied they had done their duty.

Chapter 7

After the funeral

It was three months since the sea battle was fought off Cape Trafalgar and two months since Nelson's body had been returned home. While weeks of celebrations and lamentations had preceded the actual funeral ceremony, within days of the pomp and pageantry ending, the emotions that had been shared throughout London had been exhausted. Cheeks were dry, pockets and stomachs empty, and the tens of thousands of visitors who had flocked into London to witness the special event had turned tail and escaped the metropolis.

Along with the crowds, the tiers of seating, vendors' stalls, bunting, window displays and flags had all gone. How they were conveyed out of the City so quickly was a wonder.

Of those who remained, the folks who had hugged and danced with strangers only weeks ago, now seldom exchanged an unnecessary glance, as they passed on the street. While pleasantries had disappeared, not so the piles of stinking human and animal waste that clogged the gutters, alleyways and doorways, feeding hosts of flies, maggots and vermin. It would require more than a good downpour of rain to flush the excrement into the Thames.

The streets were strangely quiet, save for the *tap-tapping* of peg-legged beggars whose source of income had dried up. The rowdy drunks, now with only holes in their pockets, had crawled back into whatever hovels they had come from. The patriotic verses the pipers had played were soon replaced by the raucous tones of fish-wives eager to reclaim their territories, along with the cries of bakers, florists and other regular street vendors.

It astounded the captain how quickly normal life resumed turning jubilation, celebration and mourning into a mundane routine with an overarching dour and heavy atmosphere. No one was talking. No one was spending. No one smiled.

Of the Londoners walking the streets, eyes failed to rise from gutter level and the name of Lord Horatio Nelson was no longer uttered. It was as though his name, titles and commands had been buried in the crypt below St Paul's Cathedral along with his body.

The men who loitered about the Thames and the entrances to the naval dockyards were mostly sailors, waiting in vain hope for a fighting ship to be repaired, re-floated and re-commissioned. But it would be a long time before that happened.

Ignored, was the fact that the war against France had *not* ended. Napoleon's focus had merely turned towards Europe; however, all Britons cared about was the fact that the threat of a French invasion on English soil had been averted.

For Oliver Quintrell, having spent many hours, sipping ale and reliving the events of the great funeral with other naval officers, and later, back in Grosvenor Square, recounting the details of the greatest spectacle London had witnessed in centuries to his sister, he felt totally exhausted.

From Ludgate Hill, the highest point of the City of London, to Whitehall by the river, and beyond, there was now a palpable air of despondency hanging over the streets. There were no words left. The news sheets and newspapers had nothing more to report. The crowds had gone and the London streets were empty.

The one exception was the Admiralty in Whitehall which saw a constant flow of officers heading in and out, all seeking commissions. Initially, their visits produced much excited chatter in the enclosed courtyard with animated voices raised in anticipation, but later that tone, like the relentless tide, turned to one of disappointment. It was no more than Captain Quintrell had expected.

From reading the *Naval Chronicle*, he was aware that the only fleet to have departed Britain in the last six months, apart from Lord Nelson's, was that of Read Admiral Sir Home Riggs Popham. His fleet of seventy-five vessels had sailed from Cork harbour even before Lord Nelson had stepped aboard *Victory* at Spithead. Heading south, other ships joined the fleet in Madeira, bringing the number to one hundred and forty ships. While Sir Home Popham's destination had been shrouded in secrecy, rumour was rife that he was bound for South Africa. The fleet had included transport vessels for 6000 soldiers sufficient to mount an invasion force.

While Sir Home Popham was not a popular commander, a berth on any of those ships would have satisfied every out-of-work seaman. But as this fleet gathered at Cork and not in an English harbour, the first to sign-on would have been Irishmen. The convoy departed the Irish coast on 28 August, 1805, eight weeks before the battle of Trafalgar even took place.

Taking up the offer of his sister's carriage and driver, Oliver was relieved to take leave of London and head back to Portsmouth, albeit making a slow journey, staying for two nights at coaching stops along the way where a meal and a clean bed provided welcome breaks.

With little Admiralty sympathy for beached seamen, every coach and conveyance, churning along the wheel ruts in the Portsmouth Road, was overloaded. With no free space on a single carriage, cart or wagon, the road was lined with streams of foot traffic, weary sailors heading to the sea ports in the hope of finding a ship to sign on. Also heading away were farm workers and country folk who had travelled to the city purely to witness the national funeral.

While trying not to appear unsociable, Oliver was reticent to discuss the recent events further and did not look forward to arriving home at Bembridge where he would be asked to relate the whole affair from beginning to end, to his wife and her companions. Despite resting at the coaching stops along the road, he still felt extremely weary and wanted nothing more than to retire to his own bed though, even when given the opportunity, sleep did not come easily.

Stepping down from his sister's carriage at the Portsmouth Hard, the captain spoke briefly with his sister's driver, and Casson, who had travelled with him. With his dunnage off-loaded, dress uniform, sword, and all the trimmings he had required for the regal occasion, placed in Casson's care, he farewelled the driver with a handsome tip and instructed his steward to procure a boat to carry them over the Solent to the Isle of Wight.

Across the road from where they had alighted, several sailors were gathered, none of whom he recognised, but noticed a young midshipman pointing in his direction. It was likely he was a clerk from the nearby naval offices.

Oliver paused and waited as the youth crossed the road and approached him.

'Beg pardon, sir. You are, Captain Quintrell, I understand.'

Oliver nodded. 'That is correct.'

The young man appeared relieved but nonetheless slightly flustered. 'I am very pleased to meet up with you, Captain, as I was about to journey across the Solent to your private residence. Your immediate whereabouts were not known to the port admiral. It was thought you had not yet returned from London.'

'Well, here I am,' Oliver said, wrapping his boat cloak across his chest, as a biting wind blew in off the water. 'Tell me, Mr—?'

'Lawrence, sir. Midshipman.'

'What is it the Admiral requires of me?'

'He requests you attend him in his offices as soon as possible.'

It was unlikely the clerk would be cognisant of the reason why his presence had been demanded; despite that, he took the liberty to ask: 'Do you know the reason?'

'I believe so, but I'm not at liberty to say.'

'Come now, Mr Lawrence, I doubt divulging your intelligence will sink the British Fleet.'

'Yes, sir. No, sir,' the young man stuttered. 'I believe the port admiral requires you to attend him regarding a ship.'

'A commission!' Oliver blurted, trying to withhold the smile that was threatening to light up his face.

The midshipman's lips remained tight sealed.

Though he had been soliciting the Admiralty since he returned from the West Indies, with a line of Admirals and post captains ahead of him on the list, he had not expected to receive news of a new command for many weeks or even months.

'What ship?' he enquired, immediately turning his head and glancing across Spithead to the assortment of vessels straining from their cables on the ebbing tide. Having not been home to monitor the shipping entering the roads, he was not familiar with the recent movements on the Solent and did not know which ships had arrived of late. A pair of large East Indiamen, a 74, a frigate, a sloop, a schooner and some fishing boats preparing to go to sea did not provide the answer. Perhaps it was one of the rated ships or a prize of war returned from Gibraltar that was currently undergoing repairs in the Royal Dockyard.

As the young midshipman struggled to retrieve a letter from his pocket, a draught of wind caught it and almost tore it from his hand. Oliver noted the young man's hand was shaking, possibly from the cold. Grasping the envelope firmly, he handed it to the captain.

Turning his back on the breeze, Oliver could not resist opening it there and then. Addressed to Captain Oliver Quintrell, R.N., it was unremarkable, just a standard letter with familiar wording, requesting him to repair to the office of the port admiral in Portsmouth at his earliest convenience. It contained no more information than that which he had gleaned from the courier.

Folding the despatch and placing it in his pocket, Oliver turned to his steward. 'Stay with the dunnage, Casson. I will return shortly.' Then he turned his attention to the young clerk. 'Come along, Mr Lawrence; deliver me to your Admiral in order that I can pay my respects.'

'Good luck, Captain,' Casson called after him.

Oliver acknowledged.

* * *

'She is a 50-gun ship, Captain Quintrell – His Majesty's ship, *Royal Standard* – currently in Cork Harbour awaiting a new captain.'

'Cork – Ireland?'

'Is there another?' the ageing officer replied, looking questioningly at the sea captain over the rim of his spectacles.

'No, sir,' Oliver replied, regretting his foolish response.

The Admiral dismissed the comment. 'She was under the command of Captain Chilcott, however, the captain was struck down by a sudden incapacity and is unable to continue his mission. Unfortunately his malady is grave. The last I heard, he was unable to communicate and can move very little.'

'Did this ailment occur in the harbour?' Oliver asked.

'No, he had set sail aboard *Royal Standard* almost two weeks ago, but only one week out from the harbour, the calamity occurred. I am informed, his injury was the result of a fall, but the doctor is unable to ascertain if the fall resulted in the brain injury or the injury already existed and resulted in the fall.'

'So the ship was returned to port?'

'Indeed, under the command of Lieutenant Brophy, a very experienced officer.'

'This experienced officer – should he not have been stepped up to acting captain?' Oliver asked.

'No,' the Admiral replied bluntly adding nothing to explain his reason and sliding a vellum pouch across the table. 'Your orders, Captain,' the Admiral said. 'You will proceed to Cork and take up your new commission forthwith. There is a packet boat, *Weymouth Lass* due to sail from Spithead, at noon, two days from now. I have arranged a berth for you. The master will be expecting you. Be on it.'

'Thank you, sir. I have one request; that my steward be permitted to accompany me.'

'I am sure that can be accommodated.' Rising to his feet, the port admiral held out his hand. 'You will receive further orders when you reach Cork. I wish you well, Captain Quintrell.'

Oliver inclined his head to the seventy year old officer who was the designated authority at the Portsmouth Navy Yard. After retrieving his boat cloak, he replaced his hat and quickly headed back to the Hard where his steward was waiting.

Under a gloomy sky, Oliver Quintrell strode smartly across the dockyard with a tsunami of thoughts rushing through his brain. The satisfaction of being granted a command was foremost, but a 50-gun ship raised questions in his mind.

Was it an old vessel? Most such ships had already seen out their working lives to end their days as troop carriers or hospital ships, sheer hulks or be razeed and sent to some disease-infested tropical location to be quickly forgotten.

As a fourth-rate, they were never built as a line of battle ship and, currently, few were being constructed for that reason. Yet, while they were grand in appearance, complete with ornately carved stern and rear galleries adorning the superstructure, and boasting spacious accommodation, their decks were only two feet longer than that of a frigate.

Of course, being in Cork Harbour, and having just returned from sea due to its captain's ill health, the ship would already have a full complement of crew with, no doubt, a fair percentage of Irish sailors, reminding Oliver of the problems he had suffered with a number of Irish seamen serving under him in the past. Yet a 50-gun ship would carry more weight in iron than either of his two previous commands, those being 24- and 32-gun frigates.

He had served as a lieutenant on a 64- many years ago but had never stepped aboard a 50-gun ship. However, he presumed it would be similar as far as deck configuration and crew numbers were concerned. He anticipated a crew of around 350 to 400 men, all being unknown to him.

Since the time of the Peace of Amiens he had commanded frigates with two hundred and forty men aboard, many of whom had followed him from ship to ship for several years.

Stepping into the shoes of a well-respected ship's captain could be uncomfortable at first – depending on the popularity of this officer who had unfortunately been obliged to stand down. Over many missions, each captain gathered men who always sailed with him. It was quite likely that this captain, who was indisposed, would have had a lot of loyal followers.

He wondered if Captain Chilcott had been popular and how the officers and men had responded to him. Certainly not something he would trouble his mind over but he could not help considering the fact.

As for himself, not only would he be unable to muster any of his own followers, it was unlikely he would know any of the senior officers or warrant officers, their reputations, experiences, backgrounds, qualities, quirks and peccadillos. But he would quickly learn.

At the present time, he could only speculate as to his destination and had no indication of the reason the 50-gun ship was departing from Cork.

Apart from the purpose of the mission, what was the ship carrying?

He had read about the large fleet that had left Cork some weeks ago under the command of Sir Home Popham. Was this 50-gun ship heading out to join Home Popham's fleet? Or was *Royal Standard* heading on an independent mission? America, perhaps?

While the victory at Trafalgar had ended the fear of an invasion on British soil, the war in Europe was escalating, with Napoleon's insatiable appetite for power continuing unabated both by land and sea. Perhaps his destination would be the freezing waters of the Baltic Sea. He hoped not.

Above all, he hoped the previous captain has been delivered into safe hands in Cork.

Hurrying, in order to keep warm, his thoughts turned back to the things he must attend to especially those he had overlooked: to thoughts about the future of young Charles Goodridge; the Doctor; Mrs Pilkington and the question of the Portuguese child. Now there was little time available to attend to even one of those things.

'I have arranged a boat to take us directly to Bembridge,' Casson called, as the captain approached. 'That will save that confounded drive from Ryde to home.'

'Good man,' Oliver said.

'When we arrive on the beach, I'll call on two of the boys from the stable to bring your dunnage back up to the house.'

With his mind still occupied, Casson's comments hardly registered and he provided an automatic response. He knew he could rely on his steward to attend to the incidentals and was grateful to know he would be heading to sea with him.

Though his mind was still churning, he resolved he would spend the evening writing letters. A letter of thanks to his sister in London. A letter to the doctor advising him of the latest developments with apologies that it would be unlikely he would see him before he sailed. He also resolved that he must take the time to pen a letter to the Portuguese lawyer who he had never met. He did not know how long it would take correspondence to arrive in Lisbon and when, if ever, he would receive a reply. Unfortunately, that would not happen until after he had sailed.

On more mundane matters, he must instruct Casson to attend to his clothing. His uniforms would require sponging and pressing. He would require his chest to be repacked with several sets of clothing suitable for his new commission, allowing for an extended period of absence, and to accommodate a climate far warmer than the one they were presently enduring.

But his overriding thought was that within a few days, he would be back at sea and all else could be forgotten.

Chapter 8

Bembridge to Cork - Late January 1806

Rising at six o'clock in pitch darkness, Oliver splashed cold water onto his face, dressed warmly, then sat down to a breakfast prepared by the cook and served by his acting man-servant, Michael Casson. It was an unlikely union that seldom occurred and, when it did, it was usually fraught with tension.

A quick glance through the window revealed nothing to see, only a little frost in the corner of the window pane. The wind was rattling the bare branches against the roof tiles, but at least it was not raining.

With his wife still sleeping, he bade her farewell from the doorway but received no acknowledgement of his presence or of his departure. Having provided Victoria with a brief outline of his commission, on the previous evening, relating only the bare details he was aware of, he took his leave. He was relieved to be heading back to sea.

After two hours, dawn was still struggling to lighten the horizon. The journey across the island was tedious, cold and uncomfortable, the carriage rattling along the hard country road at little more than walking pace. Although Casson was seated alongside the captain in the carriage, they spoke little. Casson dozed for most of the journey while Oliver's head was occupied, as he tried to evaluate the mission before him.

On arriving at Ryde, the pair stepped aboard a local craft, the boatman happy to convey them to Spithead. With the Solent's main tide working in their favour and with sufficient wind to carry them across the water, they made an easy passage. Rather than running up on the Hard or entering the naval yard, Oliver directed the coxswain to head to the sloop, *Weymouth Lass*, anchored on Spithead. As a regular packet vessel, sailing between Portsmouth and Cork with several local ports of call on the way, the ship's hold and deck were stacked high with various items – spars, cordage, paint, tar and turpentine, and chests of copper nails, plus boxes of urgent despatches to the Port Admiral at the southern Irish port.

Though the accommodation below deck was limited, *Weymouth Lass* had berths to accommodate six passengers besides its regular crew. Privacy was limited to a curtain drawn across the front of each bunk. This morning, apart from the master, mate and deckhands, only Captain Quintrell and his steward were on board.

Three days later, before first light, Oliver was woken, by one of the sloop's crew, with the news that they had raised the coast of Ireland. Being unfamiliar with the approaches to Cork Harbour, he was eager to see all he could, especially the 50-gun ship he was about to take command of. Since receiving his orders, he had pondered long and hard on what to expect.

From his initial papers, Oliver learned that *Royal Standard* was to carry convicts. Not by the hundreds, as was the case with troops, but a nominal figure of less than fifty souls. He was familiar with the fact that, since the loss of the American states, North America was no longer available as a dumping ground for British convicts – political or otherwise. New South Wales, including the island of Van Diemen's Land was seen as a suitable destination, where a free labour source could be put to good use for the period of seven or ten years, or life as was the sentence pronounced by the courts.

The recent unrest at the Cape of Good Hope, and the departure from Cork of Sir Home Popham and Major General Baird, indicated Britain's intention of wresting Cape Town from the Dutch. If so, British convicts could be put to use in that country constructing roads, government buildings and other facilities. But a handful of white convicts in a country that already received hundreds, if not thousands of black slaves from the West African traders whenever required, seemed strange. No doubt, Oliver would learn more of the political situation in South Africa when he reached that destination.

From the choppy waters of the Celtic Sea, the enclosed harbour, said to be one of the largest natural harbours in the world, brought a pleasant calm. Sailing between the fortified headlands located on the islands situated to port and starboard, the packet boat swam into the large bay with the wharfs of Cork ahead in the distance.

Anchored amongst other ships in the sheltered waters was HMS *Royal Standard*, an impressive 50-gun ship. It was certainly not an old vessel, as Oliver had feared.

'Over there, Captain,' the *Lass*'s mate called, pointing in the direction of a two-decker. 'Your ship, I think, Sir,' he said. 'We're heading to the wharf to unload so we'll sail right by her. The Master said he'll put you ashore but he reckons if the fourth rate is expecting you, they'll send a boat to collect you.'

'Thank you,' Oliver said, pulling his boat cloak across his chest. Sailing around the vessel would indeed give him the opportunity to look at her lines and see how much weed she was dragging. The opportunity to look inside her would come soon enough.

'I'll have your dunnage brought on deck.'

Oliver thanked the mate again. 'Kindly speak with my steward.'

Swimming smoothly into the harbour, *Weymouth Lass* drifted neatly to its mooring at the town dock, joining a line of traders and victualling barges that were also tied up there. Extending along the dockside were hundreds of barrels, stacked high, ready for loading onto waiting ships. The crimson coats of the marines guarding them brought a splash of colour to the otherwise dismal picture.

Gunpowder was Oliver's first thought.

At the very moment the captain was ready to step from the sloop, a naval boat from *Royal Standard* ran up alongside.

'Captain Quintrell?' the midshipman enquired. Oliver nodded. 'Lieutenant Brophy is expecting you. If you would care to step aboard, the men will attend to your dunnage.'

From his position sitting in the stern sheets, Oliver liked what he saw. *Royal Standard* was neither old, nor was she a larger vessel that had been razeed to 50-guns. She appeared to have been newly coppered and there was little growth of weed or attachment of barnacles on her hull – perhaps she had been out of the water quite recently.

Gazing up at *Royal Standard*, he was able to observe the ship from top mast to waterline. Being in harbour, most of her square sails were neatly furled to the yards, her staysails also. He was impressed. She was a fine looking ship, boasting two fighting decks. He estimated no more than six years of age with few marks upon her. He could not have wished for more, at this particular time.

She was certainly not the largest fully rigged ship in Cork's harbour, being dwarfed by a 64- and a 74-gun man-of-war, but she was slightly larger than the frigates he had commanded over the last few years. While he was eager to familiarize himself with his new commission, it appeared that several sailors loitering near the rails and lingering in the rigging were also assessing the cut of their new captain. Absorbing everything he saw, Oliver was satisfied to find the hands appeared to be sober and quiet. An encouraging start.

As the cutter rounded the stern, he was impressed with the ornate carvings around the quarter and stern galleries, reminiscent of the great ships of an earlier era. They could have easily graced any sized ship of the line. The number of gunports, piercing the sides on two decks, was equal to almost all of her 50 guns. But her length and beam fell far short of the navy's larger ships.

Having never sailed a 50-gun ship, he could only rely on hearsay. He had heard they were slow, did not sail well and were far less manoeuvrable than frigates – hence some of the reasons they were not popular. Yet, they still had a place in the hierarchy of naval vessels. Fifties were classed as fourth rates and did not stand in line in a battle.

Hopefully, on this cruise, he would not meet with much action, but with 50 guns at his command, Oliver was confident he would be well equipped to defend Britain's naval reputation, should he be called upon to do so.

Half an hour later, with his sea chest balanced across the thwarts in the bow, the naval jolly boat slid against the hull of the 50-gun ship.

Climbing the wooden steps to the entry port, Oliver stepped aboard to the high pitched peep of the boatswains' pipes. Lifting his hat respectfully to the ship, he glanced down to the waist where a mob of seamen had congregated. These men were also gazing up to assess the appearance of their new captain.

Lined up on the quarterdeck were the ship's officers waiting to meet him. A lieutenant stepped forward and presented himself. 'Brophy, First Lieutenant,' he said. 'Welcome aboard, Captain.' The Irish accent was unmistakeable.

Oliver acknowledged the officer and then, as he walked along the line, made a cursory inspection of the other officers presented to him. It was as much as he intended to do for the present. Foremost in his mind was to open his orders and then read his commission.

'Mr Holland will show you to your quarters, Captain,' Mr Brophy said. 'I have some pressing matters to attend to.'

There was no apology offered but Oliver ignored that omission, inclined his head very slightly and followed the midshipman as directed.

On turning from the quarterdeck, he noted some sideways glances from a few of the midshipmen and wondered what prompted those expressions. Was it that he was a mere post captain occupying the quarters often allocated to a commander of higher rank? Were there concerns as to the kind of captain he would be? Apprehensions? Jealousies? Perhaps. But these were not new or unexpected responses. They were the sorts any astute captain would note when he first joined a ship.

Removing his hat, Oliver ducked his head and followed the third lieutenant through the door near the helm and entered a formal dining cabin. It occupied half the width of the deck on the port side.

It was impressive. The room was light and airy but, above all, sumptuously furnished. A large polished oak table with carvel legs occupied much of the centre of the room. It was elegantly set with crystal glasses, silver cutlery, and fine china dinner plates decorated with the letters *R* and *S* in gilt paint. The table had eight settings. Standing at each end of the table was a pair of branching candelabra. The wicks of the candles had never been lit.

Moving aft through the dining room, Mr Holland opened the far door and stepped back to allow the captain access to the great cabin – a room of even greater dimensions, stretching the full width of the ship, complete with side windows to the quarter gallery and an outdoor walkway at the stern offering a 180 degree view over the sea.

The polished table in the great cabin was large enough to seat a dozen guests quite adequately, though there were no chairs around it. Currently it was bedecked only with navigational charts – two lying flat, while several others were rolled up and tied with ribbons. The door to the outside gallery was closed but, like the array of windows overlooking it and those on the side, it was panelled in glass. Oliver's thoughts flashed back to his friend, Captain Boris Crabthorne – *Boris the Florist*, who had converted his gallery into a small botanical garden.

Such space and opulence was something Oliver Quintrell had never had the luxury of before for his personal use. Negative thoughts flashed to the damage he had witnessed in ships of the line that had been raked through the stern windows – the enemy's shot having smashed through the bulwarks of the aft cabins and barrelled through to the quarterdeck, slicing through men and furnishings indiscriminately.

While he was impressed with the fittings aboard the 50-gun ship, his face revealed nothing of his feelings.

Numerous books filled the shelves, held in place by narrow polished wooden fiddles. They were, no doubt, the property of the previous captain.

'These furnishings,' Oliver asked, while admiring the velvet curtains and cherry red upholstery on the chairs, 'are they due to be removed, or do they remain?'

The young lieutenant followed the captain's gaze. 'I understand they will remain. Captain Chilcott's personal items were packed in chests and removed from the ship and delivered ashore when we were in Cork.' The officer paused. 'Might I enquire about your personal property, Captain? Will your furnishings be coming aboard shortly?'

'Unfortunately, no. News of my commission came as a surprise and with only short notice, I had insufficient time to organise anything more than my personal dunnage. My steward, Michael Casson, is attending to it. I will instruct him to speak with you.'

'In that case, Captain, let me show you to your sleeping quarters. This way, please.'

Opening the door from the great cabin, revealed a room almost the size of the dining cabin but this was on the starboard side of the ship. On entering, Oliver immediately sniffed the air, inhaled deeply then sniffed again.

The cabin was more than adequate in size, despite the black barrel of a 24-pound cannon abutting a closed gunport. His cot, hanging from the overhead beams and hiding half of the gun, was oriented forward and aft. For the present, being in port, the cot was showing no indication to swing. An elegant chair and writing desk were set against the centre wall. Another small table, with a china bowl and jug upon it, covered in an embroidered linen cloth, completed the furnishings. One door at the forward end provided for a private water closet. The second door led to a small cabin to be occupied by the captain's steward. That small room had direct access through to the quarterdeck.

But it was an unhealthy odour that disturbed the captain. It was quite overpowering. 'What on earth is that smell? Are there animals housed on the deck below?'

Mr Holland was quick to reply. 'No Captain, the wardroom and the lieutenants' cabins are directly below us. The manger is forward on the orlop deck.'

The captain was quite familiar with the configuration of ships of 50-guns or more. He sniffed again and looked across the black and white checkerboard pattern of tiles on the floor to an area part concealed from view by the gun's carriage and the embroidered white petticoat, skirting the cot.

'What is that?' he stated, pointing at what appeared to be a pile of shaggy damp rugs.

'Oh, that, Sir, that's Cecil. Were you not told about him?'

Oliver looked closer. 'And what pray tell me, is Cecil? I was not informed I was to share my quarters with some creature dragged up from the deep.'

'It's Captain Chilcott's dog, sir. It couldn't go to the hospital with him when he was carried ashore, so he made us promise we would keep him here and mind him until he returned. Then, when we heard the news that the captain had died, no one knew what was to become of him.'

'And what am I meant to do with him?' Oliver Quintrell asked.

'You don't have to do anything, Captain. Chalmers, one of Captain Chilcott's servants cares for him. He feeds him and swims him every day while we are in port. He's very loyal. He's been with the captain for three years now.'

'Who has? The dog or the servant?'

'Both, I think. Inseparable, they were – that is Captain Chilcott and Cecil. The dog always shared the captain's berth. Always slept under his cot. Never let anyone go near him without his say-so.'

'And you expect me to sleep in a cabin that stinks of wet dog. I do not think so. Get the animal out of here and send for Captain Chilcott's servant. I wish to speak with him this instant.'

'I'm not sure Cecil will want to move.'

'I beg your pardon, Mister.'

'I'll get Chalmers right away. He's waiting outside,' Mr Holland said, before heading to the door.

At the sound of raised English voices, the hairy animal stretched out its front paws, raised its head, yawned and crawled out from where it had been sleeping against the gun carriage beneath the swinging cot.

'Goodness,' Oliver heaved, 'It's the size of a small bear. What on earth is it?'

'It's a Newfie, Captain. Came from Newfoundland. That's an island in North America.'

'I am quite familiar with the geography of the world, Mr Holland.'

'Sorry, sir.'

Appearing to know it was being discussed, the large hairy dog slunk to the centre of the cabin and shook itself vigorously from head to tail. Fortunately, the coat – six inches long all over, though damp and matted, was not wet. The animal was completely black in colour apart from one short dirty white boot. After loosening its shaggy coat, it ignored the midshipman and proceeded to sniff the captain's ankles.

Not knowing how protective the canine had been to its previous master, Captain Quintrell remained still.

'Cecil,' a voice called from the doorway. 'Sit, dog.' The command came from a sailor Oliver had not seen enter.

'Chalmers,' the midshipman interrupted, as if by way of introduction. 'He's been minding the hound for some time now.'

'Indeed,' the captain replied.

'It's obvious he likes you, Capt'n,' Chalmers added. 'He doesn't always take kindly to strangers entering his room.'

'I beg your pardon,' Oliver replied, 'but I believe this is now my cabin!'

'I'm afraid the dog's been here for a long time, Capt'n, and regards it as his den.'

'Is that so? Well, it is now time to find the mongrel some new accommodation.'

The sailor's mouth dropped. 'He won't like that.'

'Won't he indeed? What about your berth?' the captain responded. 'You are obviously familiar with the animal and its needs. Perhaps it can sleep with you.'

Chalmers shook his head, 'I don't think so, sir. I rig my hammock on the mess deck with two hundred and fifty others. There's hardly room for the men to breathe in there and certainly no room for a large dog. Besides, there are already two monkeys, several pet rabbits, a cat, a goose and a parrot. I don't think they would get on too well.'

Oliver could hardly believe what he was hearing. It was apparent that other than dropping the dog over the side, the problem was not going to be resolved in a hurry. 'That is not acceptable,' he said. 'For the present, take him through to the great cabin put him out on the stern gallery. That might at least reduce the smell a little.'

'Smell?' Chalmers said. 'I keep him clean, Captain,' he argued.

'Indeed. And I say, no more swimming him. I have no wish for sea water washing across this floor.'

'If you say so, sir.'

'I do say so.'

'Might I get his rug from behind your cot, Captain? It's what he sleeps on. Captain Chilcott said the dog could have it.'

'Get it and get out!' Though barely raising his voice, the captain's tone could easily be read. Leaning down, the sailor reached for the near threadbare piece of carpet and pulled it from under the gun carriage. It looked wet and smelled as bad as the mutt, if not worse.

'Chalmers, do as the Captain says. Put the dog outside on the gallery,' the lieutenant ordered, before turning back to the new captain. 'He's popular with the men, Captain, and he's a very good ratter.'

Oliver resisted a smile and withheld the obvious question. 'That may be so,' he replied. 'However, the stern gallery will suffice for now.'

'Come along, Cecil,' the sailor called, but the Newfoundland dropped on its haunches and refused to move.

'Out!' Oliver yelled.

The dog responded with a single deep bark but made no effort to rise.

'Get him out!'

'Yes, Capt'n. Going, this minute, Capt'n.' With that the sailor leaned over the animal and wrapping his arm around it lifted it just clear of the ground and half carried, half dragged the heavy beast through the great cabin and on to the outside walkway.

Shaking his head in disbelief, Oliver watched as the dog was pushed outside into the fresh breeze.

'I can tell you, sir, that dog has been used to sharing his space with Captain Chilcott for a long time. I knew he wouldn't move voluntarily.'

Oliver shook his head again. Stories of dogs, cats, birds, reptiles and other animals being taken aboard ship by sailors and officers alike was not new. Even recently on the dock at Portsmouth, he had heard mention of Lord Collingwood's dog, *Bounce*, and both a cat and pug-dog that had been rescued from the *Santissima Trinidad* when it was sinking after the battle of Trafalgar.

He remembered reading of Captain James Cook on his second circumnavigation of the globe, being saved from near death after being fed a nourishing broth made from the pet dog owned by one of the gentleman scientists. Then he considered, Cecil – the great lump of a hound being manhandled out to the gallery. Weighing at least 150 pounds, there was enough meat on it to feed half a dozen dying men, if the necessity arose.

Then the thought of dogs served to rattle his memory. As a boy, when he sailed with his father, there had always been a dog on board – its job was to guard the ship and deter any unwanted visitors whenever they made port.

The officer interrupted his thoughts, 'Shall I ask your steward to bring you something, Captain?'

'Thank you, yes. Coffee,' Oliver replied, than added, 'and call one of the hands to mop up that pool of water.'

'Yes, right away, Captain.'

'And ask Mr Brophy to call all hands – I will speak with the men directly.'

From his cabin, Oliver could hear the peeps of the boatswain's whistle and the rumble of feet bouncing on the steps in response to the call.

By the time he emerged onto the quarterdeck, a distance of only a few strides from his quarters, he was confronted by a sea of faces lining the gangways and for'ard deck and in the ship's waist. Many of the sailors wore striped breeches and white shirts – though the shirts were mainly hidden beneath woollen jumpers, pea jackets, blankets and hand-knitted scarfs. It was a considerable company of men.

The marines, assembled along the gangways were distinctive in bright red coatees with white cross belts and tall shakos. The ship's officers were lined up on the quarterdeck. Oliver again noticed a few half smiles exchanged between the midshipmen. No doubt the Newfoundland dog was the reason for their amusement.

The first lieutenant's first words confirmed this. 'You met the captain's dog?' Lieutenant Brophy asked, with a smirk.

'I presume you are referring to Captain Chilcott's dog.'

The lieutenant lifted his hand to his mouth and coughed weakly. 'Indeed, sir. Beg pardon. Course of habit.'

Oliver Quintrell was not amused. 'Tell me, Lieutenant, what more is there to know of this canine that has not already been shared with me? I trust you don't have any other hidden surprises in store. Perhaps it has a mate or there is a litter of pups hidden in a barrel somewhere. Or a pet python in the privy?'

'The dog has been aboard for a long time, Captain. I presume it came aboard when Captain Chilcott took up his commission aboard *Royal Standard*.'

Mr Holland interrupted, volunteering an answer. 'Begging your pardon, sir, but that is not the case. The captain acquired the dog during the Peace in 1802. At the time, the Island of Newfoundland had a surfeit of the animals and several dozen were offered to various naval vessels. I was advised that Captain Chilcott was happy to take one. I was also told that several of the men would have also taken a dog but there was nowhere aboard ship to house them.'

Lieutenant Brophy was quick to respond. 'The dog's presence is common knowledge amongst the crew. It lives on a diet of rats which it catches in the hold every night.'

'Then, at least, it serves a useful purpose,' Oliver said. 'I would like to see it at work one night. Evidenced by its size, I am sure it is very industrious. Carry on, Mr Brophy.'

Chapter 9

Lieutenant Brophy

Oliver Quintrell turned to the first lieutenant. 'What is the situation regarding Captain Chilcott?'

'His personal belongings have been removed but his furnishings remain.'

Oliver nodded. 'Is the surgeon aboard?'

'Yes, Captain, Dr Hannaford came aboard early this morning.'

'Then I will speak with him in due course. But first, tell me, how many souls does *Royal Standard* carry?'

'We have three hundred and fifty names in the muster book.'

'Is that sufficient crew for a 50-gun ship?'

The lieutenant did not answer immediately. 'A dozen ran when we dropped anchor here in Cork.'

'So we are already short of that number?'

The lieutenant nodded.

'Do you regards three hundred and thirty-eight men enough to work a 50-gun ship?'

After waiting a few moments and receiving no reply, Oliver continued. 'Are most of the hands Irish?'

'Yes, they are, as are several of the officers.' Brophy said.

'Including yourself?' Oliver ventured.

'Yes, sir. Born in County Wicklow.'

'Indeed.'

'Were you aware of Captain Chilcott's sailing orders when you left port two weeks ago? Did you know where the ship was heading?'

'A course was set for the South Atlantic,' Lieutenant Brophy said. 'We had made three day's passage when the captain became incapacitated.'

'Very unfortunate.'

The lieutenant showed no sign of agreement. 'I was prepared to step up and continue along that course until the captain was fit to return to his duties.'

'But that never happened?'

Conscious of the lieutenant's reluctance to answer more questions on the subject, Oliver decided to vacate the quarterdeck. 'I believe we should continue this conversation in my cabin later. Join me when you are ready.'

Ten minutes later, the pair was sitting opposite each other at the table in the great cabin.

Tell me more, Mr Brophy. Did anything in particular prompt the captain's illness?' Oliver asked.

'He had a fall on the very day we left harbour. The doctor examined him at the time and found a lump on his head where he had struck it, but otherwise he found the captain to be well.'

'And then?'

'Two days later, the captain could hardly speak – or walk, for that matter. Though he had periods when he was quite lucid, I thought some rest would put him to rights and suggested he take to his bed for a few days. I was quite capable of stepping up to the captain's responsibilities in the meantime.'

Oliver's eyebrows rose involuntarily. 'This was your opinion?' he queried.

'Yes, sir.'

'And the doctor's opinion?'

'He was concerned about the captain's condition. In his view, he argued that his patient needed hospital care and that the ship should return to port.'

'And during his periods of lucidity, did Captain Chilcott express an opinion.'

Lieutenant Brophy paused for a moment. 'He seemed more concerned about the men held below deck – the scoundrels, thieves and brigands.'

'And what had raised that concern?'

'He had ordered the carpenter to build an additional compound on the foredeck – to serve as an outdoor exercise area for the convicts when we were at sea.'

'For a period of several months, at least.' Oliver added. 'And were you in agreement with this order?'

'Not exactly,' the lieutenant replied. The structure he wanted would have occupied almost the entire fo'c'sle and taken up the valuable time of the carpenters and other hands.'

'So you would have the prisoners confined below deck for the duration of the cruise?'

'I could see no reason not to. Not a single one of them is worth doing favours for, if you don't mind me saying.'

'And did you and the captain argue on this matter?'

'I expressed my opinion.'

Oliver did not respond to the comment. 'I would like to visit the orlop deck and see for myself the conditions the convicts are confined in.'

'But you wanted to inspect the officers and read in your commission.'

'I am not short on memory, Mr Brophy,' Oliver said, gazing at the man who he had already taken a wary dislike to. 'I repeat: I wish to inspect the conditions below decks before we sail. Do I make myself clear?'

The lieutenant nodded and moved to the great cabin door, holding it open for the captain to exit.

Descending from the lower deck, the absence of fresh air on the orlop deck was evident. With no windows or portholes or gun ports, there was not a flicker of movement in the air. Below that, in the hold, was the ship's ballast along with bilge water and barrels. The stagnant air was unhealthy – its only escape was to rise upwards to the orlop deck – the area where the prisoners were confined.

Captain Quintrell had witnessed appalling conditions in slave ships, but never stepped aboard a convict transport ship. Surprisingly, though only catering for a small number of prisoners, the conditions on the 50-'s deck reminded him of a slaver. However, as the convicts had only been brought aboard a few weeks ago, and they had spent only a short time at sea, the deck had remained relatively clean and the smell was bearable, however, he doubted it would remain in that state for much longer.

As used in the slave trade, chains ran along the boards to be attached to each man's leg irons at night. Presently the convicts, housed in the wooden cage, sat about in clusters, their wrists and ankles shackled. Bunches of spare shackles hung from hooks in the deck beams.

The simple sleeping berths consisted of large shelves fastened to the side of the hull – each shelf wide enough to accommodate three men. Apart from the sleeping berths, there were no tables or benches. There was nothing to occupy the men during the day.

In Oliver's opinion, such conditions could only foster mischievous thoughts and subversive chatter.

As most of the orlop deck was below the waterline, the hull wept constantly and shone in the light of the glim. No doubt the convicts, whose places on the sleeping berth were against the ship's hull, would constantly have wet backs.

With only one lantern swinging from the central deck beam, the gloom made it difficult to see from one end of the confine to the other. The men's dirty grey clothing, highlighted only with the stamp of a broad arrow did little to help; it merely enhanced the pallid expressions they wore. But above the noise of the men rattling the wooden bars of their compound, it was the whisper of Gaelic voices that alerted the captain's ears.

Pushing events from past missions out of his mind, Oliver Quintrell resumed the conversation with his first lieutenant from where they had broken off.

'There is no air circulating down here,' the captain commented. 'Do you not see it necessary to permit these men a little fresh air and exercise every day? Are you hoping to land all forty-six convicts alive when we reach our destination?'

The lieutenant merely looked across to the faces staring back at him from their wooden cage and sniffed.

Oliver continued. 'How many do you think will succumb to the voyage before we reach Cape Town?'

'Ain't they condemned men, anyway?' he asked.

'In your opinion, they obviously are.'

The prisoners shuffled about, no doubt taking heed of the conversation.

'I see there are boys housed with the men,' Oliver said. 'How many boys are amongst them?

'Three. That's how they arrived from Dublin. Just one consignment.'

'These men that you and Captain Chilcott argued over – are some of these felons political prisoners?'

'No, just scum brought down from *Kilmainham Gaol* in Dublin. Sentenced to transportation across and beyond the seas.'

'And their condition when they came aboard – how would you describe them?'

The lieutenant's brow furrowed, as he looked at the mob for an answer.

Oliver waited, then interrupted. 'Were they fit or half-starved and suffering from depravation and punishments? Were they manacled and how many were chained together?'

'I have a list of names for you, Captain.'

Could the man not answer a straight question? Oliver thought. 'I would appreciate your personal observations and appraisal.'

The lieutenant shrugged his shoulders before he replied. 'They all appeared to be in reasonable health when they came aboard. The doctor examined them at that time and found no signs of contagion or fever. They are all males varying in age from seven to seventy years. They were shackled, both hands and feet, when they came aboard, but when we had been at sea for a day, Captain Chilcott ordered the shackles to be removed.'

'Indeed,' Oliver said, 'and now?'

'When we returned to Cork, I ordered them to be shackled again. I was concerned for the safely of the crew should word get out that the captain was indisposed, in case they took in into their heads to run.'

'To whom are you referring – the convicts or the ship's crew?'

'The prisoners, Captain.'

Oliver sighed. 'I understand your concern, Mr Brophy, however, in my opinion, if there is going to be any attempt to escape it will occur while the ship is in port and not on the high seas. I will review the situation when we sail and speak with you about it.'

The lieutenant continued, 'One other things; we also have fifty soldiers aboard. Infantry men of the 24th Regiment. They were initially due to sail with Sir Home Popham's fleet but they arrived too late for the transports. They've been idling in Cork for over two months. It's them that are making the hullaballoo you can hear.'

'Indeed.'

'And where are both groups destined for?'

'I don't exactly know. I was never told.'

'I have seen enough,' the captain said. 'Kindly return to the deck and have the ship made ready to sail.'

'Aye aye, Captain.'

'I presume you are familiar with Cork Harbour?'

'Yes, sir, I have navigated it many times.'

'Then when the tide is running, take her out. In the morning, I will talk with the doctor, and will speak with you further about the convicts when we are at sea.'

Oliver noticed a slight curl in the corner of the lieutenant's lips and wondered what had prompted that response.

'Aye, Captain,' Lieutenant Brophy said.

The light was dimming, as dusk fell, though it was only 3.30 in the afternoon, the captain was anxious to depart before darkness engulfed the harbour waters.

With the ship's crew assembled on the foredeck and in the waist, and the contingent of soldiers lined up along the gangways, Captain Quintrell read in his commission. Having the whole crew in attendance, if not, perhaps giving their full attention, he proceeded to outline his expectations of the men and to remind them of the Naval *Articles of War*, even though most seamen knew the words by rote. With those formalities attended to, he deferred to the first lieutenant, who called all hands to stations for leaving harbour.

With only pinpricks of lights flickering in the houses surrounding the bay and lanterns swaying on the nearby ships and victualling barges still servicing some of the other vessels moored nearby, the anchor was raised from the harbour floor, staysails run up and topsails set. With the assistance of the ebbing tide, *Royal Standard* swam from the Irish harbour with ease.

A fresh north-west breeze caught the square canvas, as the ship cleared the twin forts and sailed from Cork Harbour into the grey Celtic Sea. Under a full head of sail, His Majesty's Ship *Royal Standard* headed south-west to meet the rolling swell of the North Atlantic.

Meeting the chop of the ocean was enough to fill Oliver Quintrell with renewed vigour. The sooner he had time to stand on the deck and fill his lungs with sea air, the better. But there were matters to attend to; the most pressing was to speak with the doctor.

Having visited the cockpit early the following morning, the captain had invited the doctor to the great cabin. There were pressing matters he wanted to hear the doctor's opinion on and preferred to have that conversation in private.

'Please sit,' the captain said, indicating to a chair across the table from him. Dr Hannaford accepted the invitation, flipped up the tails of his coat and sat down. He was a man considerably older than the captain, his face furrowed with the lines of age and experience.

'Tell me in your own words, Dr Hannaford, what transpired with Captain Chilcott that necessitated the ship's return to port? Was he unwell when he sailed from England?'

'I'm afraid I cannot help you, Captain. I am in the same position as you, having only stepped aboard *Royal Standard* four weeks ago.'

'Is this your first warrant?'

'No,' the doctor replied, not elaborating on his answer but sliding a bundle of papers across the desk toward the captain.

Oliver continued. 'Then I must ask for the benefit of any knowledge you have of the short time you spent aboard this ship, from leaving harbour to the time you returned only two weeks ago.'

The doctor appeared quite comfortable sharing what he knew. 'The first officer, Mr Brophy, was the one to inform me of Captain Chilcott's ill health, though he failed to elaborate as to how long he had been suffering or exactly what the malady was.'

'So the captain was already sick when the ship first sailed from Cork?'

'That may well have been the case, however I cannot say, as I never examined him prior to sailing.'

'Did the lieutenant consult you about a fall the captain had had resulting in a bruise to the head?'

'He did, but I felt it had no bearing on the malady the doctor was suffering from. Lieutenant Brophy insisted the captain would get well, saying that Captain Chilcott had suffered falls before and recovered. He was adamant there was no cause for concern and that if anything dire happened, or should the situation worsen, he would immediately assume command and proceed on the same course heading south.'

'Lieutenant Brophy said that?'

'In no uncertain terms.'

'How did this state of affairs strike you?'

'Unusual, to say the least. It was as if he was pre-empting the captain's demise. But who am I to question the operations of a fighting ship. I am merely a physician engaged to assist the sick and dying, and had stepped aboard the ship only a few days before we sailed.'

'Indeed. And, to the best of your knowledge, were you alone in your way of thinking?'

Doctor Hannaford paused for a moment before committing himself to an answer. 'I expressed my opinion quite openly in the wardroom, that the captain should have been admitted to the hospital or at least referred to a surgeon in the town before we sailed. The sailing master and the second lieutenant were in agreement. Later, when the situation worsened, they also argued with Lieutenant Brophy that the ship should return to Cork or enter a British port as they felt the captain needed more than the services I could offer.'

'Did that offend you?'

'Indeed, it did not.'

'They felt that the Captain should be admitted to a hospital?'

'That is correct. While Lieutenant Brophy, as acting Captain, said that returning to port would delay the mission.'

'In your opinion, doctor, was Captain Chilcott in a fit state to command the ship?'

'No, he was not.'

'Did you ague this point with the first lieutenant?

'Lieutenant Brophy reminded me that he was the acting captain and that he had made the decision to proceed and not return.'

'And why do you think that was so?'

The doctor was hesitant with his answer. 'Perhaps because the further we were from land, the less chance there was of getting the patient to a hospital. Or because he wanted to take charge of the ship?'

'That is quite an accusation, sir.'

'You did ask my opinion, Captain, and I gave it.'

'Indeed, I did.'

'Was the First Lieutenant conversant with Captain Chilcott's sailing orders?'

'I cannot answer that question, though I presume the Captain would have shared that information with his first officer.'

'And Mr Brophy continued to insist that the captain would regain his health?'

'He did,' the doctor said.

The captain considered for a moment. 'So who made the final decision to return to Cork?'

'It was Captain Chilcott himself.'

110

Oliver was puzzled. 'How was that possible?'

'One day, while three of the officers were sitting with him, he suddenly rallied and for a short time spoke quite lucidly. Naturally, I was called and heard him order the ship to be turned around and returned to Cork. With the order coming from the captain himself, there was nothing the lieutenant could do but pass the order to the officer of the watch to order the helmsman to alter course.'

'And the other officers accepted the change.'

'Why would they question it? It came from Captain Chilcott's own lips. As such, all hands were called and the ship was put about.'

'And did the captain remain in reasonable health until you made the Irish coast?'

'No, sir. He declined very rapidly over the next two days and was barely conscious when we dropped anchor. I remained with him for most of that time.'

'And what was the captain's condition when you transferred him to the hospital in Cork?'

'As no doubt you have heard, he died the following night. Had he remained aboard and died at sea, the first lieutenant would have got his wish.'

Oliver considered that statement for a moment. 'Thank you, Doctor, I appreciate your candour.'

When the doctor left the great cabin, Oliver pondered on the news he had just received. Taking time to examine the papers the doctor had provided, he was satisfied his qualification, character and experiences both on land and sea were admirable.

That evening, having invited the officers to join him for supper in the dining cabin, Oliver took the opportunity to relate a short anecdote which seemed fitting in the light of the loss of Captain Chilcott.

'Gentlemen, as you may have heard, I recently attended the funeral of Admiral Viscount Lord Nelson. It was a lengthy, yet stately, affair stretching over several days. As you can imagine during that time many stories were told of life in the navy and of lives that were sold cheaply on some of His Majesty's ships. However, there was a ring of truth about all the stories coming from Nelson's flag ship, HMS *Victory* and the brave men who served aboard her.

'When Lord Nelson fell, struck down by a musket ball fired by a marksman from the upper rigging of the French ship, *Redoubtable*, he passed word to his flag officer, Captain Hardy, to advise Lord Collingwood to signal the fleet for all ships, including the captured prizes, to drop anchor due to the fear of an impending storm.'

He paused and looked at the faces around him. 'That order, which Nelson had pronounced, was never officially followed, or it was ignored, or countermanded somewhere along the line. The truth of that matter is yet to be ascertained. But, no doubt, you have heard the outcome. The storm that hit the coast was said to be the worst in a century. A virtual hurricane of wind blew from the Atlantic and hit the fleet off Cape Trafalgar almost immediately after the battle. As a result, four valuable prizes that had not been secured were swept onto the lee shore or sank due to the damage they had suffered. As a result, many lives were lost.

'Having been aware of the impending storm, Lord Nelson in his wisdom, although he was dying, had the foresight to see the likely disaster about to unfold. From the ships' decks, the sailors could do nothing but watch as the prizes, they had fought hard to win, were dashed to matchwood and the prize money they should have received sank with them.'

Mumbled comments passed around the table.

'Gentlemen, I say this to you, Captain Chilcott, who I never had the pleasure of meeting, was obviously an astute man and, despite his illness, like Lord Nelson, his main concern was for the safely of his ship and the welfare of his crew. He made the correct call by ordering his ship to return to Cork.' Oliver pondered in his mind what might have happened if *Royal Standard* had not returned to port and the Captain had died at sea.

As there was no response or comment from those around the table, he considered they had missed the analogy.

'Begging your pardon, Captain, but did you fight at Trafalgar?' one of the midshipmen asked, immediately changing the subject.

'No, I did not, for two reasons. Firstly, I was serving on the Jamaica station when the fleet departed. And secondly, my recent commands had been frigates and not ships of the line.'

'So, Gentlemen, let us set our sights forward and not dwell on past events that cannot be changed. I propose a toast, to a sound ship, a safe voyage and fair winds.

'Join me, Gentlemen, if you please.'

Chapter 10

The convicts

'Thornhill, Capt'n. Ship's carpenter. You asked to see me.'

'Indeed,' Oliver said. 'Come in and close the door.'

The carpenter pulled the knitted hat from his head, releasing a tangle of brown curls belying the fact he was possibly twenty years older than Captain Quintrell. Away from his usual surrounding, swathed in clouds of sawdust-filled air, the artisan looked uncomfortable in the pristine elegance of the great cabin. As a hardy tar and integral part of the ship's company, he swayed from one foot to the other, even though the deck was relatively still.

'Relax, Mr Thornhill.'

'Aye, Capt'n.'

'I just need you to answer a few questions for me.'

The carpenter nodded – the look of apprehension continuing to weigh heavily on his face.

'How long have you been with this ship?'

'*Royal Standard*? Near on six months.'

'Indeed. Tell me about her.'

The carpenter's brow furrowed deeper for a moment, wondering why the ship's captain would ask such a question of him. Then, discounting the reason, he gave the question due consideration and spoke. 'She's sound, she is. Built in ninety-eight. Only seven years old. Been used mainly as a troop carrier, I was told. No rot. No worm. And, last time I checked, not an inch of water in the well. Stone and gravel ballast. Spars are all good and plenty of spares. Masts are sound and securely stepped. I can vouch for that.' He paused. 'But she's been lucky, Captain. Never had a broadside levelled against her. Never suffered a fire below deck or on board. Never been in tropical waters and never run aground. Bottom's clean. She was careened only a few months ago, and the copper plating is new and all in tact. I checked it myself. Not much weed to speak of. Best ship I've ever served on,' he said, then added, 'though there's them what sails her might say different.'

'And why would that be, Mr Thornhill?'

'She's not a fast sailer. Eight or nine knots at best, if you're lucky. And she can yaw a bit when running a straight course.'

'Indeed. And what of her guns?'

'Not heavy enough to make it into the line. Fifties are not popular any more. She'll probably end up carrying cargo or troops or being razeed to a hulk.'

'As for the iron – you'd best ask the gunner or boatswain, Capt'n. But I can say all the trucks are sound. I checked the wheels only yesterday.'

'I understand you erected the enclosure on the orlop deck to confine the prisoners.'

The carpenter nodded, still wondering what the questions were leading to. 'Me and me mates. We built that soon after we arrived in Cork about a month ago.'

'Have you seen the manner in which the hulls in Portsmouth harbour were converted to become prison hulks?'

'No, sir, I've only eyed 'em across the water from the Portsmouth dockyard.'

'Are you satisfied with the structure you built.'

'It's not for me to say, Captain. I just did what I was asked. It serves the purpose, but I wouldn't like to be held on the orlop for any length of time. Foul air down there.'

'I understand Captain Chilcott intended to have an exercise compound built on the fo'c'sle.'

'I did hear a murmur about it, but nothing came of it.'

Oliver acknowledged. 'I need you to construct a small compound on the foredeck with enough space for a dozen men to exercise during daylight hours. I will instruct the blacksmith and cooper to assist you. Do you have sufficient timber?'

'Yes, sir, we got plenty on board.'

'Good. I want you to start tomorrow. And when that is done, divide off an area separate from the main mob on the orlop deck, large enough to accomodate the boys. Do you understand?'

'Aye, Captain. You intend to quarter the boys on their own?'

'The captain nodded. 'Just one more question and I will not detain you any longer. Do we have a schoolmaster aboard?'

'Yes, Captain. Greenstreet is his name. Pleasant fellow. About my age. He instructs the young gentlemen – some of them barely sensible enough to be weaned off their mother's tits, if you ask me.'

'Thank you, Mr Thornhill. You have been most helpful.'

'Begging your pardon, Capt'n,' the carpenter ventured to ask when he reached the door. 'Are we likely to see action on this cruise?'

'I cannot say,' Oliver replied honestly. 'We are not chasing any action but the Frogs are ever vigilant and, no doubt, will be seeking some sort of revenge for the drubbing they received at Trafalgar.'

'Were you there, Captain?'

'Sadly, no.'

With that the chippie knuckled his forehead, pulling his woollen cap over his unruly locks and departed the great cabin.

Stepping down into the hold at the bottom of the ship, the captain adjusted his eyes to the gloom. Sitting at his horse, amidships, the cooper was constructing a new barrel. 'I understand you have a problem, Mr Larkin.'

Without standing up from his work, the cooper pulled off his hat and scratched his bald head. 'No, sir. Managing just fine.'

Oliver quizzed him again. 'Come along, man, that is not what I heard. Kindly explain yourself. I cannot read your thoughts.'

The old artisan stopped and rubbed his fist on his leather apron. 'Well, it's like this, Capt'n. Problem is that when we sailed to Ireland under Captain Chilcott, no one told me about the additional cargo I had to make space for.'

'You are referring to the convicts brought down from Dublin. Am I not correct?'

'No, it weren't that, Captain.'

'The additional soldiers, then?'

'Not that either. We'd heard there were prisoners for transportation, so them extra guards was necessary. I can tell you, none of the crew was too happy about convicts 'cause a fair few of the lads are Irish and some were sympathetic to the rebels. Most folk know of at least one person taken to *Kilmainham Gaol* during the ninety-eight and later skirmishes. Some know of those that were hung whilst in there.'

That almost a third of the crew was Irish was no surprise to Oliver Quintrell. That fact applied to most British ships. He'd been reminded, only recently, that of the men who'd fought on Nelson's flagship, *Victory*, ninety-four were Irishmen. However, the revelation that many aboard the *Royal Standard* could be Irish sympathisers surprised him. 'I trust we don't have a rebel crew on board,' he added.

'Don't worry, Captain, there's been Irishmen on every ship I've ever served on, but what they think is their affair and, for most, it's never spoken of.'

'Indeed. But if that is not the problem concerning you, what is it?'

'It was all them extra barrels we had to find room for in the hold. We loaded them off the wharf only a week ago.'

'I see no problem with a well-stocked ship.'

'No, Captain, you don't understand. It weren't wine or beer, or spuds or pease. It was powder, Capt'n. One hundred and fifty barrels of gunpowder.'

Oliver knew nothing of the nature of this additional cargo and was a little surprised to first learn of it from the cooper. He was well aware Cork was the main supplier of gunpowder to the British forces, both on land and at sea, though he had never loaded this type of cargo in Ireland. 'I was not advised about this specifically. Tell me, Mr Larkin, how many barrels does a 50-gun ship, such as *Royal Standard*, usually carry?'

'Three hundred when stowed correctly.'

Having quickly digested the figure, Oliver considered that as the 50-gun ship had not been in any action recently, it seemed unlikely it would be necessary to replace dwindling supplies of more than a dozen barrels.

'We resupplied in Portsmouth,' the cooper confirmed, as if in answer to the captain's thoughts. 'A ship of this size can take three hundred barrels – that's the quota. So taking on an extra one hundred and fifty was not easy. But Captain Chilcott said he had no choice but to accept the extra cargo as they were needed in Cape Town following the recent fighting there. That applied to the marines also,' he added.

Oliver was not concerned about the men, but stowing such a consignment of dry powder was a worry.

'Was the magazine large enough to accommodate them all?'

'No way. Not the magazine. That was already full. Lieutenant Brophy said we were to move other barrels in the hold to make space for them.'

'And that is all?'

'And to use the forward area under the fo'c'sle deck.'

'Were any special provisions made to keep the powder safe when you loaded it?'

'The lieutenant had us build a wooden fence around them – nothing metal that could cause a spark, and when all the barrels were loaded, we covered the pile in damp sacking and tarpaulins. We were told to remove the lanterns from that area and the crew were told not to go near. Oh, yes, and a sentry was posted in the hold.'

Alarm registered in Oliver's face. 'But since I came aboard, I have seen men in the fo'c'sle smoking. And knocking the ash from their pipes on the deck. Lighted sparks could slip between the deck beams. Have the crew been ordered not to smoke?'

The cooper shrugged his shoulders. 'Most of the men knew what had happened as they'd helped haul the barrels aboard and lower them into the hold. If not, they'd have seen them on the wharf or being swung cross in the netting. I reckon Captain Chilcott or Mr Brophy would have said something to them. Can you imagine if this lot went up? *Whoosh*! It'd take us all to Kingdom Come.'

'Indeed it would,' Oliver said. 'Indeed it would. I should like to see where and how you have stowed this volatile cargo. I need to satisfy myself.'

On returning to the waist, after spending more time than he had expected familiarizing himself with the locations where the powder was stowed and checking barrels, casks, chests and an assortment of other items in the hold and magazine, Oliver squinted at the brightness. Though there was little sunlight, it was far brighter in the waist than the limited lantern light glimmering in the nether regions of the ship. Once accustomed to the daylight, Oliver headed up to the quarterdeck and confronted the first lieutenant.

'Mr Brophy, I have just learned of the additional one hundred and fifty barrels of powder that are stowed in various locations below deck.'

'That's right, Captain. We took delivery of them in Cork.'

'And do you not think such an item would have been worth reporting to me?'

'I thought you would be aware of it. It was on the manifest.'

Oliver glared at the officer who he should regard as his right hand. 'Mr Brophy,' he said, without raising his voice, 'I have been aboard for less than forty-eight hours and I am neither familiar with the ship, nor what it is carrying, nor the officers and men who are aboard. I would appreciate being advised of any other incidentals that *you* might regard as unimportant – for example, a potential fuel source with the capability of blowing this vessel sky-high stored in several inappropriate locations about the vessel.' He took a deep breath before continuing. 'While the idea of taking on the enemy in a 50-gun ship came as a welcome challenge to me, I was looking forward to meeting it. However, commanding a potential fireship is not my idea of a propitious posting.

'From today, Mr Brophy, I want no smoking in the fo'c'sle and no smoking anywhere below deck. And I want no additional lanterns or open flames in the hold. I want more marines posted below and make sure they are wearing slippers.'

'That won't be very popular, Captain. The men like their baccy.'

'Damn it man, I am not here to be popular. I am here to fulfil a job, as I trust you are.'

'Mr Brophy,' the captain said, when he returned to the quarterdeck. 'I require the inventory that was taken when the convicts were embarked.'

'Inventory?' The first lieutenant returned a blank expression.

'When the convicts came aboard, did Captain Chilcott order a detailed record to be made of all the prisoners? I am thinking of a manifest with every man's details on it – namely weight, height, colour of hair and eyes, distinguishing marks – scars and tattoos plus his previous occupation, the offence he committed, the jail he came from the length of his sentence. Are you not familiar with this type of record, Mr Brophy?'

Such facts had been recorded for some years for convicts delivered to the hulks in England prior to them being shipped across the seas. A second set of records was also made when they were embarked on a transport ship.

'Were you not on deck when the forty-six prisoners were brought aboard?'

'Yes, sir, I was, as were the other officers.'

Oliver took a deep breath. 'I am not asking the other officers, I wish to know who made the inventory that accompanied the convicts and where it is now?'

'The Captain did.'

'And who wrote up this record?'

'The Captain's clerk wrote up the ship's record. He copied the details from the list that accompanied the prisoners from Dublin. The surgeon took charge of this and checked each man before he was put below.'

'And who else was present at the time?'

'Almost all the crew,' the lieutenant said. 'Nosey, as always. Didn't want to miss anything. Most of them lined the rails or sat in the rigging, ogling. They know these types of rebels will take the first chance they can to escape.'

'Ogling, you say.' Oliver frowned. 'And the marines?'

'Of course they were on deck even though the prisoners were all shackled. The captain didn't want to take any chances with them.'

'And this list we are speaking of, are you familiar with the details regarding the types of characters we have in our charge?'

Brophy shrugged. 'I didn't take much notice of it.'

'Then I suggest you locate it and familiarize yourself with the details and deliver it to me within the hour. Those men are now under my care. It would be in your interest to know who and what you are dealing with. Do I make myself understood?'

'Yes, Captain.'

The final response was less than courteous, delivered on a sigh in the fashion of it being a tedious task and with an unwillingness to comply.

'One more thing,' the captain added. 'I am interested to know the ages of the boys amongst them – they appear to be less than twelve years of age.'

'Little good-for-nothings. That's why they're here.'

'Indeed,' Oliver said. 'I have spoken with the carpenter regarding a separate compound area on the Orlop deck to accommodate the boys and an exercise area on the forecastle for the prisoners to use in the daytime in order to get some fresh air.'

'But those felons are already taking up space that could be put to better use. Using timber to make pens will use up good materials that might be needed elsewhere.'

'Let me remind you,' Oliver said, 'we are not talking about cattle. And if there is urgent demand, the *pens*, as you call them, can be taken down quite quickly. Think how easily the great cabin and bulwarks are dismantled whenever a ship clears for action.'

'But the marines will have to—' he hesitated, but did not continue. 'We will require twice the number of marines to guard them.'

'You expect them to run very far? Let me remind you we will soon be in the middle of the Atlantic Ocean, 2000 miles from the nearest land. Tell me, how many marines are guarding the prisoners currently.'

'At the present time – two.'

Oliver's brow furrowed. 'The register, if you please, Mr Brophy.'

The lieutenant did not acknowledge or raise his eyes, he merely turned and left the great cabin with a sour expression on his face.

Oliver looked to the deck beams above is head and shook his head. 'Mr Parry, where are you?' he called out loud.

The cabin door opened and Casson popped his head around it. 'Did you call, Capt'n?'

'Ignore that, Casson. I was just lamenting not having Simon Parry on board, and a few of my regular followers.'

'I can understand how you feel, Captain. Shame you didn't have time to broadcast that you had a ship.'

It was a problem Oliver Quintrell had mulled over several times since leaving Portsmouth. But even if time had been available to post notices in the street, he doubted few sailors would have been eager or able to follow him to Cork. 'I am glad to have you with me,' he said to his steward.

'Not to worry, Captain. Next time we sail, I'll make sure word is put around the town so we can muster a few of the old crew.'

Oliver smiled, 'A commendable idea, but easier said than done. First, we must return safely from the southern hemisphere and secondly, we must be granted a further commission from amongst the long list of post captains still awaiting their first command since Trafalgar. But thank you, Casson. At least you are here.' He stood up and stretched. 'At this juncture, I think I would appreciate a strong drink. Bring two glasses and we will find something to toast.'

Later in the afternoon, while walking the quarterdeck, the first lieutenant handed a list to Captain Quintrell but made no comment.

'Is this the list I requested?' Oliver asked.

'It is.'

'Have you spoken with the prisoners recently, Mr Brophy?'

'Only to order them to be quiet. I promised them they would be put on half rations for the rest of the cruise, if they didn't pipe down.'

'And did that have any effect?'

'For five minutes, maybe.' With that, the officer left the deck.

Shaking his head, Oliver returned to the cabin to study the detailed information that had been recorded when the convicts were boarded in Cork.

Studying the list in front of him, Oliver considered the details, noting a few names and occupations of several prisoners who could possibly serve a useful purpose on deck rather than being left below to languish in shackles.

Returning to the deck, he found Lieutenant Brophy at the binnacle.

'I have prepared my own list,' the captain said, handing Mr Brophy a short list with only eight names on it. 'I wish to speak with these men. Kindly have them brought on deck.'

'Now?'

'Yes. Now.'

'I don't think you will get much sense out of them,' the first lieutenant grumbled.

Oliver glared at him.

'I'll have to muster the marines.'

'Mr Brophy, I only wish to speak with eight men. Do whatever you think necessary.'

Reluctantly the first lieutenant passed the list to the midshipman standing nearest to him. 'You heard what the captain wants.'

Ten minutes later, the prisoners were formed into an untidy line on the quarterdeck. Not having been in fresh air for several weeks, they turned their faces to the wind and breathed deeply, then, looking around, their eyes widened, as they gazed at the expanse of ocean spread out around them.

With the second lieutenant alongside him and half a dozen marines standing at a distance, Captain Quintrell spoke. 'If you are not already aware, I am the ship's captain and, like you, I only boarded this vessel in Cork.

'My Admiralty orders are to sail to Cape Town – that is near the Cape of Good Hope in South Africa. There, you will be disembarked and escorted to the colony's prison. At that location, you will continue your terms of hard labour – the period being determined by your sentence, be it seven years, fourteen years, or life.' He paused and looked at the men.

The convicts were more interested in the scene around them than the words the captain was uttering.

'However,' he continued, 'I have questions to put to you all. I expect your full attention and want you to answer honestly. This is not a test or trial.' He looked to the faces. Most now appeared to be listening.

'The record I have in my hand informs me that some of you men had connections with the sea before your convictions. Raise your hand if that is so.'

Three hands went up – cautiously.

'You,' Oliver called, pointing to one of them. 'Step forward.' The convict looked around sheepishly to the others in the group before taking a tentative step forward. The chains on his ankles and wrists rattled as he did.

'What is your name?'

'O'Leary. Michael O'Leary.'

Oliver Quintrell referred to the names before him. 'Seven years for stealing. Is that correct?

'If you say so.'

'And what do you say, O'Leary?' The captain waited for the man to provide an answer.

'I was pressed in '01. Then when the Peace came and we were discharged, I headed back to Ireland so the press gangs couldn't get me again. But what I found when I arrived was the British had left us nothing. They'd taken the farm. Torn down the house. My mother was dead and my sisters starving. I'd been paid off and collected my wages but that didn't go far. Only way to survive was to thieve.'

'And you were caught?'

'Seven years, the beak gave me. Seven years.' He shook his head. 'He might as well 'ave hung me there an' then.'

'You,' Oliver said, indicating to the man who had been standing next to him and had also raised his hand.

'Facy, Captain.'

'You were a seaman, Mr Facy?'

The man nodded.

'What ship did you serve on?'

'*Delia*, Capt'n. Transport. Sixteen guns.'

'And you,' to the third man who had seemed undecided whether to raise his hand of not. 'Name?'

'Paddy Cronin.'

'Your past occupation, Mr Cronin?'

'Deck hand on a local fishing boat,' he replied, then quickly added, 'It wasn't my fault we foundered.'

'So how was it you ended up in the assizes court?'

'The captain's money went down with the ship and he said I took it. But I never touched his money, I can swear to that. But no one believed me.'

Oliver passed to the next man in the line. 'Name and occupation?'

'Byrne. Patrick Byrne. Shipwright.'

'Have you ever served aboard a ship, Mr Byrne?'

'Only worked on the ones I had a hand in building. Never been on the water, just on the stocks before they were slid into the sea.'

He moved on. 'You, what is your name?'

'Daniel Davies.'

'It says here you were a fisherman also.'

Davies nodded. 'Yes, and a damned good one at that.'

Growing up on the deck of a fishing boat, Oliver Quintrell felt at ease talking briefly about catching herring. 'So how did you fall foul of the law, Mr Davies?'

'It was my father's boat,' the Irishman claimed. 'That was until the day the British invaded in ninety-eight. It was taken by the redcoats. They promised he would get it back, but, of course, he never did. Soon after that, my father was murdered, our house burned to the ground and the family turned out on the streets. We all near starved. I stole to buy bread and milk to keep us alive. And I'm not ashamed. I was only sixteen at the time.'

'And what of your family now?'

'How am I to know?'

Oliver turned back to his list. He had two men remaining in the line but three names on the list. 'John Kemp,' he called. 'Where is John Kemp?'

The men looked at each other but no one answered the call 'He's not here,' one of the remaining men volunteered. 'He's still below. He's one of the youngsters.'

'It says here he was charged with smuggling. What do you know of that?'

'That's a lie. He's my nephew. A good lad, he is. We got taken together collecting flotsam from a beach – stuff washed up from a wreck. We was both charged with smuggling and brought up before the magistrate. When we were taken down, I swore to my sister, I'd take care of him.'

'You had a boat?'

Kemp nodded. 'Don't know what happened to that.'

'And what is your name?'

'Andrew Kemp. I'm the lad's uncle.'

Finally, only one man remained. 'You are Denis O'Donaghue, I believe?' the captain said. 'Wherryman?'

The man was surprised and looked around.

'Tell me Mr O'Donaghue, did you work on the sea?'

The prisoner shook his head. 'Not me, captain. The Liffey was my pond.'

Captain Quintrell strode back along the line scanning the dishevelled group before him. It was obvious their hair, faces, hands and clothes had not seen water in weeks.

'It appears that most of you are comfortable on the water.'

The response came in nods with the words, 'sir' and 'captain' drifting from a few throats.

Apart from the beggars on the back alleys of most English ports, Oliver had not seen such a bedraggled, moth-eaten, vermin-infested bunch of individuals since he walked through the slave markets in Peru. Six weeks stuck in a cage on the orlop deck had done nothing to improve the prisoners' appearances.

'Now listen carefully to my considerations. Much will depend on what lies ahead of us, which none of us can foretell. However, one thing is for certain, we are short-handed. A ship of 50-guns, if called to action, will require more than the three hundred men who are currently aboard.

My orders are to sail *Royal Standard* to Cape Town, to deliver marines and powder to assist the British forces who are presently engaged in reclaiming that territory. If all goes well there, from Cape Town, I will return to Portsmouth.

'My proposal, which may in time come into effect, is that you work on this ship by day alongside the regular hands but at night you will be returned to your compound. During the day you will eat in the mess and receive the same rations as the regular hands.'

'Including grog rations?' O'Leary asked, through a half smile.

Oliver chose to ignore that remark. 'If however, we come into action, you will be expected to stand to a gun and fight as required.'

'And die,' one Irish voice mumbled.

'Indeed,' the captain agreed, 'as we all will, if the ship is taken.'

The men looked puzzled.

'What choice do we have?' Paddy Cronin asked.

'Let me put this to you: if you accept, and my proposal should go ahead, you will be given clean slop clothing – the sort supplied to the regular tars. If you perform your duties to the best of your abilities and when, and if, we reach the Cape of Good Hope without incident, I will recommend to the Navy Board, that you are signed onto another ship for a period of five years in place of being returned to jail.'

'Can you do that, Captain?' was a tentative enquiry.

'I can promise nothing, but I can try. However, I am aware that in some English courts a quota system exists whereby prisoners are given the choice of serving in the British Navy or going to jail. If you accept this offer, you must prove yourself deserving by doing all that is asked of you. The first sign of misbehaviour or proof that you have disobeyed the *Articles of War*, you will be slapped in irons and thrown in the hold with your backs stained red from the cat's claws. Do I make myself clear?'

The prisoners looked at each other. 'And what if we don't want to do this?' one asked boldly.

'You will remain under lock and key on the orlop deck and be held there until we raise the Cape. You have ten minutes to consider my proposal.'

There was little discussion. For the prisoners who had spent months and sometimes years in Kilmainham Gaol – the newest, yet perhaps the harshest, coldest and dampest prison in the British Isles – the sniff of freedom right under their noses was sweet. Not knowing what ports the ships might touch on as it headed south, the possibility of jumping ship was even sweeter. Accepting the Captain's offer was the easiest commitment they had ever made.

Acting as spokesman, O'Leary turned to face the captain. 'Begging your pardon, Capt'n, but the lads have one question.'

'Speak,' Oliver said.

'The men are afraid the regular crew won't like it.'

'They may not,' Oliver replied, 'but unlike you, the crew will not be given a choice.'

Soon after the prisoners had been dismissed and returned to their confines on the orlop deck, Oliver put his proposal to his first officer. Not unexpectedly, the response he received was less than positive. It echoed the same concerns expressed by the convicts.

'The crew won't like it,' the first lieutenant said. 'Imagine the hands hauling on a brace alongside men unwilling or too weak even to coil a rope. Or leaning against the bars of the capstan worrying that the man behind him might crush his skull with a length of timber.'

'Mr Brophy, I will evaluate the men's fantasies if and when the need arises, in the meantime, all men will be expected to put in their best efforts no matter what the challenge and without question or quibble. Any man, be he convict or able seaman, will face the same discipline.'

'I just don't think the regular hands will be happy.'

'Perhaps a masquerade ball or quadrille on deck would tickle their fancy,' Oliver said, walking away, peeved with himself for being hooked into a confrontation that he saw no value in.

Chapter 11

Young Gentlemen

At 8-bells, Oliver Quintrell was looking forward to a tasty meal with vegetables and meat still fresh after being loaded at Cork. Quite a treat on a naval vessel.

For a week, *Royal Standard* had been sailing well on a following sea however, the wind that had carried them south all morning had now almost died. The Bay of Biscay was proving docile on this occasion. Taking the opportunity of dipping pen in ink on a steady writing desk, Oliver turned his attention to his personal log adding comments and observations of the events of the previous few days.

He had also taken time to observe the ship from stem to stern, poop deck to hold, and to wander the decks casually observing the men as they went about their duties or during their time off watch. It was obvious his close attention was not appreciated. However, all in all, he found the conditions on board *Royal Standard* satisfactory. He was pleased to find the carpenter had completed work on the compound on the foredeck so groups of eight or ten convicts could be aired at least once a day. That several youngsters were still confined with the men had yet to be addressed.

Despite the gallery windows being left open there was insufficient wind to draw a breeze from the stern gallery. With no rain during the past week, the dog, Cecil, had accepted his designated place outside the great cabin. And, for the present, with no sign of a change in the weather and heading into slightly lower latitudes, the air was less chill than when they had left Ireland.

Calling for Chalmers the previous afternoon, Oliver had suggested the dog should be shorn. 'Enquire if we have a shepherd amongst the hands,' he had instructed, 'or a barber, who can shear the beast. It will look tidier and will be more comfortable. Hopefully it will also smell less without all that hair.'

'I'll enquire, Captain.'

'And pass the hair to one of the men who is able to spin yarn. I would like to see a hat or jerkin knitted from it.'

Chalmers raised his eyebrows and nodded. 'I'll let you know, captain.'

'Good man.'

Chalmers padded off, the sway of his movement resembling that of his charge. Oliver hoped to see him return very soon to whisk the dog away and for it to return later measuring half its present dimensions.

After scratching his brow with the tip of his quill, the captain returned his pen to the well and exchanged his position for the velvet upholstered wing-back chair. Though elegant, the piece of furniture, bequeathed by Captain Chilcott, showed signs of stain and wear especially in the places where his weary head had often rested. Not intending to allow himself the luxury of sleep at this hour of the day, Oliver's thoughts drifted and inevitably his eyes closed. Sleep was an insidious temptress.

How long his mind swirled in a dream-like state, he did not know, probably only a matter of minutes, but his senses were not dulled enough to block out the sounds from the ship that surrounded him. The thump of feet running around the deck and along the gangways reverberated through the very timbers of the hull. That sound echoed urgency and usually meant only one thing.

The captain shook his head and berated himself. *Had he slept through the call? He had not heard the beat of drums or shrilling of the whistles? Had the officer of the Watch not thought to call him to the deck? Why had he not been informed? Was the ship in danger? Were they under fire?*

'Casson,' Oliver called, jumping to his feet. Not waiting for an answer nor reaching for his coat, he bounded out, through the dining cabin to the quarterdeck.

On opening the door, he was met by a scene of apparent calm. The officer of the watch was standing beside the binnacle, the schoolmaster beside him. From the rail, stretching to the far horizon, the sea had a glassy surface that rolled with the smooth and gentle undulations of a woman's body. The slow moving wash, curling from the bow, clung to the hull but could not be seen unless standing by the rail. With the canvas begging to luff the sailors were gazing upwards and waiting.

That brief moment of peace was quickly shattered when a stream of boys, aged nine to thirteen, thundered down the larboard gangway. Elbowing, pushing and shoving each other for position, they turned onto the quarterdeck and headed across it to the starboard gangway and then headed aft. The herd of over twenty-five stampeded around the deck like the Hounds of Hell were on their tails. With heads down, they did not notice the captain when he stepped on deck.

One of the middies, balanced on the ratlines, immediately saw him and interpreted the expression on his face. Attempting to draw the attention of the officer of the watch, he coughed loudly into his hand, but he could not distract the young officer and the two warrant officers from the conversation they were deeply engaged in.

Stepping forward three paces, Oliver stopped dead in the centre of the quarterdeck.

Having run around the forward deck, the pack was now stretched out with the stragglers unable to keep up. They rounded to the quarterdeck from the gangway, with those at the front running full tilt into the ship's captain. The older and taller boys in the lead pulled up abruptly, but those making up the bulk of the mob failed to see any reason to slow and ran into the backs of their mates, several falling to the deck and being trampled on. As the pile disentangled itself, some of the boys moaned as they rubbed their bruised ankles or knees. The sounds some of youngsters emitted resembled a back-alley cat fight.

Only then did the spill attract the attention of the officer of the watch and the others at the binnacle.

'Apologies, Captain,' the sailing master said, when he saw the captain surrounded by flailing arms and legs.

'What is going on here?' Captain Quintrell demanded. 'Are we under attack?'

'Begging the captain's pardon,' Mr Brannagh said. 'I considered the young gentlemen needed some exercise to burn off a little of their excess energy.'

'You,' Oliver said, calling to the tallest youth who had been leading the throng.

Tossing his head back and allowing a stream of blonde curls to flow across his shoulders, the boy looked straight at the captain. The cherubim like pink cheeks and wide blue eyes were at odds with the resentful expression on his face. As he stepped up, a smirk quickly developed on the downturned lips.

'Name?' Oliver demanded.

'Angus Dorrington, Captain. My grandfather is Admiral Dorrington.'

'I am not concerned with your heritage, sir. Your father may be King Neptune for all it matters at this moment.'

Turning his attention back to the sailing master: 'Mr Brannagh,' he said, 'in my opinion, there is little to be gained by running these precocious gentlemen across a flat deck. Let us see how agile they are in the rigging.'

'Aye, Captain.'

'Line them up in an orderly fashion. Let Mr Dorrington lead them off – up the port rigging to the main topgallant, across the yard and down the starboard side – no sliding down the stays, I might add. Double around the foredeck, then up and across the foremast t'gallant yard and down; along the gangway and back to the quarterdeck. Mr Holland, can keep a tally to ensure all the boys complete a full dozen.'

'Aye, Captain.'

'Mr Dorrington, you will report to the sailing master when you have completed that exercise by which time he will have decided on your next exercise.'

'Yes, Captain.' The reply was mumbled. The bravado was diminished but the arrogant expression had not been extinguished.

Despite the undercurrent of complaints, the sailing master shuffled the boys into single file with Dorrington at the head. 'You heard the Captain,' Mr Brannagh said. 'One at a time. No pushing.

133

And silence. Off you go. Fast as you can. A dozen times around the ship.'

Within seconds the ratlines were swaying, as the young gentlemen reached for a hand-hold, scurried up, pulling and pushing for position, behaving more like Barbary Apes than members of the gentry. The ones in the lead set the pace, eager to impress both their superiors and inferiors. Climbing down proved slower and after half a dozen laps the speed of the leading group had slowed noticeably. It was further obstructed by the smaller, weaker and less confident youngsters who they had overtaken after only three laps. Elbows again came into play, as the bigger bullies barged through anyone obstructing their passages almost dislodging a couple of the weaker ones.

When Dorrington and three of his immediate mates dropped to the deck after completing the required twelve rounds, their cheeks were ruddy; sweat trickled down their faces and forearms; and their white shirts were stuck to their backs.

'Finished!' Dorrington announced triumphantly, to anyone who might be listening. After bouncing from the rail back to the deck, Dorrington glanced around the ship to the youngsters who were struggling to complete the sixth, seventh or eighth lap. His mates, however, had gathered around him and were eagerly congratulating each other.

'Gentlemen,' the captain called quietly.

The boys expected praise.

'On a fighting ship,' he said, 'seamen work together as a team. You haul together, you furl together, you mess together, and, if you are unlucky, you die together. One thing you do not do is sit back and relax when your mate is still working. Get up there now and continue climbing until the last of the boys has completed his final round.' Oliver ignored the murmurs and a growl from one of the throats.

'Did I not make myself clear?'

Several boys nodded. 'Yes, Captain,' Dorrington murmured, glancing at his companions.

'Then go.'

It took another turn of the half-hour glass before the last of the small boys finished the exercise and the deck was littered with sweaty bodies.

'Mr Holland, have a pump brought up on deck. These boys are not fit to return to their quarters in their present state. Hose them down before they go below.'

'With pleasure, Captain.'

It was an extra duty the deck hands would enjoy. The Captain did not remain on deck to witness the event.

The knock on the door of the great cabin was hardly audible.

'Come,' Oliver called.

The sailing master entered and closed the door.

'It does not pay to be soft with these young coves be they lords or gentlemen or whatever they wish to call themselves,' the captain said.

The experienced officer merely nodded.

'They will deserve my respect, when I witness them showing courage in the face of danger. But not until then. There is no title that will equip them against an enemy, either on land or sea. In the smoke and noise of a sea battle, a strong arm on a line or a steady hand on a length of quick-match, can belong to anyone.' He paused, realising the warrant officer did not merit any rebuke.

'So, tell me, Mr Brannagh, how many of these young men has the Admiralty blessed us with on this vessel?'

'Thirty, Captain.'

Oliver shook the revelation from his head. 'And what program have you set for them?'

'Apart from the formal class-room tuition in mathematics and navigation with the schoolmaster, they spend an allocated time with each of the petty officers. The boatswain instructs them in knots and splicing, the sail maker in palming and stitching. From the quarterdeck, the midshipmen instruct them in use of the sextant. They take the noon reading daily. From the topmen they learn how to make and reduce sail, heave to, and handle clews and bunts. The first lieutenant endeavours to imprint the *Articles of War* into their brains. And I introduce them to maps and charts. I don't doubt most of them have brains, but most are lacking in common sense?'

The sailing master did not comment but continued. 'Then there are the domestic duties to tackle, if they are placed with an officer – laundering, pressing, sewing, polishing shoe buckles, and the bright work around the ship.'

'Bright work – a daily chore usually undertaken by the hands is it not?'

'Yes, Captain.'

'And do they all participate in these chores?'

'Yes, sir, though grudgingly. Not all are eager to partake in menial tasks. Much also depends on the nature of the officer each young gentleman has been assigned to. Those allocated to the warrant officers also spend time learning the manual trades.'

'And what are your thoughts on this current group aboard *Royal Standard*?'

The sailing master hesitated.

'Come along, that is not such a difficult question. I want your honest opinion.'

'I think, before stepping on the ship, a few of the boys were molly-coddled by their own servants to such an extent they could not even tie their own neck-cloths, and certainly could not thread a needle or sew on a button or shine a shoe-buckle. As you know, there is much for them to learn regarding the demands of seamanship.'

'And life itself, it seems. And how many servants was Captain Chilcott personally allocated?'

'Twelve, captain. The Admiralty allows four servants to every one hundred crew; therefore with a crew of three hundred, you have twelve young gentlemen at your disposal.'

'I wish to see a list of all the boys on board with names, ages and details of which officer each boy has been assigned to.'

The sailing master nodded.

'In the meantime, I advise you keep a watchful eye on Mr Dorrington. I fear he could stir up trouble amongst the more vulnerable souls.'

'There's always at least a couple of bad apples in a batch, but I hope you are wrong, Captain.'

Chapter 12

Gun practice

Two days later, with the hands called on deck, only the gun crews from five of the guns on the upper deck were needed. The other hands were allowed to stand down.

There was an undercurrent of grumbles from those who were called, as they were not sent to their usual stations – to the guns they always stood to. Every gun crew was familiar with a particular gun, with its faults, and foibles. The gun captains knew just how much priming powder his particular gun needed; exactly how long it would take for the flame to carry down the quill to ignite the cartridge. And each man in the team knew his job and his position near the gun. Above all, he knew how hard his gun would kick, and exactly where to stand to keep well out of its way. On this occasion they were ordered to man five of the 24-pounders on the upper deck they were not familiar with.

'Quiet,' Mr Holland called. 'Stand to your gun and wait.

They didn't have to wait long until Mr Keath came down the companionway ladder from the quarterdeck. Behind him were three of the young gentlemen also known as volunteers, boys – third class or officers' servants. The group was resented and despised by the regular hands, for their aristocratic breeding, educated, arrogant behaviour and general uselessness aboard a king's ship. They were regarded as young snobs who *still needed their own servants to wipe their arses for them.*

Of the thirty *volunteers* who had joined *Royal Standard* in Cork, they were aged between ten to fourteen years but having been fed on the finest foods since birth, they were already as tall as, if not taller than, most of the regular hands. To add to the sailor's frustrations, they were told to teach these boys who, one day, would be walking the quarterdeck and giving them orders.

Conversely, the young gentlemen had no time for the types of riff-raff who made up the crews on his Majesty's ships.

Having been disappointed with the boys' behaviour earlier, Captain Quintrell had decided to give three of them the opportunity to redeem themselves and prove their capabilities.

Mr Keath directed them to their stations. 'Mr Dorrington, you will serve on that gun. Mr Price is the gun captain. You will follow his orders. Do you have gloves or mittens?'

'No, I don't.'

The midshipman moved on to the next gun also on the starboard side of the deck.

'Mr Witcher and Mr Chittenden, you will take orders from Mr Marsh – he is the gun captain here and won't stand any messing.'

They were interrupted by raised voices on the previous cannon.

'What is going on, Mr Price?' the midshipman asked the captain of that gun.

'This 'ere whipper-snapper says he don't want to stand at the back of the gun. He says he wants to stand where Albert stands and load the shot into the barrel.'

'What did you tell him?'

'I told him, if he doesn't stand where he's put he can sling his hook. He's not going to mess up my crew and I've no time to argue.'

'Mr Dorrington. Stand where you are stationed. Do not grumble or object. Have a look around at the pock marks and dents in the bulwarks and beams. Some of those are from shots that came through with a man's head or arm caught on it – a man who had been standing in the wrong place at the wrong time. Now go where you are put and stay there. One more word from you and you are off the deck.'

Stepping around the bare capstan which was situated amidships, the midshipman headed across the deck to the three 24s on the larboard side. The crews of six men were standing in silence by their guns – their expressions spoke of not looking forward to receiving their quota of young lubbers but only three had come down with the middie.

With the sound of footsteps coming up from the deck below, the crews looked and waited. Appearing from the companionway coming from the lower gun deck, two marines stepped up first and positioned themselves at either side of the stairs. They were followed by Mr Holland then by seven men wearing prison grey uniforms indelibly stamped in black ink with the broad arrow. Another pair of marines, with muskets in hand, followed behind. Everyone aboard *Royal Standard* had heard of the mob of felons being held below on the orlop deck, but very few had seen them.

After lining the convicts up, the midshipman ordered six of the men to go to the three larboard guns. The one who remained was sent to the starboard side to work alongside Mr Dorrington.

'Now listen, and listen well.' The midshipman's voice carried easily the full width of the deck. 'You will receive your instructions from your gun captain. You will ignore everyone else. Do as you are told, learn and remember. You are here for gun practice. This morning we will be firing cannon filled with rags. Tomorrow we will fire 24-pound round shot. I trust you understand the difference. If you are to survive on a gundeck you must keep you eye on the gun at all times – it has a kick far worse than an angry mule, and keep your hands off it if you value your skin. Don't interfere with the man next to you, or ask for help. In fact do not utter a word once the practice begins. After tomorrow, the next time you are called to *Royal Standard*'s gun deck, the ship may be under fire.

'Gun Captains give your orders clearly. You have fifteen minutes. And if any man is injured, I will hold you responsible.'

When Mr Holland stood back, the crews followed the routines they knew. The gun ports were flung open and secured in place. The openings on the starboard side allowed beams of morning sun to shine across the full width of the deck. The tompions were withdrawn from the muzzles. The inclination of the barrel was adjusted, the barrel given a quick swab, though the gun had not been fired and was clean inside. There was no cartridge on this occasion. Then a wad was rammed home and after that an extra large wad of rags in place of a cannon ball. Finally the contents of the barrel were rammed in ready to be fired.

The breeching lines and preventer lines were released, the order given for the gun to be moved forward on its wooden trucks till its muzzle was poking out through the side of the ship.

The men then waited for the order to fire while the gunner followed his oft repeated ritual. On *Royal Standard*, some of the guns had been fitted with flintlocks while others still needed a linstock or a length of slowmatch to ignite the powder in the bowl.

'Keep clear,' a voice called from one of the starboard gun. The young gentleman working opposite the convict quickly stepped back a pace, only just in time as the gun fired. Had a cartridge, full of powder been lit, the gun would have bounced off the deck and be held by the preventer braces, to stop it from careering across the deck and into another gun on the larboard side.

'Reload,' Mr Holland ordered.

While the regular hands from the gun crews treated the exercise with distain, the practice of saving gun powder during gun practice was recommended by the Admiralty. *Royal Standard*, however, was not short on that commodity.

The following morning, gun practice began immediately after breakfast.

Apart from the recruits who had participated on the previous day, five of the smaller boys – the youngest of the young gentlemen – were led down to the magazine and given instruction from the gunner in the magazine of their duties and of the dangers they faced when servicing the gundeck as a powder monkey.

'Not only can you be blown to Kingdom Come, if you allow a spark to float into your satchel and ignite the cartridge you are carrying, but you could be struck by a splinter when a gun port is blown to matchwood. I would remind you, the splinters we get down here are not the size of those you get under your finger nails. Our splinters are great chunks of wood, big enough to cut a man in half, impale him to the mast, or slice off his head without making a sound.

'And mind you don't step in the path of a gun that is being fired. It could pick you up and throw you out of the gunport on the other side of the ship and no one would ever miss you until many hours later.

'And when you are not running the deck with powder, there are practical jobs you can do, like sprinkling sand on the deck near the guns.'

'Might I ask what that is for?' one of the young gentlemen said politely.

'To soak up the blood and prevent you from slipping on it. Now if you see a man who has lost a hand or arm, or a leg, stick one of these on him and call for the stretcher bearers to take him to the cockpit.'

Holding up a tourniquet, it was obvious the boys had never seen one before and would not known how to use it. The gunner demonstrated.

'And if your mate is dead, drag him well out of the way. You don't want to have to step over him every time you run the length of the gundeck. But if he falls near an open port – push him through it.'

One of the young gents being only about eight-years-old tottered a little but managed to keep his feet.

'The main thing to remember, when you come down to the magazine is to bring your leather satchel, and when you come to enter, you must wear felt slippers. You must give your name to the guard outside, and remember to fasten your satchel when you have the cartridge in it. What ever you do, don't let a spark or a flaming floater fall into it.

'Apart from that, it's an easy job. Just remember to keep running and don't dilly-dally.'

On the upper gundeck, the hands stood to the same guns and the three young gentlemen and seven convicts joined them, taking up the positions they had been allocated on the previous day. The regular crew were more relaxed than they were the day before, even though, on this occasion, they were to fire live shots.

'You and your mates are all Irish, aren't you?' The voice had an Irish lilt and came from the gun captain who was at the other side of the barrel to Danny Collins.

The convict, however, kept his lips closed. He was loath to talk, for fear of being reprimanded and sent back to the wooden cage on the orlop deck.

'Where are you from? You can tell me,' the gunner said in a low voice.

'*Kilmainham*,' Collins said under his breath.

'I know that,' the older man said. 'Where before that, where are you from?'

'The young convicts looked across, as he helped haul the cannon up to the open port. 'Kerry,' he said.

'I thought so,' he whispered. 'Have you done this before?'

The young man shook his head. 'Not on a ship.'

'Army?'

'In ninety-eight, during the rebellion, we managed to pinch a British gun and defend the village. I quickly learned how to fire one.'

'A bad time, eh?'

'We gave it all we could, and more. But we failed.'

'Quiet there, no talking,' Mr Holland said, as he walked past.

'And you ended up in *Kilmainham*?' the gunner whispered when he saw the midshipman head over to the guns on the starboard side.'

'A place I'd rather forget.'

That was the end of the conversation and though the other men in the gun crew had heard what was said, there were no comments.

Danny Collins nodded to himself. For once in a long time, he felt as though he was amongst friends.

After two rounds had been fired, the ship's waist was blue with smoke and it was impossible to see across the gundeck.

The wet swab was used to sponge the barrel and kill any flames that remained from the pervious ignition. Then a wad was rammed home, followed by the cartridge, handed to him from the powder monkey. Another wad was rammed into the barrel on top of that. Then the gun was hauled forward and the gunner pricked the cartridge, added priming power to his bowl and waited for the word from the division captain – Mr Holland.

Peering through the rising smoke, Captain Quintrell leaned over the rail from the gang boards. Your report, Mr Holland,' he called.

'Slow, Captain,' he replied. 'But the new men understand what is required. They will serve alright.'

'Mr Keath,' the captain called, though he could not see the other midshipman till he emerged from the smoke.

'Just getting the young gents into order,' the midshipman replied.

'Too slow,' the captain said. 'The time it is taking your gun to fire, your crew would have been blown off the deck along with half of the ship unless you can return fire more quickly.'

'Aye, aye, Captain.'

The next time, however, as the gun exploded, shooting orange flame from the muzzle, the young gentleman jumped in fright and, in trying to cover his ears, one boy lost his balance. As he went down, the breeching line caught his legs. The crack of the bone was sharp and clean. The scream was ear-splitting.

'Mr Keath, get that man off the gundeck!'

'Aye, aye,' but before he could call for help, one of the stronger fellows in the gun crew picked the boy up from the deck and carried him down the companionway heading for the cockpit, the screams followed him all the way.

From across the deck, Dorrington laughed, as though the accident to his fellow young gentleman was amusing.

'And remove that man also,' the captain called. 'He is not fit to serve on a gundeck. Return him to his quarters, immediately.'

For Oliver Quintrell, the exercise to utilize several of the convicts had proved very satisfactory. He was not disappointed with a single one of them. He only wished he had time to employ all forty-six of them in one occupation or another. But with only a few weeks' sailing time remaining before they reached Cape Town, there would be insufficient time. However, the young gentlemen were another matter altogether.

'Can you credit these young gentlemen,' Mr Holland said, later in the wardroom. 'They have little understanding of the world and seem to have very little imagination to boot.

'The gunner, in the magazine, sent one of the young gents to get some cheeses for the gun, as he had used the last one.'

A *cheese* was the name he gave to the wads rammed into the cannon to hold the ball in place when firing. Because they were made of a circle of rope with rags bound around them – the shape and size resembled that of a cheese. After half an hour of being missing, he sent one of the other hands to find the boy.

'Having headed straight down to the galley, the young gentleman asked for some cheese. The cook had queried the request and sent him to the purser. The purser couldn't understand why the gunner had asked him to get some cheeses and had sent him to the division captain to get clarification.'

'By the time the mystery had been unravelled. The young gentleman was a laughing stock on the gun deck and word of his mistake quickly spread.'

'Serves him right,' the young officers in the wardroom agreed.

The rest of the company around the table appreciated the joke.

Chapter 13

Heading South

The rising sun was encircled in a burnished halo created by the hot desert winds of the Sahara. Every morning, the same orange haze tarnished the eastern sky, stretching from north to south as far as the eye could see. Yet no sign of the coast of Africa itself was sighted, it being over seven hundred miles away. After being becalmed in the Doldrums for seven days, patience was wearing thin.

'It's possible that sandstorm may reach us,' the sailing master said. 'I've heard that those winds can carry for 2000 miles. Shame a little of it can't blow in our favour.'

The captain nodded and paced across the quarterdeck to the larboard side. Fifty yards off the beam, a pod of pilot whales swam by heading north, their black dorsal fins slicing the water but never making the slightest splash. Flying fish, stirred by the presence of the predators, shot from the water. Their whirring wings glistened in the sunlight as they darted across the tops of swell for thirty to forty yards before slicing the crests and disappearing into the sea.

The ocean's broad horizon was smooth and endless making the curvature of the earth a reality and dispelling the myth long held by certain sceptics that the world was flat.

While every dawn was a perfect copy of the previous day's, there was nothing to inspire the sailors, as they dragged themselves on deck whenever a change of watch was called. With little wind, the sultry air drained the spirits. The morning chores on deck were a repetition of duties performed day after day to surfaces that showed no need to be cleaned. As a result, the men moved in a sluggish fashion, much to the ire of the division captains.

'Put your backs into it, you lazy good-for-nothings!' was the call, but even that was merely a repeat of the previous day's order.

At 8-bells of the larboard watch, the hands went below for breakfast. The couldn't-care-less attitude was repeated in the expressions of the starboard watch that replaced them.

'It's the Doldrums,' the sailing master said. 'When we are stuck in that belt, for any length of time, the men get infected with its lassitude. And when we eventually pass through it, their brains are unable to cast off the fog of lethargy. I've witnessed it several times before.'

'An interesting observation,' the captain said, 'though I believe it is caused by plain boredom. With no change in the wind or weather, and sailing set on a constant course, they are not called upon to do anything.'

To the delight and relief of the whole ship's company, the following dawn brought with it a light westerly. Sails were set and trimmed and *Royal Standard* swam south picking up on the course it had previously been following. With the wind freshening, the topmen lifted their chins to feel the rush of air on their faces. On deck the mood that had persisted for days, disappeared even before the men had been for breakfast, contrary to Mr Brannagh's opinion.

Turning about to attract the attention of the first lieutenant, the captain was alerted by a call from the lookout on the foremast.

'Deck there! Sail. Sail on the starboard bow.'

That single word directed every pair of eyes, first to the mast head and then out over the ocean on the starboard side.

'Where away?' was the call from the officer of the watch who reached for the glass, left the binnacle and strode briskly over to the rail.

Before he reached the gunwale he received his answer. 'Two points off the starboard bow.'

Resting his hip against the rail for balance, the young midshipman opened the telescope and scanned the horizon off the bow.

'Two sail of ships. Maybe three,' the lookout called.

'Mr Weir, go up top and report what you see.'

The second lieutenant swung himself up from the deck and scrambled up the ratlines. While every pair of eyes followed him as he climbed, the captain was anxious for more information.

Duplicating the actions and stance of the lookout, the lieutenant peered through the glass for a moment then made the call. 'Four sails. Square riggers. Hulls not up fully yet. Could be more. Heading north.'

'Thank you Mr Weir.'

By now, the captain and sailing master's interest had been piqued. *How many ships were there? Were they part of a large fleet?* they wondered.

Studying the line of the horizon, there were no deceptive clusters of clouds resting there, so the flecks of white tinged with a dull orange glow and slowly rising from the sea could be nothing other than a convoy of ships.

'Maybe a dozen or more,' the lookout called. 'Spilling over a wide area.'

'French fleet or East India men?' the sailing master queried. 'Let's hope it is not a French fleet returning home.'

'What colours?' Oliver hailed and waited for an answer.

'Can't see, Capt'n. Too distant.'

'Should we change course?' Mr Brophy asked.

'Let us not be hasty. I wish to know their heading. But call all hands, quietly now – no drums or whistles.'

With orders circulating the ship, sailors appeared on deck, some half-dressed, pulling on their shirts and fastening handkerchiefs around their necks or foreheads. With a temperature heading towards 100 degrees, the cloth helped soak up the sweat running down from their scalps.

The quarterdeck was soon occupied with every officer on the ship craning to get a view. The buzz of whispers in the fo'c'sle was to ascertain why all hands had been called, then to argue their opinions as to the nature and intent of the approaching fleet. The picture consisted of several ships, hulls up and more appearing from the horizon every minute. Within an hour, the number had risen to forty and the monotony of the last few days was broken.

'Raise the ensign,' Captain Quintrell ordered. He watched as two middies collected the flag from the deck lockers and headed aft. Moment later the huge flag was fluttering in the light breeze.

As the ships grew and slowly sailed closer, it was clear four were men-of-war carrying 64- to 74-guns each. The other ships, however, appeared to be carrying cargo with little weight of metal.

'An East India fleet, I suggest,' Oliver said, 'returning home from Batavia or China, heavily laden with spices, tea, timber, silks and more. Individually, such vessels would be a tempting target to any hungry privateers patrolling the region. But with a convoy of over forty ships there was no fear of attack.'

A pair of 64-s, a 74- and a 50-gun ship accompanying the heavily laden merchant ships, were on hand to provide protection if and when required. There was always strength in numbers. Some merchant fleets numbered as many as ninety ships.

From his home garden, Oliver had often watched them gathering at Spithead and St Helen's Road. He was aware that the largest John Company vessels carried as much weight in guns as some British naval ships. And the sailors aboard them were skilled at their job, many having served on rated vessels.

'Reduce sail but maintain the heading,' the captain called to the officer of the watch. 'I would speak one of the ships if the opportunity arises. I have mail for the Admiralty. I shall go below and collect my correspondence.'

'Aye, Captain.'

It was two hours before the last of the Company vessels sailed by. They was an assortment of craft, – the largest being equivalent in size to a 74-gun man-of-war, to sloops, snows, schooners and brigs. Not all were East India Company ships. Some were independent traders that had paid to sail with the fleet for protection.

'Captain,' the midshipman called from the door of the great cabin. 'There's a chance to speak one of the ships. I have hailed her already.'

'Thank you, Mr Aitcheson, I will come on deck.'

With both vessels hove to at close quarters, a brief conversation was made without the use of speaking trumpets. But Oliver had little interest in discussing the ports the ship had stopped at, or the weather faced in the Indian Ocean. Those details were of little consequence to him. His main concern was news of any opposition encountered in the latter part of their voyage. Also, what the present state of affairs was in Cape Town and whether the South African territory had been ceded to Britain or remained in the hands of the Dutch. He was also anxious to know if Admiral Sir Home Popham and the marines were still in Port or if they had already departed. The state of health within the colony was also of concern. He had no desire to sail into a den of infection or quarantine.

Captain Yollander, master of the brig sloop, *Indigo*, said he would be only too pleased to provide Captain Quintrell with answers to his enquires and update him with the affairs of the Cape Province. So, with relatively calm seas, Oliver invited the master to step aboard and share a coffee with him. No sooner had the offer been accepted than a boat was lowered and the visitor rowed across to *Royal Standard*.

As news travelled slowly to the east, Captain Yollander was eager to learn of the recent fighting in Europe, particularly the battle of Trafalgar, its triumphs and tragedies, and to hear of Nelson's death and funeral. Even though it had happened months earlier, much was new to the fleet that had been at sea for many weeks. Napoleon's advance into Europe was also of particular concern to ships of the East India Company.

Of significance to Oliver and *Royal Standard* was that, only a few weeks earlier, Sir Home Popham had been preparing to leave Cape Town Bay with a large fleet. It was transporting a large number of soldiers under the command of Major General Sir David Baird. His destination was Buenos Aires in Argentina. He was intent on seizing control of the area from the Spanish Viceroyalty. The Spanish however, had no intention of relinquishing their colonial lands on the Río de la Plata to the British. They would also welcome any chance to defeat the British after the drubbing Spain's navy took at Trafalgar.

The good news was that, in January, under Home Popham, Britain had resumed control of the Cape, having wrested it from the Dutch, and that the changeover had been peaceful. The British jack was now flying in Cape Town.

There was little time for the two ship's captains to sit down to refreshments, however they managed a toast to the East India Company's safe return home after a long and tiring voyage and to *Royal Standard* – a safe and successful mission.

For almost half an hour the two captains exchanged stories, the conversation flowing back and forth non-stop after which time, Captain Yollander gave his apologies, thanked Oliver Quintrell and returned to his ship. As the fleet were sailing well, he did not want to be left behind.

As soon as the visiting boat cast off, the call went out for all hands. The yards were braced around, the helm responded and the breeze filled the belly of the canvas returning *Royal Standard* to the heading it had originally been on. Though the wind was light, it was better than no wind at all.

That afternoon, spirits were piped up later than usual but a double ration of rum was issued. It was gratefully received by every man and boy. The servants, volunteers or young gentlemen, as they were referred to, hovered around the scuttlebutt and were the first in line when the ration was served. Were it not for the eagle eyes of the boatswain, a couple would have crept back for a second serve and chanced having a taste of the boatswain's starter.

Re-joining the captain, the sailing master asked, 'Should we take a more westerly bearing. We might find more wind.'

'Thank you, Mr Brannagh, but I have no desire to encounter the Doldrums again. Continue south on this heading to the Verde Islands.'

'Wood and water?'

'No. Once we reach that latitude, set a course south-south-west and maintain that bearing until we cross the Equator. From there we shall head due south.'

'St Helena?'

'I think not. Ascension Island is my choice.'

The destination was met with a questioning look. 'Are you familiar with that island, Captain?' the sailing master quizzed.

'Only from what I have read,' Oliver replied. 'It's an uninhabited barren outcrop and seldom visited but it will serve us well to break our journey for a few days. I think we will not be troubled there.'

'I heard it was a God-forsaken place,' the sailing master added.

'Indeed. But it is British and of no strategic interest to our enemies.'

'Is there a garrison there?'

'No garrison and no settlement. To the best of my knowledge, it is unpopulated but has ample fresh water springs and a good supply of goats and sheep running wild, courtesy of the early Portuguese explorers. Plus, it is visited by giant sea turtles around this time of the year. They come ashore to lay their eggs. Plenty of fresh meat for the taking. A party of marines and marksmen should be able to supply the galley with enough fresh meat to feed us till we reach Cape Town. What say you?'

'Most acceptable. I never say no to a bowl of turtle soup. Perhaps, also, a chance for the men to bathe and scrub their clothes and hammocks, and in this heat the ship will have a chance to dry out a little. But it will take a month of sailing to fetch us there.'

'Do you have another pressing engagement?' the captain asked glibly.

The sailing master smiled. 'No, sir. Ascension Island it is.

Chapter 14

Ascension Island

Clouds of black volcanic dust rose from the broad stretch of loose cinder scree that covered half of the distant hill, as a mob of boys padded across it. Above it were inhospitable rugged cliffs and, scattered below, the jagged volcanic rocks that had, long ago, been vomited from the volcano's mouth. Not a tree or bush could be seen on this part of the island, nor any other living thing. Like the pimpled face of a pubescent schoolboy, the island was marked by dozens of cone-shaped hills – the forty extinct volcanoes that had once formed the island's landscape.

'Captain Quintrell,' the second lieutenant hailed from the quarterdeck rail. 'The young gentlemen are heading back. I can't see the schoolmaster but he must be amongst them.

'How many? Oliver asked.

'All of them, I think. I counted twenty.'

'Thank you, Mr Weir. I shall go ashore to speak with them. I am interested to hear what they have learned from their venture across the island and if they have made any significant discoveries. 'My boat, if you please, Mr Weir.'

With an hour of sunlight remaining, the returning party were making no effort to hurry. Some sauntered, walking arm in arm, totally immersed in their conversations. One or two stopped to examine a plant or pick up a stone to add to already bulging pockets. A pair ran about taunting, teasing and annoying their companions. A couple made balls of scree and threw the black dust into their companion's faces, much to the annoyance of those who were targeted. Time meant nothing to any of them.

As the boat was being lowered from *Royal Standard*'s davits, the captain examined the group carefully through the lens of his glass, taking note of their less than gentlemanly appearance – the unruly hair, the neckerchiefs tied around their foreheads, collars unbuttoned, shirt tails flying, stockings rolled down to their ankles, while sleeves were rolled up higher than the elbows in the fashion of a common wharf worker. While he could not see their features clearly, he assumed they would be carrying as much dirt on their faces, hands and shoes as on the roots of the botanical samples they had set off to collect.

In the days prior to embarking on the excursion, the schoolmaster had introduced them to the geography of the island and to its volcanic origin. Having ascended from the sea bed many millennia ago, it had been given the name – Ascension Island. To inspire their interest, Mr Greenstreet had assured the young gentlemen it was quite possible for them to discover some un-named variety of plant that could be credited to them and presented at a future Royal Society meeting, or to Kew Gardens later in the year.

If nothing else was achieved, the captain conceded that at least the boys would expend some pent-up energy during their time on land, rather than causing a disturbance aboard the ship. Unfortunately, the disruption caused to nesting birds and crabs was an unavoidable incidental. Being inspired and engaged would be a bonus.

From *Royal Standard*'s hull it was only a short pull to the small beach and the ship's cutter, where one of the midshipmen and the boat crew had been idling their time all day waiting the return of the young gentlemen in order to ferry them back to the ship.

Relaxing in the balmy atmosphere, the peace the boat's crew had been enjoying for several hours was disturbed only by the sound of birds and the gentle lapping of the waves. Finding any shade from the overhead sun had been the sailors' greatest challenge. When the captain's boat was seen approaching, the group quickly rose to their feet and dusted themselves down.

'Anything to report, Gentlemen?' Oliver asked when he stepped ashore.

'No, Captain, just enjoying the scenery until a few moments ago when we thought we heard the young gents returning.'

From a distance, the high-pitched cries from young voices heralded the disorganised mob as they drew closer. The sound increased, as the group ran helter-skelter to the beach. It was quite evident from the faces that each one was eager to relate what had happened. Weaving between the boulders, they arrived exhausted at the shore, immediately dropped their knapsacks and threw themselves headlong onto the soft warm sand. Panting, they rolled over and sprawled out as if dead.

Oliver considered the dishevelled mob of precocious manhood but reserved his judgement. 'Where is Mr Greenstreet?' he asked.

The response came in unison from at least a dozen voices each trying to out-shout his mate with the news.

'Silence,' the captain called, before pointing to the tallest boy sitting in the sand closest to him. He repeated the same question to him.

'He's back there, Captain.' The boy stood up and pointed and, as if prompted, the whole group turned their heads and extended their arms to point back up the track they had come down. 'He's following behind us.'

Oliver turned to his second lieutenant. 'Mr Weir, kindly ensure the young gentlemen attend to their dress, dust off the sand and return to the ship immediately. I shall return to the ship with you and speak with the schoolmaster later.'

'Aye, Captain. On your feet, all of you,' Mr Weir ordered. 'Do as the captain said.' Dragging themselves up from the sand, picking up their knapsacks, and dusting themselves off, there were a few low grumbles but, with the captain standing within earshot, they complied with the lieutenant's orders. The sight of the midshipman pulling the boatswain's starter from a red bag emphasised the call.

'Any more disruption and you will all be kissing the gunner's daughter before the day is out,' he growled.

The threat of punishment worked a treat. With nothing more said, the boys helped the sailors drag the cutter from the sand, climbed or fell into it and sat silently on the thwarts or in the bottom of the boat, not daring to make a murmur until the boat crew pushed off.

Eight oars splashed each time they dipped into the crystal clear water disturbing the shoals of tiny fish that were unused to intruders. As for the boys, their expressions became doleful as they neared the ship's hull. The eyes of the captain, watching them from the stern sheets, didn't leave them until they climbed to *Royal Standard*'s entry port. Throughout the time, not a word was uttered.

It was almost twenty minutes before the schoolmaster returned to the beach. Hardly able to walk and in a very distressed state, he was supported by two of the stronger young gentlemen. His face was etched with the pain of his journey. His neckerchief, blackened with blood, was wrapped around his ankle and secured with a bandage made from his stocking.

On seeing him, two sailors from the waiting boat, hurried along the track to meet him and carried him the rest of the way to the beach. The boys who had supported him along the track were totally exhausted.

'Welcome back, Mr Greenstreet,' the midshipman said sympathetically. 'The men will help you aboard.'

'I would prefer to sit for a moment, if that is in order. Did the boys tell you what happened?'

'Indeed,' the midshipman admitted. 'The boys arrived full of wind and a cacophony of voices that I was hardly able to interpret. Perhaps you can explain.'

'I must report to the captain urgently,' the teacher said, struggling against his aching limbs to raise himself up. Gazing across the narrow strip of water to where *Royal Standard* was anchored, he was obliged to admit, 'I have lost three of the boys.'

'Lost,' the midshipman repeated. 'Are they headed this way? Were they following you and perhaps gone off the track?'

'I wish that were the case. No, they deliberately took leave on their own, early in the day, and failed to return. I have no knowledge of where they are. I have searched without success and must convey this information to the captain so he can decide what must be done.'

'All in good time,' the midshipman advised. 'You must sit for a while and rest. Wait for the captain's boat to return.'

Anxious but relieved, Mr Greenstreet rested on the beach leaning against the boat with the crew gathered around him. They all listened intently as he explained what had transpired.

'All went well, at first, until eight of the boys ran ahead of the group. Despite my calls for them to wait, reminding them to show some semblance of respect for the other fellows, my pleas fell on deaf ears.

'After only half an hour,' he continued, 'five of the younger boys returned, deflated and full of apologies. If truth be told, they had been unable to keep pace with the three biggest boys who were intent on heading off on their own. Fearing being lost and never being found, the youngsters were relieved to return to my care.'

The midshipman, who was not much older than the young gentlemen, chose not to comment. 'As you are aware, the majority of the boys reached the ship well before you. They were spurred on by their exuberance to convey the bad news.'

'That three of the boys were missing?'

'Indeed, that was the story they shared only half an hour ago. And the captain was on the beach at the time.'

'Oh!' was the schoolmaster's only reply.

Sitting down on a black boulder that had once been spewed from the vent of an active volcano, he stared at the sea, shaking his head.

'Water for Mr Greenstreet,' the midshipman called.

The man drank thirstily. 'Thank you.'

Though there was not a cloud overhead, the sky was suddenly darkened by a reeling mass of thousands of birds returning to the island for the night. The sound was ear-splitting. Over the years, the squawking and squealing had been likened to the haunting calls of the souls of sailors lost at sea. The sound grew louder as seething masses swooped lower and circled the ground eager to return to their nests and reunite with their eggs.

'Time for us to leave,' the midshipman said. With the return of the Captain's boat, two of the sailors helped the schoolmaster to his feet, assisting him across the sand and into the cutter.

The water in the cove was still as any pond as they were rowed back in silence to *Royal Standard*.

When the boys and Mr Greenstreet had been safely delivered back to the ship, the captain requested one of the middies return to the beach and remain there until the three lost boys returned. Mr Adams, who had stayed aboard *Royal Standard* all day, was happy to volunteer to go ashore. But he did not go alone. Six sailors from the boat crew and two marines accompanied him.

On the beach, the sailors immediately collected driftwood and built a large bonfire to serve as a beacon for the lost boys. It was thought unlikely they would attempt to trek across the island in pitch darkness. While there was no danger from natives or wild animals, the volcanic terrain was treacherous, the surface littered with holes from which sprouted bushes bearing evil thorns.

As the evening progressed, the sea turned black and the contours of the island disappeared under a heavy veil of grey. Despite the clear southern sky being dotted with a multitude of stars and a bright moon shining, undertaking even a short journey across the island would have been foolish for anyone to attempt.

During the night, the sailors took turns to stand watch, the only interruption was the sighting of two large turtles. Having hauled themselves up the beach, they proceeded to dig holes in the sand and deposit their eggs into them.

Waiting quietly, in the flickering light of the dying embers, the sailors and marines watched the creatures until their job was completed and, after flipping sand over their nests, they turned and dragged themselves slowly towards the sea. Catching the pair was easy, but their weight made it difficult to flip them onto their backs. In the morning, they could be lifted into the boat and hoisted onto the ship's deck. Remaining upside down, the turtles would stay fresh until the cook was ready to use them. In addition to turtle meat, the sailors collected a sack of fresh eggs to present to the ship.

'Damned young fools,' Oliver Quintrell cursed.

Sitting with him in the great cabin, Mr Greenstreet merely inclined his head in agreement. Having exhausted his thoughts, words and constant apologies, his face was white and drawn.

'Which boys are they?' the captain asked. 'Do you have their names? Is Dorrington one of them?'

The schoolmaster looked surprised. 'He is.'

'The ringleader, I don't doubt.'

'You are right, Captain. I believe he convinced two of the other boys to go with him and, from the onset, had no intention of following my instructions. I was told Dorrington's plan was to climb to the top of the highest point on the island so he could get a 360 degree view of the ocean.'

'He said that?'

'So I was told.'

'Has he not discovered he can achieve the same by climbing to the top of the main? Perhaps I shall remind him when he returns.'

'I should have stepped in,' the older man said apologetically. 'I'd heard them whispering and ignored it but, some time later, discovered the three boys were missing.'

'You should have taken two marine guards with you,' Oliver said. 'However, it is too late now.'

'With your permission, Captain, I will head off in the morning and take a party along with me to conduct a thorough search for them.'

'I think not. You are not fit to walk on that injured leg. In the morning a search party will be raised. You will draw up a rough map with instructions of the route you took and advise the possible locations where you think the boys might be.'

'But I should accompany the party. Those boys were under my care. They were my responsibility.'

'Let me remind you, Mr Greenstreet, as captain of this vessel, those boys are my responsibility. I can assure you, however, they will be found, even if it takes us a week to find them. This rocky outcrop, in the middle of the Atlantic, measures only eight miles in both width and breadth. And while the terrain is not easy, there are no wild beasts, to my knowledge, and nothing harmful except perhaps a few snakes. At these latitudes, it is never cold so they will not freeze. Also, it hardly rains but, if they are thirsty, by all accounts, there is good water rising in springs on the higher ground. They will just have to search to find it. And if they have a modicum of intelligence they will not starve. They can feed on land crabs and nesting birds to their hearts' content.'

'You think so?'

'Indeed, I do.'

'What will you do with them when they are found?' Mr Greenstreet asked.

The Captain chewed over the question for a few moments. 'That depends on several things. If some accident has befallen them, then I will deal with them sympathetically and leniently. But, if I find that they have blatantly disobeyed the instruction they were given, then I will regard their deliberate actions as tantamount to desertion. And you know the penalty for desertion from one of his Majesty's ships.'

Oliver paused and sighed. 'Unfortunately, I find myself in a difficult situation. These boys are very young and, as *servants*, are officially not yet in the King's service, therefore I cannot deliver them to a court martial nor hang them,'

The schoolmaster was shocked.

'But mark my words, any report I write about their behaviour will be submitted to the Admiralty. That might mean they will never make it to midshipman on a fighting ship.'

'Dorrington's father is a cabinet minister in the government – a close friend of the Prime Minister,' Mr Greenstreet advised tentatively.

'I don't care if he is second cousin to the Prince of Wales! I will not tolerate this type of behaviour.' He took a deep breath. 'But first, you must allow the surgeon to attend to your lower leg. Obsidian rock is as sharp as glass and can cut deeply. After that, I advise you to take to your bed as soon as you have eaten. We will speak again in the morning.'

The schoolmaster has hardly left he great cabin when Lieutenant Holland asked to speak with the captain.

'Enter,' Oliver said. 'Is there a problem?'

'No problem, Captain. I'm sorry to disturb you so late, but I thought you would like to see this.' In his hands was a large bone, which he handed to the Captain. 'What do you make of it, sir?' he asked.

Gazing down, Oliver turned it over in order to view it from all sides. He closely examined the bulbous ends. 'It's not fresh,' the captain observed.

'That's exactly what the surgeon said when I showed it to him.'

'And what else did the Doctor say?'

'He said it is a human bone. A leg bone.'

'Where did it come from?'

'From the island. The captain's dog must have dug it up somewhere. He carried it to the beach and tried to bury it in the sand. He wasn't too happy when one of the hands took it from him.'

'Do you know where he picked it up?'

'No one knows. Chalmers took Cecil ashore for some exercise after the party had left to search for the boys. But Cecil took off on his own.'

'Following them?'

'No, Captain,' Mr Holland said, 'I'm told he headed north along the coast, not inland. Chalmers tried to catch him, but the dog was too quick.'

Oliver studied it again. He had seen bones on beaches before, some from beached sea creatures, seals, whales and turtles. He was also familiar with the human toll claimed by sea battles including the dire reports from Trafalgar, and the report of ships lost in the storm where damaged prizes sank with all hands, and where bodies of the dead, or near-dead, were tossed overboard from ships of all nations. Many bodies had floated ashore to await a Christian burial that never came. Slowly the relentless tides washed the remnants of clothing from them, while crabs and seabirds made a feast of any

161

flesh that was available. Eventually the beached carcasses were torn apart by wild dogs, foxes or vultures, their bones scattered across the countryside. Few traces would be left after only a matter of weeks.

This bone, over a foot in length, was bleached white from long exposure to the tropical sun. The only marks on it were minor scratches. With no foxes on the island, they were probably inflicted by Cecil's teeth or claws. The marks were fresh, clean and only superficial.

'The surgeon called it a femur. He can't put an age to it, but says it once belonged to a healthy individual. He said it shows no signs of prior breaks or wounds. But it is not fresh and would not belong to any of the crew.'

'Interesting,' Oliver said. 'With no dirt on it, I do not think it had been buried. More likely, it was merely laying on the surface when the dog found it. With no scavengers to tear it apart and being too large and heavy for a bird to carry it off, it is possible other bones were still with it. I would like to know if that is the case and precisely where, on the island, it came from.'

Returning the bone to the lieutenant, Oliver continued. 'Mr Chalmers appears to be able to relate to the dog. I suggest you take Chalmers, the bone and the hound back to the beach in the morning and see if it can lead you back to the spot where he found it. Tell Chalmers, to rig up a long line to tie around the dog's neck to prevent him from running away again.

'Also take a couple of the youngsters who did not go with the schoolmaster on the expedition.'

'Aye, Captain.'

'I suggest you make an early start in the morning.'

By dawn, the bonfire built on the beach had died. Only the embers remained. Overnight the tide had filled, delivering drifting clouds of foamy bubbles along the beach. The gentle breeze lifted them and rolled them further up the sand.

Everything was silent. Then, as if responding to a wake-up call, the thousands of birds that had arrived on the island the night before emerged from their burrows and took to the wing blotting the sky in great roiling clouds of living blackness. The sound of beating wings and squealing cries was deafening. Then almost as quickly as it had happened, the swirling murmurating mass rolled away and the sound faded to silence.

It was promptly broken when one of the ship's guns fired, was reloaded and fired again. Three times in all. The explosion was sufficient to carry the noise across the island. It was intended to provide direction for the missing boys to follow and to spur them into returning to the ship.

An hour later the search party was assembled on the beach. It consisted of a lieutenant, a midshipman, two sailors and four marines. The captain insisted the surgeon also accompany them along with his loblolly. A folded hammock with two pikes was carried with them to be used as a stretcher, if required.

On a roughly drawn map, Mr Greenstreet had marked where the boys split from the rest of the group, and the location of the island's highest point that had once been its main volcano. While the schoolmaster continued his protestations that he should go along, Captain Quintrell was adamant that he did not leave the ship. The surgeon also insisted that Mr Greenstreet rest his leg, as the injury was far worse than first considered.

Within half an hour of the search party setting off, a second smaller group, led by a recently shorn Newfoundland dog, left the beach in search of human remains. Several hours later that group returned. Though the search had proved fruitless, the dog and the boys had all enjoyed the ramble which took them to the northernmost coast of the island.

On return, as a treat, Cecil received a bowl of knucklebones from the cook.

'Were you expecting us to find something?' Mr Holland asked when attending the captain in the great cabin.

'It was a vain hope,' Oliver replied. 'Several years ago, the newspapers related the story of a sailor who was deliberately marooned on Ascension Island and left alone there with only minimal supplies. Some years later, his knapsack was discovered and evidence was found of a campsite he had built. But the sailor was never found. Perhaps that bone is all that remained of his body. Or perhaps he was not the only man to be marooned on the island over the years.'

'What crime did he commit?'

'What other? Sodomy.'

The lieutenant thought for a moment. 'What about a shipwreck and bodies washed ashore?'

'It is possible,' the captain said, 'but one would expect to read of such events in the *Naval Chronicle*. I think we will gain nothing by searching for old bones. Pass this one to the doctor. He might like to keep it as a souvenir.'

It was early evening when the party returned escorting the three young gentlemen with them. This time, there was no shrieking or cheering. The boys were filthy, thirsty and hungry and bore numerous scratches on their bare arms and legs. Their fine white shirts and breeches had been ripped to ribbons. Their lips were cracked and swollen, their noses blistered, their cheeks almost the colour of a marine's coatee.

If Dorrington and his cohorts had expected to receive a rousing welcome on their return, they were sorely disappointed. Once aboard ship, the three were immediately separated, taken below and placed under lock and key in three small cabins. Apart from water to wash in and a cloth to dry themselves with, they were each handed a clean shirt and breeches, given water to drink, a bowl of broth and a hunk of bread to eat, but nothing more.

Despite several demands from the oldest boy to speak with the captain, Oliver Quintrell preferred to allow them time to simmer. Four hours later, he had the three boys ushered into the great cabin.

Seated at his desk, Captain Quintrell was making an entry in his journal. A lantern burned from the overhead beam, without the slightest movement in the flame. A glim was also lit on the captain's desk close to where he was working.

The boys sneaked a look at each other, grinned and fought the urge to giggle. The captain looked around and glared. 'You find something amusing, Mr Dorrington?'

The tall youth, thirteen years of age, cleared his throat. 'No, sir.'

'And what about you, Mister?'

'No, certainly not, sir,' the second boy's answer was full of confidence but not convincing.

The third boy sniffled.

'Then why is it, the three of you are struggling to hide your emotions.'

'Not, sir,' Dorrington piped up. 'Just pleased to be back.'

'I don't doubt you are – as are the men who were despatched to search for you. Let me inform you that your irresponsible and disobedient behaviour has caused considerable disruption to the ship. It has taken up valuable time, and created additional cost and, not least, resulted in a serious injury being suffered by Mr Greenstreet, who you treated with utter disrespect. You ignored his instruction and as a result he could have died. If any of you three *gentlemen* were ever told you had the potential qualities to rise to the rank of midshipman, let alone advance through the ranks to serve as a lieutenant, then you were sorely mistaken. I am sure your fathers will be less than thrilled when they receive my report and an account of the problems you have caused, not to the mention the time expended and cost incurred in returning you to the ship.'

At the mention of the word *fathers*, the three faces transformed, as if a death shroud had been slipped over their heads. Any residual expressions of bravado, bluster, pride or superiority immediately dissolved.

'Might I say something?'

Oliver looked at the smallest boy with the mop of ginger curls and the face that on any other occasion was the epitome of innocence.

'Speak.'

'It was Dorrington, Captain. He said we should go with him and forget about Mr Greenstreet.'

The second boy in the line nodded his agreement.

'And the pair of you went along with that foolish and deceitful suggestion? Have you no backbone, either of you? Have you no mind of your own? Do you not know right from wrong?' Rising from his seat, the ship's captain glowered at the three boys. 'Let me remind you, in His Majesty's Navy you must obey orders at all times. Perhaps this fact slipped your mind, or perhaps you did not heed the *Articles of War* that have been read to the ship's company after every Sunday service since you stepped aboard. Did you think those rules did not apply to you? Perhaps you closed your ears and did not even listen. Or perhaps you thought it was a joke and scoffed at the naval regulations.'

'No, Captain,' the youngest boy muttered and was about to continue.

'Silence. For the rest of this cruise you will no longer have the privilege of sharing quarters with the midshipmen, instead you will eat and sleep with the hands in the mess. I can assure you the regular crew will not tolerate any mischief or misbehaviour from the likes of you three. The quartermaster will allocate a number on the overhead beams where you will hang your hammock. Now get out. I do not wish to see you again!'

It was inevitable that during the reprimand, Oliver Quintrell, when looking directly at the three young gentlemen, had compared their manner, demeanour and personality to young Charles Goodridge, the orphan who had come aboard his ship, two years earlier, in Gibraltar.

At eleven years of age, Charles's knowledge of the construction and workings of a fighting ship was equal to that of most midshipmen and seasoned sailors. And, at that young age, his selflessness, ingenuity and bravery had played a major role in saving one of His Majesty's frigates and its crew, on a previous mission.

He wondered how Charles, being of humble birth and parentage, was contending with the likes of these young aristocrats. Would such company at the Naval Academy forge his character for a bright future in the navy or would such associations dim his resolve and break his will in the process?

Did Charles really want to go to sea – to study at the Naval Academy – to serve time on one of his Majesty's ships, sit for examinations and rise in the ranks with the added prospect of promotion, prize money and a comfortable life? These were the questions the captain had puzzled over for some time. Not being born into gentry would always stand against the boy.

Or did Charles want to go to the university in Scotland, following in the footsteps of Dr Whipple and study to become a physician? That decision would be made when he returned to England.

'Marine,' he called, when the boys were dismissed. The sentry posted outside the cabin door responded. 'Pass the word to Mr Brophy – I intend to sail at first light.'

Chapter 15

Scorpion sighted

With a fresh westerly blowing, the 50-gun ship was sailing well making a steady seven knots.

Relaxing in the warm air, some sailors of the starboard watch rested against the rails, while others sought shade on deck beneath the billowing canvas. There had been little call on them for the last two hours.

At eight o'clock, the bell clanged from the belfry, stirred the crew and sent them below for supper. On the ratlines, the topmen of the starboard watch descended as the larboard watch scrambled up to take their places. Nothing was said as the men passed each other. From the quarterdeck, Oliver observed the smooth change of watch.

Within minutes of the fresh lookout reaching the top of the foremast, he cupped his hands to his mouth and shouted to the deck. 'Sail, ho!'

Every ear that heard the call from the masthead turned in the direction the lookout was pointing.

'Where away?' the officer of the watch, called back.

'Four points off the port bow.'

'What do you see?'

There was no immediate response.

Mr Holland repeated his question.

'I can't be sure. It's a ship alright. The hull's half up and it looks to be the size of a frigate, but there's something mighty strange about the way she's sailing. Looks like she's dragging her anchor.'

'Hardly likely, in mid ocean,' the sailing master scoffed.

The lookout heard the comment. 'Well, she ain't going nowhere with her canvas furled on the fore and main yards. Only cloth that's loose is the fore t'gallant, but its shredded and waving like half a dozen pennants in the wind.'

'A glass, if you please,' the second lieutenant requested. A telescope was handed to him by the shipping master. Unable to see much from the quarterdeck, he snapped the glass shut, leapt onto the rail and headed up the ratlines to join the lookout.

The captain waited a moment. 'What do you see, Mr Weir?'

'It's as the lookout said, most of her sails are furled. It's likely the others have been unbent or torn away. But she's dead in the water. No stays'ls set. Just rolling on the swell. Can't be sure from this distance, but I don't believe there's anyone on the deck.'

'And the helm?'

'No one there either.'

'Obvious damage?'

'Starboard rail partly gone. Can't speak for the larboard side.'

'Shot holes? Other damage?'

'Too far away to be sure, but I don't think so.'

'Thank you, Mr Weir. You can return to the deck.'

Within minutes, the lieutenant jumped down from the ratlines and joined the captain on the quarterdeck.

'What colours is she flying?' the captain asked.

'She don't appear to be flying any.'

Without colours it was impossible to know if she was friend or foe, though the opinion bandied across the quarterdeck was that she was French-built.

Even the name on the transom – *Scorpion*, revealed nothing of the mystery, but all agreed it was a tidy vessel.

'What is your opinion, Mr Weir?'

'A bit too far to see clearly, but it's as the lookout said, she just don't look right. She ain't sailing, just rolling on the swell.'

'How many guns?' the captain asked.

'Possibly twenty-four.'

'And the gun ports?'

'All closed,' the officer said.

Despite the fact not a soul had been seen on the ship's deck, Oliver remained suspicious. It was an unlikely trap, but he could not be too careful. On the other hand, if the vessel had been abandoned, the question remained – why? Considering it was still

169

afloat thousands of miles from any naval port or dockyard proved it had a sound hull, so if it was deserted, why was that so? Without stepping aboard, it was impossible to know the answers.

'Any other ships on the horizon?' Oliver asked.

'I didn't see any.'

'Do we run out the guns?' Mr Brophy interrupted eagerly.

'Not yet,' the captain replied. 'However, beat to quarters. All hands on deck, if you will. I intend to take a closer look at this wandering albatross. Bring us to within a cable's length of her starboard side. If she fails to respond to our hail, put a shot across her bow. Let us see what that brings.'

'Aye, aye, Captain.'

The high pitched squeal of the boatswain's pipe and the *rat-a-tat* on the drum's taut skin spilled the sailors from the hatches and onto the deck; many still chewing on lumps of tough meat.

'Put a shot alongside her, Mr Brophy.'

'*Scorpion*,' the sailing master read out, as *Royal Standard* closed on her and the gold-painted letters on the transom became easily legible. 'Single deck. Twenty-four or twenty-eight-guns, I would say. And riding low in the water.'

Fifteen minutes later, the silence was shattered and the forward deck reverberated to the recoil from the cannon. Smoke engulfed the forecastle as the barrel spewed orange flame and the muzzle spat out an 18-pound ball on a tongue of fire. Hissing through the air, the shot stayed low and splashed into the sea twenty yards from the stranger's bow.

There was no response from the ghost ship, it merely continued pitching and heeling gracefully to the easy roll of the broad troughs of the Atlantic.

The hot barrel was sponged out, the gun carriage hauled back and the crew stood ready waiting for further orders.

'Take us in closer, helmsman,' Oliver Quintrell called. 'Boarders, make ready. I want marines at the rails and sharp shooters in the tops.'

The deck suddenly sprang to life with an undercurrent of excited anticipation.

'She's maintaining her course,' one of the young midshipman announced.

Oliver turned to the young man. 'She is not following any course, Mr Aitcheson, she is drifting on the current. Look closely at the helm and see if it is running free.'

A glance confirmed the wheel was spinning in response to the movement of the rudder in the swell. 'What do you make of it, Mr Brannagh?' the captain asked.

He shrugged his shoulders. 'Something amiss there, Captain. But as the gunports are closed, there's no danger of her firing on us without warning.'

'The name *Scorpion*, does that mean anything to you?' Oliver asked.

'Nothing. Perhaps she was one of the ships that escaped from Trafalgar after the battle.'

'Not so,' Oliver answered. 'The four ships that ran from the battle were captured off Brest within days. I heard they were quick to haul their colours and were taken into Portsmouth as prizes.'

Oliver looked again at the ghost ship's name. 'There was a *Scipion* at Trafalgar – a French man-of-war. I thought perhaps this was it, but the name is not the same and I believe that was a seventy-four.'

The sailing master considered the vessel without the glass. 'She's sitting low in the water, Captain,' he added. 'She might have been holed below the waterline.'

'I agree,' Oliver said. 'I fear she has a bellyful of water though not enough to sink her. As we are presently seven hundred nautical miles from the coast of West Africa, she could hardly have reached this latitude had she suffered any major damage to her hull. It may be waves breaking over her or slow seepage that has filled her up. I want you and the carpenter to accompany me when I go aboard.'

'Are you going to take her, Captain?'

Oliver smiled, 'It appears, she is there for the taking – how can I refuse?'

'Tread carefully, Captain. Make sure she hasn't been booby-trapped before going below.'

'Thank you, Mr Brannagh; I will heed your warning.'

'Bring us alongside, Mr Brophy,' the captain ordered. 'Ready the boarding party and a dozen marines. The ship appears to be empty but, until we board her, we can't be sure. I want a thorough search conducted below deck and a full report on what is found – bodies, cargo, contraband, provisions, victuals, weapons and more. And bring the cooper along to check the barrels.'

Lieutenant Brophy took a step forward. 'I would like to volunteer to go with you.'

'Thank you, Mr Brophy, but you will take charge of the deck here. I intend to go over myself. Maintain our present position until I return. Is that understood?'

'Yes, Captain.'

'Now kindly organise the boats and men. Let us visit this ghost ship. I want half a dozen marines in each boat and sharpshooters in the rigging. As quick as possible, if you please. Let us do this while we still have light.'

With most of the crew lining the sides, the men allocated as boarders waited for their order. The tops were decorated with the striking scarlet coats of the marines.

'Boats ready,' the boatswain called.

'Grappling irons and cutlasses ready, Captain,' one of the division captains called.

'I doubt the latter will be necessary,' Oliver replied, though memories of slicing through a plague of live rats infesting another abandoned ship flashed through his mind.

The ship's boats lifted and fell against *Royal Standard*'s hull riding the easy troughs of the slow ocean swell. With everyone aboard, the painter was tossed into the bow and with a call from the coxswain, the oarsmen dipped their blades and made quick work of covering the distance between the two ships. With sailors and marines in the first boat, the captain, sailing master and carpenter were in the second boat. Spray splashed from the bows and oars as the boats swam across the pond.

Receiving no fire from the empty ship, some of the young boarders behaved as though this was a game, brandishing their cutlasses and pretending to strike the man sitting opposite. The sort of make-believe boys would play when pretending to be pirates.

'Save your energy,' Oliver shouted. 'Once you reach the deck, tread carefully and keep your eyes scanned for trails of gunpowder.'

The mention of powder immediately dampened the eager spirits though a few were still spurred on by the earlier rumour of prize money.

Even with no sound from within the ship, or response to the boats bumping alongside, or the clatter of the grapples as they landed on the deck, the first few boarders climbed cautiously. No sooner were they aboard, than a rope ladder was rolled down the side of the hull. Oliver Quintrell was the first from the second boat to climb aboard.

When he stepped onto the deck, he ducked his head to avoid the slow but lethal pendulum-like swing of a lump of *lignum vitae*. 'Secure those blocks,' he ordered. 'And lash the guns.'

On the deck, two 18-pounders along with their carriages were missing from their positions. It was obvious they had worked free, careered across the deck, smashed through the gunwales on the far side and dived into the ocean. A second barrel was on its side, having fallen from its carriage – the truck wheels broken. The remainder of the deck was clean, save for loose lines and lengths of dried kelp entangled around the carriage wheels with bundles of seaweed clogging the scuppers.

But there were no bodies or body parts or even old blood staining the timbers on the ghost ship, and the deck itself was relative clear save for an empty leather water bucket and two cannon balls rolling back and forth, caught up at times on the loose frayed hempen lines squirming about like live serpents. After a quick inspection, the boatswain confirmed the guns showed no signs of being purposely spiked or tampered with.

'Cut those rags down from the fore t'gallant yard. And unfurl the main t'gallant if it is still sound. But warn the men to step carefully on the ratlines and foot ropes, they may be rotten and need replacing.'

While the courses were neatly furled to the yards and the gaskets still holding tight, it was impossible to say how long they had been subject to the rotting elements of burning sun and salty sea spray. But to bend on new sails would necessitate finding replacements in the sail lockers. If the depth of water in the hull was as great as the captain feared, the water-logged sails would prove near impossible to haul onto the deck.

'The canvas on the fore t'gallant is shredded to ribbons, Captain,' the lieutenant called, only confirming what the captain could see for himself. 'And the ship's boats are all gone,' the sailing master added, 'apart from the jolly boat.'

Had they been washed away or taken by the crew when they departed the ship and left it to the elements? Oliver wondered.

'The forward hatch is open,' Mr Aitcheson called, and I can hear water washing around below.'

'Mr Weir, come with me. I want to investigate the main cabin and the hold. Kindly look for a manifest. I want to know what cargo this vessel was carrying. With memories of a hold full of dead slaves from a previous mission, he was prepared for anything.

However, the captain's cabin revealed very little. Oliver concluded, although most of the contents were missing, the cabin had not been pillaged. This was not the work of pirates. More likely, a systematic and concerted effort had been made to remove everything portable before the crew abandoned ship. Charts, instruments, clothing, pistols and ammunition were all gone. Every cupboard and drawer had been emptied.

'Where do you think she's come from?' the sailing master asked.

'I hope there is something here to tell us that,' the captain replied. Stepping gingerly, Oliver turned to a chest of drawers and pulled out each drawer in turn but they were all empty. There was no log or journal amongst the scattered debris. The books on the cabin floor had come from the shelves whose wooden fiddle had broken. A glance at the pages of one of the volumes indicated that it was a French ship. The other books were in the same language.

'I need the boatswain and the sail maker to check the canvas and the rigging. I want to know if this ship is in a fit state to sail. We must take advantage of the fair winds. They may not last long.'

Having been constantly washed by waves breaking over the ship and sluicing through to the deck below, the cabin was damp and had an unhealthy smell about it. But with the bulwarks and furnishings still in place, it was obvious *Scorpion* had not been cleared for action, confirming it had not come under fire at the time it was abandoned.

From the cabin, the captain headed for the hold. Four steps down and his feet were in water. With no light, it was impossible to survey the items stored there. With no small barrels visible, it appeared that anything that could be carried had been removed by hand, while the large barrels and leaguers containing water and ship's supplies, had been left. They were now being washed in an ocean of brine mixed with bilge water along with rotted sacks that had long since disgorged their spoiled contents. An occasional rat provided the only movement, paddling vigorously across the swaying surface. With only numerals stamped on the barrels, and with no inventory to refer to, it was impossible to know what they contained – wine, beer, potatoes, pease, chocolate, slops or silver.

'Get the cooper to check the integrity of these barrels. I must know if the drinking water is potable and if any of the stores are still edible.' Oliver was unable to reach the magazine in the bottom of the ship. If the barrels stowed there had been underwater for any length of time, the damp would have ruined the black powder and it would be useless.

The order was relayed for the cooper to join the captain.

'Seven feet in the well,' the carpenter said popping his head up from below. 'I'm surprised she's still afloat.'

'And the pumps?' Oliver turned to the midshipman at the top of the steps. 'Mr Holland, get some men on the pumps immediately.'

'I can't see where the water has come in from, Captain,' the carpenter called. 'There are no shot holes. There is some damage to the hull, port side below water level – but not much, mind you. A copper sheet might have been ripped off and the caulking gauged out. I'd wager a big sea lifted her onto a reef and she got lodged there. The crew would have attempted to get her off but eventually decided she was wrecked and accepted that they would never retrieve her. So they took what they could carry before they left her. Who knows how long she might have sat there – days, weeks or months. Then later, another rogue wave would have washed her off and sent her back to sea. That's just my opinion, Captain.'

'Thank you, Mr Thornhill. You may well be right. In the meantime, monitor the level. There will be hands on the pumps as soon as possible, and when she's sitting a bit higher in the water, kindly do what you can to stop her leaking.'

'Aye, Captain.'

'Good man.'

There was little in the main cabin that was worth salvaging. It had obviously been stripped of anything of value. There were no instruments, no sextant, compasses, charts, clocks or watches, not even a pencil. There was no clothing – uniform jackets, great coats or tarpaulins, no boots – and no charts.

'The ship must have met with a disaster and the crew decided to abandoned her and save themselves before she went down,' one of the sailors said.

'But she didn't sink,' Mr Holland noted.

'No, indeed she didn't. Kindly go below and see if you can find anything of value in the wardroom and the officers' quarters,' Oliver said.

'Aye, Captain.'

Mr Weir was quick to return. 'The carpenter's shop, boatswain's locker, sail lockers and magazine are all half submerged. I can't say what we have that's good. I guess we won't know until she's been pumped out. It's not safe in the hold at the moment with some of the barrels swimming back and forth. A few have smashed. There's salt beef and rotten potatoes floating about, and a strong smell of beer. There's plenty of wine on board. Those barrels look tight.'

'The men can attend to those later. Pumping is the first priority.'

Returning from below, Captain Quintrell turned his attention to the sails.

'Captain,' one of the sailors called from the bow.

'What is it?'

'The cable through the hawse hold is slack. She's not anchored in these waters. She must have cast the anchor somewhere else.'

Oliver thought that was fairly obvious, being mid-ocean, but he said nothing.

'Haul in that cable and let it dry on the deck, and check the other anchors are secured. I want to get this ghost ship underway as soon as possible.'

Chapter 16

The Captain

'Well, Mr Brannagh? What are your thoughts?'

'It appears we have netted a tasty catch, Captain. Will you be taking her into a British port?'

'Interesting question,' Oliver replied. 'I have no intention of returning to Cork or Portsmouth and, as to our present destination of Cape Town, I am a little unsure. If we find that the Cape has been returned to Britain by the actions of Admiral Sir Home Popham, I will deliver this vessel to the hands of the naval authority there. If, however, *Scorpion* is not accepted there, we will take her back to Portsmouth.'

The sailing master looked troubled. 'Who will take command of the frigate for the rest of the voyage?'

It was a question Oliver had already considered. 'I will give that honour to Mr Brophy. Apart from myself, he is the oldest and most experienced naval officer aboard. He has had many years of service and is eminently capable of assuming command.'

'A role he has been hankering after for some time,' the sailing master said, with a note of cynicism in his voice. 'Have you spoken to the lieutenant about this?'

'Not as yet.'

'He will be happy to have command but I'm not so sure what the men will think about it.'

'The men will have little choice in the matter. What is it you are suggesting?' the captain asked.

'Not suggesting anything, sir, just stating a fact. Captain Chilcott was a born gentleman, astute and shrewd, and a good and generous man. He'd been at sea for most of his life, seen plenty of action and was popular with the crew. Lieutenant Brophy, on the other hand, lacks breeding, charm and diplomacy and has made several enemies amongst the officers, the warrants and the crew.'

'Enemies, you say. That is a strong word. Be careful who hears you say that.'

The sailing master shrugged his shoulders. 'It's common knowledge in the mess and fo'c'sle. At times, Lieutenant Brophy is hard on the men, especially the younger and less experienced ones, even the middies. He expects new hands to know the ropes, even the lubbers straight from the Press, if you understand my meaning. And he's quick to recommend the cat. I think he likes to see it scratch a man's back till it's raw. But that's just my opinion, Captain.'

Oliver cringed at the comments. 'You have said enough, Mr Brannagh, too much, in fact. I will put what you have said aside and form my own opinion. For the present, however, Lieutenant Brophy is the logical and only choice to take charge of the frigate as we head south. With his years of service and rank, I believe him to have more knowledge of navigation and seamanship that all the young officers put together.'

The sailing master could not disagree.

'However, as acting captain, Mr Brophy will require a sailing master and a couple of midshipmen to serve with him on *Scorpion*. I prefer that you stay aboard *Royal Standard* with me, but I want you to nominate one of your mates to go over to the frigate and support him. His job will not be without some major challenges, not least the ones you have mentioned, therefore I suggest you nominate a man who holds Lieutenant Brophy in high esteem. Apart from that, I shall send two of the midshipmen to support him, and call for volunteers to make up the balance from which Mr Brophy can select the men of his choice.'

'How many crew will he take?'

'The more pertinent question is how many men can I spare from *Royal Standard*? Currently the muster book lists three hundred and thirty-eight names and every one of those men is essential to the smooth operation of a 50-gun fighting ship. Ideally, a 24-gun frigate carries over two hundred men but I cannot spare that number. I will allocate eighty men to *Scorpion* leaving over two hundred and fifty here.'

The sailing master acknowledged.

'Let us pray we do not come into any close action as we head south.'

Mr Brannagh agreed.

'Furthermore,' the captain continued, '*Scorpion* has been stripped of all its stores, and will require provisions for at least three months at sea. We can resupply in Cape Town when we are there. The transfer of men and victuals to the 24-, however, must be made as soon as possible while this relative calm persists. As we sail south from the tropics to the Southern Ocean, we will fall into the band of conflicting winds and currents, and conditions are likely to change. The most important consideration is that the two ships sail in convoy and do not part company.'

'I understand,' Mr Brannagh said.

'This evening, I will speak with the officers and give them their orders. Please pass the word.'

The great cabin was indeed the largest area Oliver Quintrell had enjoyed for his sole use. With quarter windows and glass casements stretching along the stern, it appeared even roomier. The view of ocean, horizon and sky was not wasted on him. The pair of cannon, one on either side of the deck had to be ignored. On this occasion it was the venue for the evening meal, the chairs had been brought up from the hold and the table was set for fourteen guests.

While the meal was cooked in the main galley and delivered to the dining room, Casson, with the assistance of a small contingent of young gentlemen volunteers, took charge of the preparations and service.

At eight o'clock, the officers of *Royal Standard* took their seats around the table. In addition to the lieutenants, there were five midshipmen and six warrant officers, including the purser, the sailing master, doctor and schoolmaster. A handful of the young gentlemen were permitted to assist at the table. Mr Greenstreet had provided his recommendation of the most suitable boys to nominate.

After a round of drinks, the dishes arrived. Turtle soup followed by roasted young goat. The meat was fresh having been slaughtered on the ship and hung for several days. Boiled tern eggs were served with some of the vegetables, delivered fresh to the ship in Cork that had retained their colour and flavour – such a welcome change from salt pork and six-month-old sauerkraut and swedes.

Eyes widened, mouths watered and stomachs tightened as the senior officers were the first to be served. For two of the young middies, this was their first trip to sea and their first time at the captain's table. The two young gentlemen who had assisted the sailing master on the island were allowed to take a plate when the others had been served.

When the meal began and the glasses had not yet been refilled, the conversation centred on the ship's previous missions. Lieutenant Brophy was eager to relate some of the action he had been involved in, which he claimed was aboard *Royal Standard*. Yet, from the captain's earlier conversation with the carpenter, and the state of the ship, the claim of battle action was at odds with the advice he had received – *that the ship had never faced a broadside*. Considering the congenial atmosphere, Oliver chose to remain silent about the matter.

It was before the dessert was served, the captain tapped his glass and drew the attention of the company.

'Gentlemen, as we sit down together, I take this opportunity to speak with you all. I apologise that this gathering is long overdue. Being given command of *Royal Standard* was a surprise to me – a welcome surprise, I might add, however, not so for you, the death of your previous captain and change of command happening suddenly must have come as a shock.

'First, I must remind you that we all serve His Royal Highness King George. While facing unexpected challenges, we operate on a system of well-tried and tested routines, and it is that stability, reliability and trust which welds the Navy together. The punishments that are meted out on some ships are often the result of a chink in our own defences, to failings and shortcoming along the way. But without the regulation set down in the *Articles of War*, without following orders and abiding by those principles laid down for us all, the system is in danger of falling apart. I shall say no more. I do not want to spoil your appetites.'

The captain received some muted applause.

'I am not here to remind you of your duty. Looking around I can see that some of you have served for several years, though the majority of you are fairly new to the service. Whatever, I am sure your behaviour on the loss of your previous captain was met with the dignity desired, as indeed was the welcome you gave me when I came aboard, and the condition in which I found the ship. I commend you all.

'Now, however, we have a new challenge – namely we have adopted a frigate that has floated into our path. Whether we truly want it or indeed, need it is of no matter. It has become our responsibility. As you are probably aware, *Scorpion* is a French ship of 24-guns.'

Mr Adams leaned forward in his chair. 'Begging pardon, Captain, but might I ask where you think it came from and how it came to arrive at this point?'

'Those are difficult questions to answer on which one can only speculate. However, being French-built, she may have been serving the French islands in the West Indies. I suggest that during one of her voyages, she sailed into the path of a hurricane and was in danger of sinking or ran aground somewhere, at which time her crew considered her unsalvageable and proceeded to strip and abandon her. It is likely fate played a hand. If, some time later, another storm re-floated her, the Gulf Stream would have carried her north and sent her on a meandering drift around the Atlantic's laterals – skippered only by the prevailing winds and sea currents.

'From there,' the captain continued, glancing at a map of the world on the far wall, 'the North Atlantic swell would have driven her south towards the Equator. Once she reached the tropics she would have been dependant on the Trade winds and perhaps became a little confused.'

'Until we found her.'

'Correct.'

'She's a nice prize,' the youngest of the midshipman whispered to his mate.

'A prize, you say, Mr Adams?'

Not realising the captain had been privy to what he'd said, the young man blushed.

'I am sorry to disappoint you, and while others may be of the same opinion, this 28-gun ship, albeit French built, is not a prize of war. We did not win her in battle. She is a salvage vessel and, if the Navy Board deems her to be so, we will receive only one eighth of her value, if we are lucky. They will decide her fate and it is possible we may not benefit one iota either from the value of the ship or its contents.'

The look of disappointment showed on several faces particularly those who had already mentally spent the prize money they had expected to receive.

'But, consider this,' the captain said, '*Scorpion* is not a wreck. Far from it. Her condition is sound and, once pumped out, she will perform well with the likelihood of making more speed than the vessel we are sailing on. Consider also, if we had met up with any French or Spanish ships while sailing alone, our chances of defending ourselves and coming away unscathed, was not good, however, with two ships and a combined total of 74-guns, we will be a formidable force to be reckoned with. Depending on the size of the enemy, the tables may be turned in our favour putting us in a position to capture a real prize or two.'

Feet stamped on the floor and hands tapped on the underside of the table in approval.

'However, any French ships crossing our path will be eager to take back one of its lost frigates. I do not intend to let that happen.'

Oliver looked around the cabin at the eager young faces listening to his every word. 'Currently, the dilemma I am faced with is that we have insufficient men to serve two fighting ships. It will be impossible to man all 74-guns and work both ships simultaneously, so I will depend on the division captains to make best use of the numbers allocated to them.'

The captain glanced to the man sitting to his right. 'As you may have heard, Lieutenant Brophy will take command of *Scorpion*. And, as we head south, the two ships will sail in convoy until we raise Cape Town.

'Presently there are men working on the pumps. If the water can be eliminated and the carpenter can stop the seepage in the hull, I believe *Scorpion* will prove to be a speedy sailer and *Royal Standard* will be hard pressed to keep pace with her.'

The cabin remained silent.

'With the sailing master's assistance, I will chart our course, as we head south. Hopefully, we will stay clear of the French shipping lanes. But these waters still remain the haunts of Portuguese slavers, not to mention pirates and privateers. My advice is to make sure you always keep a sharp eye on the horizon. Apart from that, Gentlemen, enjoy your meal and I wish you good health.'

The choice of seamen to transfer to *Scorpion* came first from a call for volunteers. Initially, there were some hands who were eager to serve on the smaller and faster frigate, while others wished to remain on *Royal Standard* and were not prepared to leave. The rumour that they were sitting atop a powder keg changed a few minds, until the captain advised that a portion of the gunpowder would be transferred to *Scorpion*'s magazine.

Where the volunteers consisted of groups of mates who served together on gun crews, the captain intervened. He could not risk depleting the gun crews on *Royal Standard*.

Apart from those who volunteered, Oliver insisted that amongst the *Scorpion*'s crew, a carpenter's mate, boatswain's mate, cooper's mate and the loblolly boy should be included in the transfer, along with four good topmen. As the ships would be sailing in tandem, mutual assistance could be given from *Royal Standard* at any time, if needed.

The selection of a sailing master was made from Mr Brannagh's mates, while a lieutenant and two midshipmen were allocated by Captain Quintrell.

To replace Mr Brophy as first lieutenant on *Royal Standard*, Mr Weir was appointed to that post. Of the officers remaining aboard the 50-gun ship, two of the midshipmen were stepped up to serve as acting third and fourth lieutenants. Two of the older and more sensible *young gentlemen*, were allowed to stand as acting midshipmen under the supervision of the sailing master. It was Captain Quintrell's intention to include the eight convicts he had interviewed earlier, into the ship's working crew with the proviso they remained on *Royal Standard*.

Though both ships were badly undermanned, the overall result was that each ship carried an experienced crew.

The final tally in *Scorpion*'s new muster book was eighty-one souls leaving Captain Quintrell with a crew of a little over two hundred and sixty – sufficient to man a small frigate. But with fair winds and seas, and sound hulls, the two ships should have no problems making Cape Town in a few weeks' time – providing they did not encounter any French ships along the way.

Because *Scorpion* had been stripped bare of provisions when it had been abandoned, it took four days to complete the transfer of men and sufficient victuals from *Royal Standard*.

The following day, with Captain Brophy in command of the French frigate, work on the outstanding repairs proceeded immediately and seemingly without incident. For two weeks the ships headed south, sailing in tandem. But being within earshot of the 50-gun ship, men and officers on both vessels were aware they were under observation.

The first flogging, however, surprised everyone.

When *Scorpion*'s company was called on deck to witness punishment, Captain Quintrell immediately despatched Mr Holland to attend and report on the circumstances. The fact it was only two dozen lashes was not excessive, but the offence – *being late on watch after breakfast* – seemed fairly extreme and was taken badly by the rest of the crew.

Soon after that, requests from the men to transfer back to the 50-gun ship started filtering across the pond, but Oliver would not hear of it. South Africa was only a few weeks' sail away and, in the meantime, both ships would have to contend with affairs as best they could. It was up to each captain to handle any situation the way he felt fit.

Chapter 17

Storm at sea

With the intention of maintaining the officers' good spirits, Captain Quintrell invited them to take dinner with him again in the great cabin. This time, he was unable to include Captain Brophy and *Scorpion* officers in his invitations.

After having partaken of a hearty course, the steamed pudding arrived with hot syrup running down its sides and swimming on the platter. The smell reminded the youngsters of home. With the decanter filled for the third time, the chatter grew louder. Cigar smoke curled to the overhead beams and hung suspended in a blue haze. While the midshipmen tittered and coughed at their own private jokes, the anecdotes and ditties, delivered by the older members of the company, commanded everyone's attention. Assisted by two of the officers' servants, Michael Casson supervised the clearing of the table, the last of the dishes being carried out when a low rumble reached them only moments before havoc unleashed itself on the ship.

Being otherwise occupied, no one at the table had looked at the sky or the barometer in the last hour. The blast of hurricane force wind hit *Royal Standard* on its starboard beam and heeled it over. The main yard sliced into the sea taking the forecourse with it. That acted as a sea anchor and swung the hull around to port. The reverberation through the wooden ship was like a full broadside from a man-of-war.

'Hold tight!' the captain yelled, though his voice was lost in the thunderous clatter as every man and object that was not fastened down was sent crashing over.

'Oh, God! We're done for,' a voice screamed before it was muffled.

Any item remaining on the dinner table, including the cloth itself, slid off. The huge table remained upright, surviving the ninety degree tilt only because its legs were nailed to the deck. The officers, however, and the chairs they had been seated on were thrown across the cabin. Even the heavy sea chests, the middies had been sitting on, rolled over, one landing on the legs of one of the unfortunate youngsters, pinning him to the deck. Without warning the door flew open delivering Casson and one of the other servants back into the great cabin sluiced in on a torrent of seawater. At the same moment, the gallery windows on the larboard side exploded and broken glass and water gushed into the great cabin. The two great guns bounced on their trucks, but fortunately did not break from their lashings.

As the officers fought frantically to get themselves upright, the ship struggled to do the same – stretching every fibre of its timbers, twisting every joint and plank under the pain of being drawn and quartered. With no help from sails or helm, *Royal Standard* slowly began to right itself.

The glass panels in the lantern swinging overhead had been smashed, scattering fragments all around, the flame had gone out blinding the men who found themselves in total darkness. A match was lit. The lantern's wick reignited.

'What happened?' one of the middies yelled. 'Did we hit something? Are we sinking?'

'I'd wager it was a rogue wave,' Captain Quintrell advised calmly.

'Why didn't the lookout give a warning?'

Oliver glanced to the barometer swinging like a pendulum from a nail on the wall. The pressures had dropped significantly since he had last looked. 'Who is officer of the watch?' he asked.

'Mr Holland.'

'Then, God help him and every other man who was on deck. I trust the crew had time to go below, but I fear not all will have survived this catastrophe.'

A cry of pain came from one of the young gentlemen and the captain knew not all the injuries would come from the deck.

'You there, lend a hand. Get this chest off Mr Knox's legs. Mr Weir, Mr Aitcheson, I want everyone on deck to lend a hand. Mr Brannagh, you too. Reduce all sail and check the rudder. Find the carpenter. Tell him to check the well. And get some hands onto the pumps. Mr Weir, you are now acting first lieutenant, are you not?'

'Yes, Captain.'

'Take the deck and relieve Mr Holland. Mr Greenstreet, check on the convicts. You will, no doubt, find them in pitch darkness. Take a lantern and release any men that are injured and have them brought to the cockpit. Being closely confined in their compound may have cushioned them. They cannot have fallen too far. However, the shackles may have inflicted some injuries to their legs. Ask the cooper to remove the rivets in their irons. I will speak with the Captain of the Marines and instruct him to put his men to work.'

Finally, Oliver looked to the gallery windows and seeing the broken glass scattered all over the floor, he thought of the dog. 'Someone call Chalmers. If the dog has survived, tell him to bring him inside. He can put it into my sleeping cabin for the present.

'Mr Weir, pass a message to *Scorpion*. I want a report from Captain Brophy as to their damage, and an injury count, as soon as possible. I will be on deck in a moment.'

Despite the mess and confusion in the great cabin, Casson remained calm throughout, assuring his captain it would all be attended to in *quick-sticks*. Oliver did not linger, after locating his boat cloak and went through to the quarterdeck.

On the starboard side, young Mr Holland, who was officer of the watch, was crumpled against the gunwale with the doctor leaning over him. Two of the topmen had a firm grip on the helm. The wind was still strong while the sea, whipped into huge white caps, was rushing across the full width of the deck.

'Report please, Mr Holland. What happened?'

'It came out of nowhere, Captain,' the lieutenant replied between gasps. 'One minute we were commenting how well she was sailing and then *boom* – it was upon us. First we saw was the line of heavy rain bouncing up off the water. It was coming from the west directly for us like a herd of galloping horses, stirring up the surface with a thunderous roar that carried on the wind. Above it were curtains of black clouds even darker than the night sky. As

189

for the sea, we didn't see it, hear it or feel till it rose up and hit us. It was a giant wave like I'd never seen before. It reared up to the height of the topmast then lifted the ship and threw us over like a toy boat in a raging river. I sent men up top to shorten sail, as soon as we saw it coming but that wasn't soon enough and the men weren't quick enough to do anything or even to get down. God knows where they are now. I pray they were able to hold on. We were carrying a full head of sail when it hit so when she went over, I feared the canvas would drag us under. Thank God, she managed to right herself.'

'A thought I feared also,' Oliver murmured. 'Let's get those sails close reefed. I doubt we will get a repeat of that wave but cannot be too sure. And the man on the helm? How did he fair?'

'He hung on while the water took his feet from under him till another hand grabbed a rung and the pair saved the wheel from spinning. The rudder is answering, Captain, I've been told.'

'Good man,' Oliver said. 'Mr Larkin, kindly go below and check on the state of the barrels. But, mind, no lighted lantern near the powder kegs.'

For the first time, after checking his ship and his men, Oliver took time to scan the horizon. Looking around, he could see no sign of *Scorpion* even though it had been sailing no more than two hundred yards from *Royal Standard*'s starboard quarter. In Captain Quintrell's mind, the frigate would have taken the full force of the wave and suffered a similar fate, if not worse. With most of the ship's lantern glasses broken, he was not surprised that he could see no lights lit on the frigate.

'Where is she?' he asked, to anyone who was listening. 'Where was the 24-gun ship before this weather hit?'

Standing within arm's length, the topman, whose hands were still firmly gripped on the helm, answered: 'She was a cable's length off the starboard beam, Capt'n. But she was drifting to the south-east. The officer of the watch had made a signal for her to close up. I think it was sent twice but there was no answer.'

'Did she continue to drift?'

'I can't say, Captain, I wasn't looking out for her.'

Thanking the midshipman, Oliver listened and tried to make sense of the situation.

'The frigate must have gone straight down,' the sailing master declared. 'There's not a sign of a spar or sail or single piece of debris – or any survivors. What say you, Captain?'

'I say it is too dark to see anything, so one can only speculate.' Turning to his first lieutenant: 'The forward carronade, Mr Weir. Make a signal. If *Scorpion* is afloat she must surely hear it and respond. A blank shot, I suggest. We don't want to sink her if she is out there in the darkness.'

'Aye, aye, Captain.'

The sound of the powder exploding in the big gun brought several seamen onto the deck, thinking *Royal Standard* was under fire. Standing on the quarterdeck, the captain, sailing master and first lieutenant waited for sufficient time for a gun to be run out on the 24's deck and a shot to be fired in reply. But other than the water thumping on the bow, cracks and crackles from luffing sails and the hum of the wind in the rigging, there was no reply.

'As I said,' the sailing master insisted. 'I think *Scorpion* went straight down.'

Oliver was not ready to accept that suggestion.

'Tell me, Mr Brannagh, in your opinion, if she stayed afloat and made sail, how far could such a wind drive her from us?'

'More than a dozen miles,' he replied. 'Maybe double that. She'd sail until it blows itself out. Certainly out of earshot in this gale. And in the darkness, her lights, if she had any left, would be invisible for any distance more than thirty yards. You still contend she sank?'

The sailing master hesitated. 'There should be some flotsam – sea chests, bodies, rigging but we didn't see any.'

'And if she ran to escape the weather, would she know where to locate us?'

'If she ran, she might not want to locate us.'

That was hardly the answer Captain Quintrell was expecting. 'What are you insinuating, Mr Brannagh?'

'I'm not saying nothing, Captain, just postulating.'

'Mr Brannagh, are you suggesting the acting captain has taken the ship. What would lead you to that preposterous idea?'

The sailing master shrugged his shoulders. 'Couldn't say.'

'Couldn't say. Wouldn't say. But if you were pressed for an opinion?'

He shrugged again.

'Then I am pressing you right now, Mr Brannagh. This is not the first occasion you have expressed concerns regarding Captain Brophy's integrity.'

'Then, in answer to your question, I would propose it is the very nature of the acting captain that was the cause, sir.'

'You say: *the nature of the acting captain*. Please explain?'

The sailing master shuffled uncomfortably for a moment. 'Captain Brophy desperately wanted a ship of his own. What I'm suggesting is that if he got separated from us in the South-Atlantic, for a time, at least, he would have been granted his wish. And, after all, it wasn't really a king's ship, was it? You said it yourself. It was merely a salvage vessel.'

'*Hmm*! But fully rigged, fully armed and adequately crewed courtesy of my men, it was damned close to one. Hopefully, most of those men had no allegiance to Mr Brophy, or did they? I find your proposition hard to swallow.'

'Like I said, Captain, you pressed me for my opinion.'

'Indeed, I did.'

'You don't have to heed anything I say, Captain. Wait till the night clouds clear, and, lo and behold, you'll find *Scorpion* hull-up on the horizon with her canvas hanging out to dry. Then we shall know I was quite wrong.'

'I trust that will be the case,' the captain said, wondering at his sailing master's perspicacity.

It was during his very first meeting with Mr Brophy, Oliver Quintrell had decided that he was not partial to the attitudes and opinions expressed by the ship's first officer, but he had tried to maintain an open mind. Prejudice was a quality he disliked. But, until this moment, he had not considered the lieutenant's subtle innuendos could be a forerunner of mutinous behaviour.

'What on earth was he thinking,' the captain said. 'He might be able to make more speed than a 50-gun ship, but he does not have sufficient crew to work the ship, the sails and the guns. Most of the powder in his magazine is likely to be spoiled. And he has a crew who are more likely to mutiny than follow him. I promise you, he will not escape. I will find him.'

'Where do you suggest we look for him?' the sailing master asked.

Oliver sighed, as he considered the question. 'Because *Scorpion* was a French ship, she would not head for any French territory. Nor for a British port as, without orders and a full British crew the captain would fall under suspicion. Let us not forget, if he has deliberately taken the ship, he must now be branded as a pirate. I suggest, therefore that he would head for a Portuguese port – Rio de Janeiro perhaps, or Batavia or India.

'I promise you, Mr Brannagh, if I catch the blackguard, I will delight in taking him back to England in irons to face Admiralty Justice.'

Having had his fill of this unsavoury topic, the captain called on his recently appointed first lieutenant. He needed to concentrate on the current problems facing his ship. 'Mr Weir, kindly have the carpenter report to me. I need to know how much water is in the well. Also, if the ship sustained any damage to the hull when it went over. Go down to the cockpit and enquire if the doctor needs assistance. I fear the storm will have left him with his hands full. And have someone check in the galley. Make sure the fire was extinguished and didn't discharge embers into the mess.'

Finally, 'At 8-bells, call all hands and splice the mainbrace. I think a tot of rum might help raise spirits, albeit for only a short time.

The break of day brought a hazy sun rising from a misty grey horizon. Overnight the storm had passed, the wind had blown itself out and the sea calmed. A thorough search of the area could not turn up any evidence that the smaller ship had sunk. It was agreed by everyone that any debris washed from its deck could have drifted miles away by now and would never be found.

Under the present conditions and repairs underway, making three knots was all *Royal Standard* could manage.

Leaning over the table, studying the chart from various angles, the captain was discussing his proposed course with Mr Brannagh.

'I believe Captain Brophy was familiar with my sailing orders,' the captain stated. 'I trust that, if *Scorpion* is still afloat, she will be in Cape Town when we arrive. Let us hope for the best.'

'Amen to that.'

Chapter 18

The Jolly Boat

Heading south, with almost 2000 miles to sail before raising the Cape of Good Hope, the air on deck was warm, despite the cold waters of the Benguela Current flowing northwards beneath the ship. The usually busy route for vessels sailing to the East, was quiet, and since departing Ascension Island, and the *débâcle* surrounding *Scorpion*, not a single ship had been sighted. For a few nights, the captain was able to sleep at nights, if only in short bursts.

Early on the fifth day, he was interrupted from a deep slumber.

'Beg pardon, Capt'n.'

'What is it, Casson?'

'Mr Weir says there is something you would want to see.'

Swinging his legs down from his cot, Oliver Quintrell slipped on his shoes and reached for his coat, though quickly decided against it because of the heat. He nodded briefly to his steward as he passed him and headed out to the quarterdeck.

After rubbing the salty sleep from the corners of his eyes, he glanced around the dark and empty horizon. He felt reassured. The ship was not under threat. 'What do you see?' he asked the young officer.

A group of sailors congregating around the entry port had obviously been attracted by something in the water.

'Over the side, Captain,' the second lieutenant said.

Though it was unlikely, his first thought was that one of the deckhands had jumped or fallen. Visits from porpoises were a regular sight and even a close encounter with a blue whale did not demand the captain's attention. *A green turtle, perhaps? Worth netting to make more soup.*

His thoughts were answered, when the matted head of a sailor appeared from the steps. The way the man struggled to pull himself aboard made him look drunk. He was grabbed by the arms to prevent him falling back and helped onto the deck by his mates.

Once aboard, he crawled up against the gunwale, his eyes immediately closing and his chin dropping onto his chest. Another sailor followed slowly behind him, and then another, both conducting themselves in the same manner. Oliver didn't recognise the individual faces, but behind them was young Midshipman Keath. He looked gaunt and dishevelled with salt or tears staining his cheeks.

'There are two more,' the middie uttered, his voice barely audible. 'They need help.'

'Quickly now,' Mr Weir called. 'One of you men, climb down. Lend a hand and secure the jolly boat until we are able to hoist it aboard.'

Looking over the rail, Oliver immediately recognised the small boat as being from *Scorpion*. It was the only craft that had remained on the frigate when it had been abandoned. In it, sprawled between the thwarts were two bodies that appeared lifeless.

'Rig up a sling,' Captain Quintrell ordered. 'Hoist those men aboard. Mr Holland, we need blankets and warm drinks for these sailors. And call Dr Hannaford to attend.'

Mr Holland responded instantly.

'Mr Keath, when you are recovered, kindly attend me in my cabin. I need to hear what transpired to deliver you here in this manner.' Oliver's immediate thought was that *Scorpion* had foundered after the storm and that these men were the sole survivors of the sinking.

With a cup of brandy in warm milk cupped in his hands and a blanket wrapped around his shoulders, the young midshipman, seated in the great cabin, was unable to stop shivering.

'How long were you in the boat?' Oliver asked gently.

'Three days, Captain. This was to be the fourth. I don't know that we could have lasted much longer.'

'You had water?'

'We had taken a small barrel, but we had no mast or sails only a single pair of oars, and no compass.'

'Had *Scorpion* foundered?' the captain asked.

'No Captain. I took the boat,' he admitted guiltily.

The answer was a shock. 'You headed out into the Atlantic so ill provisioned?'

The young man merely nodded his head.

'So, where were you heading?'

'East – to the coast of Africa. I thought it nearer than South America. My only hope was that we would see another ship and be able to hail it. It was a vain hope, but it was the best I could do.'

'How many men were in the boat?'

'A dozen, including myself.'

'Did everyone survive?'

The midshipman looked down, his eyes clouding over. 'Amos Bickersdyke, cook's mate, took sick the first day. He was so sick his throat swelled and he couldn't even swallow water. Two days ago he sank into a deep sleep and never woke.' He paused and breathed deeply. 'We surrendered his body to the sea and I said a few words for him.'

The captain remained silent.

The young midshipman raised his rheumy eyes and continued. 'On the second day we saw a big fleet of ships heading north; East Indiamen, I think. We were desperate to attract their attention, but we were too far away for them to see us and had no means of signalling, apart from waving a shirt tied to an oar. The men yelled until their throats were sore. They prayed and cried but all to no avail. We watched for hours as the whole fleet sailed by and disappeared over the horizon. Can you imagine how desolate the feeling was?'

There was no answer to that question.

Taking a breath, the midshipman continued. 'Then, yesterday, late in the afternoon, we saw a sail rise on the horizon. We didn't know it was *Royal Standard*, and when night fell we lost sight of it. Then early this morning, after almost running us down, you saw us. We thank the Lord, for being saved.'

'Amen to that,' Oliver said. 'You are indeed lucky men.'

Casson entered quietly with a mug of steaming hot chocolate on a tray. He placed it in front of the young man. 'Can I bring you anything, Capt'n?' he asked.

'Thank you, no, Casson.' Pausing, only a moment, the captain allowed the young middie time to sip the drink slowly until the pot was empty.

'Now tell me how you came to be aboard the jolly boat. What happened to *Scorpion*? Did she sink after the storm or is she still afloat?'

'Lieutenant Brophy,' he began, then corrected himself, '*Captain* Brophy has taken the ship and is heading to China. At least that is what he claims. He would brook no argument from anyone and listen to no sense. Anyone who raised his voice against him was punished.'

Oliver Quintrell was astounded. 'Did he not realize that by taking the ship he would hang?'

'"Only if I am caught,"' he had boasted.

'What!'

'Those were his very words and I was not the only one to hear them. You can ask the other men. It was terrible aboard the frigate after the ships parted company. The captain was drunk most of the time, shouting orders at everyone. For those who did not jump to his command he had them bound up to the gratings and lashed. No one on board liked it – apart from two of his loyal followers. He appointed them as his lieutenants. Any man who refused to follow their orders was put in irons. As for the rest of the crew, rations were cut. The situation was dire.'

Oliver was aghast. 'Had the man taken leave of his senses?'

'That was the opinion of all the men you put aboard. No one wanted to remain. The only ones he did not bother were the carpenters and the other hands who were working below decks repairing the ship. He insisted *Scorpion* be made seaworthy.'

'There must have been rumblings in the mess.'

'Indeed there were, sir. But what were the crew to do? If they disobeyed Mr Brophy's orders, they were likely to be flogged or worse.'

'Did the men not consider overpowering the acting captain and wresting the ship from him?'

'Only in whispers, but there were plenty of calls for action – everything from abandoning the ship, to murder. But the men were afraid. Every seaman knows the penalties for contravening the *Articles of War* – being reminded of them weekly. Some argued that if they went against the captain's orders they would be found guilty of mutiny. After all, despite the treatment he meted out, Captain Brophy was a commissioned Royal Navy Lieutenant and the ship's acting captain. For most of the men, his word was law. Plus they still regarded the salvaged ship as a prize which would guarantee money in their pockets when they got back to England. Because of those arguments, they could not agree on what should be done.

'The idea of taking the only remaining boat was suggested, but it could only carry a dozen men and there were eighty of us. Plus, the crew knew that by taking the boat they would be stealing from one of His Majesty's ships and could be subject to a court martial according to the *Articles*.'

'But that is just what you did, Mr Keath.'

'Yes, Captain,' the young man answered reluctantly. 'Rightly or wrongly, I formed my own opinion and decided to take the jolly boat. Several of the men were of the same mind. I warned them of the possible consequences but assured them that if we were lucky enough to survive the sea, we would get help and pass a message to the Admiralty.'

Captain Quintrell studied the face of the lad in front of him. Sandy haired, pimpled cheeks and brow, and barely old enough to have need of a razor. 'It was a bold decision. Did you take charge?'

'I did. There was no one else with authority. The idea of running was not popular with all the hands but some agreed it was the only option.'

Oliver remained quiet.

'So we waited until after midnight – four nights ago – when Captain Brophy and his followers were sleeping. Then we lowered the boat, put water and some ship's biscuits aboard and pointed the bow to the east.'

'How old are you, Mr Keath?'

'Seventeen, Captain.'

'From what you have told me, I think these men owe you a debt of gratitude.'

With eyes closing, it was unlikely the young middie had heard the captain's response.

'Just one more question before you take to your bunk, I must know the condition of *Scorpion* and how far the frigate is ahead of *Royal Standard.*' Oliver shook his head. 'I find it hard to believe that the acting captain had his sights on China? That is a long distance away.'

The young man attempted to shake the tiredness from his head. 'I can't rightly say how much work the carpenters have done, but when we took to the boat, I was aware some of the hands were still at the pumps day and night and were getting heartily sick of it. During the terrible storm, when the ships became separated, the foremast came down but the crew were able to rig up a jury mast and bend a sail to it. We were making four knots and the bearing was south-east. We were heading for the Cape of Good Hope, but I'd heard Captain Brophy say he would take a broad reach around it. He had no intention of making landfall there.'

'Thank you, Mr Keath. Go eat and then sleep. I will speak with you again in the morning.'

'Thank you, Captain,' the young man mumbled, stumbling as he rose from the chair in an attempt to stand upright. He leaned his weight on the furniture as he crossed the room but made it to the door unaided.

Having sat silently at the rear of the cabin throughout the interview, the sailing master did not rise from his seat until the midshipman had left.

Joining the captain at the table, he watched as the brandy was poured and accepted a glass.

'God Almighty,' Oliver swore. 'What do you make of it?'

'Nasty business,' the sailing master said. 'I never did like that fellow from the time I first set eyes on him, but to do anything as stupid as to take a ship and His Majesty's men, mostly against their will, beggars belief.'

'Those are my men,' Oliver reminded, 'and I am responsible for them. As for that unfortunate ship – I care not a jot for it. What I know is that it is my duty to find that pirate and deliver him to a court martial.'

'A noose on the end of a rope might be more fitting – and would be far quicker and cheaper.'

'*Hmm*! We must find him first, Mr Brannagh. Where is he in this great ocean?' Oliver questioned out loud. 'Is he ahead of us or following us?'

'If *Scorpion* is sailing under a jury rig, we are probably making better time than he is,' the sailing master added. 'We should arrive in Cape Town before him.'

Oliver wasn't convinced.

'At some point, he must touch land. Though the ship was provisioned from our stores, he does not have enough supplies to take him to China. Apart from victuals, he will need wood and water. But I doubt he will dare to go into Cape Town or even False Bay, as half of the crew are likely to run. And if he comes under enemy fire, he does not have enough men to work the guns.' Oliver thought for a moment and drained his glass. 'We shall maintain our course, Mr Brannagh. I intend to sail into Cape Town Bay, discharge the convicts and marines and enquire if *Scorpion* has been sighted by any of the ships in the harbour.'

'And if there is no news?'

'Then I intend to wait for his arrival, or continue around the southern tip of the continent and search for him.'

'It will serve Brophy right if he encounters Vanderdecken and his ship.'

'*The Flying Dutchman*?'

'I doubt the phantom would treat him with mercy.'

On deck, Oliver Quintrell was anxious to know how the repairs aboard *Royal Standard* were progressing.'

'Going well, Captain,' Lieutenant Weir reported. 'The carpenter and his mates are still working but say there is nothing that will delay us. The wrights have completed their work on the rudder so we can make good speed.'

'In that case, I intend to put some of the convicts to the test again and will need you to assist me.'

The furrows in the sailing master's brow deepened. 'Are you sure about that, Captain. There are some ugly-looking coves amongst them.'

'There are also some sailors amongst them and we are short of about a hundred hands. I cannot use them all but believe a few of them will be prepared to work rather than being held below.'

The following day the same seven convicts who had been tested previously were brought on deck. With two marines guarding them, along with the captain of the foretop and a boatswain's mate, they were given instructions as to what was expected of them. After proving their competence in being part of a gun crew, there were other jobs on the ship they could be put to. The four convicts, whose records showed that they had sailed before, were taken into the rigging under the supervision of the captain of the top. Once they had shown they were capable of climbing, they were observed as they trod the foot rope, furled a sail and secured the gaskets. The other three were assigned to the sail maker and shown how to use a palm and needle.

Eager to prove their worth, and glad to fill their lungs with fresh air, they trained throughout the day and when spirits were piped, were allowed to join the end of the line after the rest of the watch.

Returning them to the compound on the orlop deck that night was not well received by the other prisoners. The situation was not ideal but with no time to resolve a better alternative, it had to suffice.

After sailing 2000 miles due south without another sail being sighted, *Royal Standard* stood to within ten miles of the entrance to Cape Town Bay. The mist-shrouded top of Table Mountain could be seen in the distance.

With each passing mile, and no change to the helm, whispers spread around the ship that the captain was pursuing a fool's mission and it did not take long for those mumblings to filter back to the quarterdeck.

'The men are not too happy,' the sailing master said. 'They fear you will follow *Scorpion* all the way to China.'

'Let them speculate all they will,' the captain said. He had made his decision. He was intent on finding *Scorpion* along with the rogue lieutenant who had pirated it. His aim was to return both of them to England and to deliver Captain Brophy to the Admiralty Court.

There was a chance *Scorpion* may have crept into Cape Town Bay before them. The captain doubted it, but it was worth checking.

'Three days ago, I spoke with you about entering Cape Town Bay in the hope of finding the missing frigate

Mr Brannagh nodded.

'Having given the matter some thought, I have decided we must search first. If we linger, even for a few days in Cape Town, we provide *Scorpion* enough time to slip by us. Once she enters the Indian Ocean, we will have no chance in finding her. We must intercept her with all haste.'

The sailing master was doubtful they would have any chance at all. 'It's a vain hope, Captain.'

'Consider this,' Oliver said. 'Apart from the need for wood and water, if *Scorpion* has the problems that Mr Keath described, 'Captain Brophy may have no alternative but to run her up on one of the southern beaches, before heading across the Indian Ocean.'

The sailing master was less than convinced. 'That's a dangerous coast, Captain, rocky headlands and the sea is thick with kelp. Besides, even if he finds a sheltered cove, the lieutenant doesn't have enough men to careen the ship.'

'True, but he has a damaged ship combined with not a logical thought in his head. Perhaps he will search for shoal waters. Anything is possible. With that in mind, I intend to make an effort. We will head around the south coast and sail in as close as is safe. If we cannot locate *Scorpion* within seven days, we will head back to Cape Town and deliver our charges. I may not be brought to account for losing a salvaged ship, but I will have to face the consequences for forfeiting seventy of my men.'

As he spoke, the gravity of the situation was driven home. 'Damn the man,' he said.

Chapter 19

The search

Table Mountain loomed over the town, shrouded in a cloth of white cloud as it so often was. The bay itself was milling with merchant ships, many being part of another East India convoy along with trading ships flying various national flags.

From the ocean, the town could be clearly seen; the neat white-painted houses gleaming in stark contrast to the black rushes that thatched their roofs. The spacious streets, built in an orderly fashion, criss-crossed the settlement and led down to the small congested wharf, where an assortment of ships of various sizes were tied up four or five abreast.

On the harbour, two large merchantmen and other smaller craft, unable to find space along the jetty, were swinging from their anchor cables. All manner of provisions, including live cattle, pigs and poultry were waiting to be conveyed by the lighters that were ferrying back and forth from the busy wharfs.

A British jack was flying in the town's centre.

For most of the vessels arriving from the East, the administration of the colony would have changed since the time they passed through on their way to the Indies creating confusion.

On board *Royal Standard*, the officer of the watch echoed the captain's order to heave to. It was relayed along the deck. Yards were braced around, causing the vast expanse of the forecourse to luff and crack and bring the ship to a virtual stop. *Royal Standard* would need a berth along the dock to discharge its human and other cargo; however, Captain Quintrell he had no intention of wasting time and was intent on continuing his search.

'What do you see?' Oliver asked of the sailing master, standing next to him on the quarterdeck.

The older man was screwing his right eye as he twisted the scope for clearer vision across Cape Town Bay. 'More ships still arriving. But I do not see *Scorpion* in the harbour.' He was aware of the Captain's preoccupation with the missing frigate. 'Shall we bide our time here for a short while?' he asked.

The captain did not answer immediately. His attention had been distracted by a 64-gun man-of-war heading into the bay, having recently rounded the Cape of Good Hope.'

'A moment,' Oliver begged. 'I would speak this ship when it passes. Mr Weir,' he called, 'kindly make a signal and draw their attention.'

'Aye, Captain.'

After acknowledging the request from the 50-gun British ship, the 64-'s sails were backed allowing it to drift to a halt only fifty yards from *Royal Standard.* The officers and seamen of the larger ship crowded along the rail eager to find out what was happening.

From the quarterdeck, Oliver Quintrell waited until the ships were close then wandered over to the rail where the lieutenant hailed the ship and asked the uniformed officer on deck if any sighting had been made of a frigate recently, possibly sailing under a jury rig and probably heading east.

After relaying the message, the speaking trumpet was handed to another officer standing by the rail. 'We have not seen it, but a local boat, we bought fruit from only a day ago, advised us that such a vessel was beached or grounded in a cove on the southern coast.'

'What ship was it?' Mr Weir asked. 'What condition was it in?'

'It was described as a small ship of war,' was the reply. 'From the description, it could have been a frigate,' the officer continued. 'The master of the local boat thought it had run aground.'

Oliver took the trumpet. 'Was there any report of men or bodies on the beach? Had any distress signal been seen?'

'No signals were mentioned, but the master said that sailors were seen on the shore waving as if to attract attention. But it was late in the day and he had to make Cape Town before dark, he did not stop. It is my captain's intention to report those facts when we anchor in the harbour.'

'Thank you kindly. *Royal Standard* will head south and investigate. Hopefully, I will return in due course with news.'

Oliver closed the glass and handed it to his first lieutenant. 'Mr Weir, make sail. We head south then east hugging the coastline sailing as close in as possible.'

The sailing master repeated his warning. 'Be wary of the kelp. And there are conflicting currents and winds around the Cape of Good Hope and Cape Agulhas where the two oceans meet.'

'I'm quite aware of that, Mr Brannagh, and I am sure *Royal Standard* is up to the challenge.' The captain smiled briefly. 'It appears Lady Luck may have glanced in our direction for a change.'

With all hands to a rope or line, the main brace was hauled around allowing air to fill its deflated canvas. And with its beak pointed to the southern tip of the African continent, the 50-gun ship began its search. Once the lines were tied off, all hands were ordered to stand to their guns. If *Scorpion* was found, it was impossible to know what condition it would be in and what reception *Royal Standard* would receive from those on board.

'Let's take the bite out of this scorpion's nippers once and for all,' Oliver said. He was looking forward to the opportunity.

When night fell, *Royal Standard* hove to on a heaving swell with extra lookouts posted on the fore and mizzen masts. The captain was intent on finding the stolen ship and had no intention of letting it slip out of his fingers.

The following morning the 50-gun ship rolled and pitched unnaturally on a cross sea caused by the conflicting currents delivered around Agulhas. With little wind to carry them over it, the passage was uncomfortable. Resuming their hunt, however, the ship followed the rugged coast examining each bay and inlet for any trace of the French frigate.

Forward progress was slowed this time, not by the current, but by the great forests of kelp that clogged the sea and ran for hundreds of miles around the bottom of the continent. With roots set in the ocean bed several fathoms below the keel, the trailing fronds grew up to the surface making it impossible to sail close to the shoreline in many areas. However, Captain Quintrell was not deterred.

That evening, when the starboard watch was about to go to dinner, the call came down that a mast could be seen in the next inlet. It was a sheltered cove enclosed between two headlands. The mast was not upright but laying at a slight angle. It was obvious, the 24-gun frigate was not going anywhere. Everyone on board recognised it immediately and a relieved cheer went up from the crew.

Had Scorpion *been holed and run up on the beach then keeled over? Or had it purposely been careened for repairs?* Oliver wondered but was confident he would soon have the answers.

On closing on the inlet for a better view, it became evident that the storm that had struck both ships several weeks ago had inflicted more damage on the salvage vessel than on *Royal Standard.* Although the shipwright, carpenter's mates and other artisans who had been transferred on board, had succeeded in making *Scorpion* seaworthy enough to sail to the tip of Africa, something was now preventing her from continuing her voyage across the Indian Ocean to China or Batavia, or whatever destination Captain Brophy had chosen. Oliver wanted to learn more.

Ever unsure of the reception he would receive and being wary of possible armed lookouts in the rigging, Captain Quintrell insisted on caution and dropped anchor half a mile from the shoreline. From a vantage point, it was easy to see the frigate's situation. *Scorpion*'s stern was being lapped by gentle waves while its bow was buried deep into the white sand.

When *Royal Standard* had sailed around the headland with the British standard flying from the stern post, it had been quickly recognised. The sound of huzzas and welcome cries carried across the water.

'What height are the tides here?' Oliver asked, but before he received an answer, sailors were seen jumping down to the beach from the frigate's sides and running towards the surf calling out and waving their arms or whatever bits of rag they could lay their hands on.

'Who's giving the orders, I wonder?' the sailing master asked.

'Is any one giving orders?' Oliver mused.

With the mob on the beach growing in number every minute, their spontaneous behaviour was an outpouring of relief. Two of the sailors dropped to their knees and spontaneously gave thanks to the Heavens. The mob numbered about sixty.

'I shall go ashore,' the captain said. 'Put away the boats. You have the deck,' he said, turning to Mr Holland – the officer of the watch.

'Mr Brannagh, be so kind as to accompany me. I want half a dozen marines and the carpenter and boatswain to come also. Call the Captain of Marines to have his men stationed in the rigging and along the rail. I swear I will tolerate no more tricks from this pirate.'

With all eyes to the careened ship and the rugged interior rising up not more than a cable's length behind the beach, the cutter and launch were swung out and lowered to the water. The boat's crew quickly dropped into the launch and took up their oars. The Captain and his party joined them.

It was an easy row to the beach, the gentle surf lifting them on their way. On touching the sand, the gunwales were grabbed by a dozen waiting hands and the boat dragged up onto the beach to the rousing call of huzzas. But Captain Quintrell still remained cautious. Scanning the faces both on the beach and the ship for his ex-lieutenant, Oliver looked at every one of them but the face he wanted to see was not there, nor were those of the midshipmen who had also been put aboard *Scorpion*.

'Who is in charge?' Captain Quintrell asked, as he stepped from the boat, his feet sinking into the wet sand.

'Me, sir.' The voice, hardly broken into manhood, came from a fresh faced lad. 'John Aitcheson, midshipman.'

'Where is Captain Brophy? Is he injured?'

'No, sir. He's gone.'

'Gone? Gone where? Please explain.'

A group of weathered seamen, gathered around the young man, as if to give him moral support.

'When we ran the ship up on the beach, four days ago, the captain had us attempt to refloat her, but even with the kedge anchor and all hands, and the aid of the tide, we couldn't budge her. Then another big wave came and washed her further up the beach and the bow dug in. We needed another big one to float her off, but it never came. Now the whole keel is sinking and she's taking water again. I had the men on the pumps but it's hopeless.'

'Thank you, Mr Aitcheson; I commend you on your efforts. But where is Brophy?'

'He left three days ago, on foot. He took some provisions with him and said he would make Cape Town in two days and get help. He said it was only fifty miles away. He told us to remain on the beach.' The youth glanced to those around him for confirmation. 'We hoped he would have been back yesterday or today with a ship. When we saw you sail around the headland we thought it was Captain Brophy returning.'

'A bold venture,' Oliver commented, looking at the blank faces around him. 'But fifty miles of unknown hinterland is a foolish trek to attempt. Did he know the Dutch farmers have little respect for English uniforms? As to the Hottentots, I heard they do not take kindly to anyone on their land. Did he go alone? Was he prepared to fight?'

He took Midshipman Durling and one of the seamen. They had a rifle each and a cutlass.'

'Thank you, young man. Considering what you have told me, we will wait here for two or three days for his possible return. In the interim, the carpenter will evaluate the damage and assess if *Scorpion* can be made seaworthy once again. If so, my men will dig her out and tow her from the beach, stern first. But we will need a high tide to assist us. If she floats and remains upright, I intend to sail her to the prize agent in Cape Town. She may still be of some value.'

Sighs of relief spread through the men, whose hopes of rescue had been getting slimmer by the hour.

'Mr Keath, return to the ship. Tell the officer of the watch to raise two working parties and send them ashore as quickly as possible. Tell him also to alert the lookouts for a ship, in the event Mr Brophy returns by sea; however, I doubt that will be the case. For now, those of you who are able, I need you to dig a channel around the keel. If you don't have tools, then find a rock or dig with your hands. Now, set to it.'

No one objected to the orders they were given. The men were conscious of their dire situation and eager to take any measures that might help deliver them to safety.

Stepping aboard *Scorpion*, with the carpenter alongside him, Oliver inspected the work that had been done following the storm and considered what additional work was needed before the ship could be put to sea again. In its present condition, it would never make an ocean-going voyage but, with fair winds and seas, handled judiciously under tow, it could make the short distance to Cape Town. The captain's greatest concern was the fickle nature of the currents flowing around the southern coast. This concern, he kept to himself.

'Do you have sufficient rations for the men?'

'Enough for a week, at least, Captain.'

'And water?'

The midshipman nodded. 'Ample.'

'The carpenter estimates the work will take several days. From then on, we will be dependent on wind, waves and weather.'

'Mr O'Brien, check *Scorpion*'s hold and magazine. If you find ammunition and dry powder, transfer it to *Royal Standard*.'

'Aye, aye, Captain,' the boatswain replied.

'It is possible Mr Brophy will return but it's more likely any activity on this beach will be from local tribesmen or wild beasts. Are the sentries aware the local natives could attack from the jungle? And that there are lions roaming these hills? I do not know which would be more threatening.

'Finally, any man not employed can collect dry wood. We need fires burning around the ship. Everyone must keep a close

211

watch and, before nightfall, I want all hands to return to *Royal Standard*. No one is to remain aboard the frigate. We can keep a watchful eye on her from the water.

'I have lost this ship once,' the captain added. 'I do not wish to lose it again.'

Six days later, with *Scorpion*'s keel sitting in a shallow man-made lake on the sand, cables were run from *Royal Standard*'s stern and attached to the frigate. All that remained was to wait for high water and sufficient wind to fill the 50-'s canvas.

With suction gripping the frigate's hull, *Royal Standard* strained to release it, stretching the cables to the limit. Finally, by adding more sail, *Royal Standard* succeeded. A cheer rose from the sailors both on the beach and on the ship's deck as the frigate was slowly hauled from the beach and slid onto the water. No time was wasted, once it was afloat. With the crew returned aboard, and with *Scorpion* put in tow, both ships made sail, headed around the Cape of Good Hope and back to Cape Town.

Having regained almost all of his original crew after retaking *Scorpion*, Captain Quintrell was only minus his first lieutenant, plus Midshipmen Durling and an able seaman: Andrew Wallis.

Because of the loss, he had been happy to step Mr Weir to the position of first officer to replace Lieutenant Brophy. Though only a young man, Weir had been aboard a Royal Navy ship since the age of twelve. He knew the routines and respected naval discipline, and he could be relied upon to uphold the *Articles of War* to the letter. He only had two problems. The first was his tender age compared with that of most of the hands, many of whom were twice as old and knew every devious way of wheedling their way out of duties. The second was that that his father was a clergyman and he was not born a gentleman. But he was intelligent, industrious, and had manners and charm which in the captain's eyes were more than enough to compensate. Hopefully time would prove him right.

Chapter 20

Cape Town

Since 1488, when the first European explorer rounded the Cape of Good Hope, the perils of the passage have been legendary. Portuguese navigator, Bartolomeu Dias, had named it *Cabo das Tormentas* – the Cape of Storms. Despite the hazards created by conflicting oceans and surging sea currents, Cape Town, near the gateway to the Indian Ocean, had long been an important provisioning stop and a haven for repairs. With the Peace of Amiens in 1802, the colony of South Africa was handed back to the Dutch by Britain. Now, with the Cape's strategic value fully recognised, Britain had sent Sir Home Popham to re-instate British sovereignty at the Cape.

Having achieved that mission, Sir Home Popham had departed the Bay on the 15th of April, only days before *Royal Standard* rounded the Cape. Popham was now heading across the South Atlantic, with several battalions of soldiers, commanded by Major General Sir David Baird. Their mission was to wrest control from the hands of the Viceroyalty of New Spain in Buenos Aires. Some considered it an ambitious proposal and unlikely to succeed.

Sailing into Cape Town Bay was not without challenges. The years of wild seas and disputed possession had left a legacy of shipwrecks that littered the harbour floor.

At low water, the masts of wrecked ships poked up from the bay. Without warning, a ship's hull could be scraped by a spar, capable of ripping strips of copper from its hull, gouging a groove in the worn timbers and thus inviting the ill-reputed worm to feast on its rich wet timber.

When *Royal Standard* sailed into Table Bay, the wharfs and jetties were already busy. Fortunately, the fleet of over fifty British East

India Company ships had departed on its journey north. With only an American whaler, a Baltic timber trader and a Chinese spice ship anchored on the bay, little attention was paid to the two British ships when they entered, even though one was under tow.

It was unusual for a Royal Navy ship to bring in a damaged vessel but *Scorpion* was in a poor condition and would not make the journey back to Portsmouth. Captain Quintrell's main worry was that it would sink while moored against the town jetty. In his estimation, *Scorpion* was only fit for the wrecker's yard. And the sooner it was taken there the better.

After speaking with the port admiral, regarding the prize agent, the captain was obliged to wait for a response. Not knowing for how long, he turned his attention to the various commodities *Royal Standard* was carrying: gunpowder, marines, convicts and several unmarked chests that had been stored in the hold.

The first and easiest to disembark were the soldiers. Mustered on the deck's gangboards, their swaying green kilts created considerable interest from the locals. Wearing tall plumed shakos, the troops of the 42nd regiment appeared almost a foot taller than the average British sailor and, as such, they reminded the populace of the newly re-instated British rule in the colony.

Following a brief inspection, the marines were marched to the barracks in the town. They were a welcome addition to the colony.

After delivering a box of despatches from Whitehall to the port admiral's secretary, Captain Quintrell moved to the bond store to arrange for the receipt of six cases of specie. The wooden chests of coins had been sent from the British Treasury to assist the colony's new administration and bolster the flagging finances of the province. Oliver required the items to be removed from *Royal Standard* as early as possible.

The following morning, in the pouring rain, six unmarked chests were hoisted from the ship's hold and swung out to the dock, where six artillery wagons were lined up to receive them and deliver them to the treasury. Most of the coins consisted of Spanish doubloons, pieces of eight and guilders. They would replace the need for written promissory notes. The consignment was escorted by foot soldiers and mounted guardsmen.

Oliver smiled to himself. Although the coins had come aboard during Captain Chilcott's command, and Captain Brophy had, no doubt, seen them when they were stowed in the hold, he had been blissfully unaware of their contents and made no effort to examine them. No one else on board knew of the contents but, when they were carried ashore, it took four men to lift each one. Their weight alone raised a few eyebrows.

When one hundred and fifty barrels of gunpowder were being hoisted from various parts of the ship, Mr Larkin supervised their unloading. On deck, three midshipmen were posted to ensure that none of the sailors lit a pipe or struck a flint on or near the ship. Later in the day, convoy of bullock wagons rumbled along the dock to transport them to the ordnance depot. Oliver Quintrell was relieved to see them go also.

On gaining an appointment with the port admiral, an ageing naval officer – it took a considerable amount of time explaining the details of the discovery of the abandoned French frigate, *Scorpion,* its subsequent loss, and then the eventual recovery of the same vessel. Having had the forethought to document all the facts and have his secretary prepare an accurate copy, Oliver had to content himself with leaving the details and the matter of the ship's future in the hands of the Admiralty's officer in Cape Town.

While salvage money usually amounted to only one twelfth of a vessel's value, he realised any resolution about *Scorpion*'s value could take longer than usual. Even then, any remuneration for the recovered vessel was unlikely to be made before they departed the port. And, whatever figure was offered, it would be nominal, meaning it was unlikely the crew would benefit greatly, if at all, from it.

On arrival in port, the captain had seven men and three boys separated from the other convicts and removed from the orlop deck and held in the recently erected compound on the foredeck.

Speaking to the prisoners, he outlined his concerns, fearing rejection of his proposal by the port admiral. He presented them with two alternatives. Firstly, they would to be delivered to a Cape Town jail and face years of hard labour under ruthless overseers and toil till they dropped from exhaustion under a burning African sun. Or, secondly, they could return to England and face British justice once again. It was his intention, once on English soil, to write to the Board of Transportation to plead the commutation of their sentences to five years of maritime service. Such offers had been made to prisoners in the past, allowing them to choose between a prison term and five years service in the Royal Navy. But this offer was usually made at the time of conviction and reflected the inconsistences in the judicial system. As such, he emphasised that he could make no promises. The best result would be that they could serve out the rest of their time on a British ship. The worse outcome would be that their original sentences were upheld. That being the case they would be returned to jail to await transportation again.

Without exception, every one of the prisoners chose to return to Britain with the ship in the hope of service in His Majesty's Navy.

Equipped with the names of the convicts who had been delivered to the ship in Cork, Oliver Quintrell presented all the information to the port admiral, informing him that of the forty-six convicts who had boarded in Cork, he had lost none during the voyage. But, because the ship had been short-handed, he had made use of ten of them. He added that these men had filled valuable roles aboard *Royal Standard*, and were needed for the return voyage to England. Oliver asked the port admiral to accept only thirty-six prisoners.

Having been at his post for only a week, the admiral was bewildered. Denying any prior knowledge of the expected arrival of the convicts and being unaware of whose jurisdiction they fell under, he washed his hands of the whole affair. In his estimation, because the original sentences had been pronounced by a magistrate in Ireland, he was not prepared to interfere with those rulings.

With that decision being final, Captain Quintrell repeated his proposal of returning the ten prisoners to England, assuring the admiral he would refer the matter to the courts as soon as he reached home. Reluctantly, that was agreed to.

Satisfied with the outcome, Oliver returned to *Royal Standard*.

With ankles and wrists manacled, and eyes screwed to the bright sunlight, thirty-six convicts lined up on the wharf. They were dirty and dishevelled, dressed in the same tunics they had worn when they were put aboard in Cork. On his return to the ship, Captain Quintrell ordered the seven men and three boys, who had served on the guns, to remain in the compound on the foredeck temporarily. He did not give the reason.

Half an hour later, a group of armed prison guards collected the convicts from the wharf and Oliver Quintrell heard nothing more about them. He intended to release the selected prisoners when the ship sailed and let them take up active duties as would any able seaman or lubber on a ship.

On the second day in port, news quickly spread through the town and to the wharfs of a massacre that had occurred in the hinterland some days earlier. Unfortunately, it was often the hard working Boers – the Dutch farmers, who were set upon by natives who objected to them usurping their land. As this type of occurrence was not-uncommon, it did not create much of a stir in the town.

As was the usual practice, the remains of victims having been collected were brought into town on the back of a wagon. In this instance, the decapitated heads had been impaled on stakes; the torsos torn to shreds by spears, and little more than bloodied fragments of clothing hung from the three bodies.

With no reports from the local farmers of missing field hands or workers, the soldiers who had delivered them turned to the ships in the harbour to enquire if any of the crew had deserted.

Fragments of blue cloth and the cockade from a bicorn hat led them to the only naval ship in dock. With no local police, it fell to the military to handle the local skirmishes.

Captain Quintrell was called and asked if he could identify the bodies.

It was a sickening task. The condition of the remains was appalling but, with the help of Dr Hannaford, the identifications were made. The decapitated bodies belonged to Captain Brophy and Midshipman Durling, the third man was an able seaman – his name was Andrew Wallis.

When asked why the three had been trekking inland across the country, Oliver Quintrell explained that their ship, *Scorpion*, had run aground and he had learned that its captain had set off on foot to reach Cape Town to seek help for the rest of his crew.

Those facts were truthful and, as such, were reported in the daily newspaper the following day. What was distasteful and untrue, were the editor's comments that Captain Quintrell of *Royal Standard* deeply mourned the loss of the senior British officer.

Unfortunately, that was not the end of the matter. The next day, the captain was obliged to attend the burial of the deceased. Dressed in full uniform and with the sailing master, Lieutenant Weir and two midshipmen alongside him, Oliver Quintrell fulfilled his naval obligation. He deeply regretted the loss of the young midshipman and the sailor. Both men had unwittingly been dragged along by the whims and wiles of Mr Brophy. As for the Irishman, Oliver was satisfied he had eventually received his due deserts.

Before leaving Cape Town, *Royal Standard* took on fresh victuals, exotic fruits, and eight beasts for slaughter, plus four pigs, and several geese and chickens. At least for a few days the officers and crew would eat well.

A week later, the 50-gun ship sailed out of Cape Town Bay with slightly more crew than when it had departed Cork. Ten Irish names had been added to the muster book, while the word *dead* was marked against four names – those of Brophy, Durling, Wallis; and Amos Bickersdyke, who had died in the jolly boat when escaping from *Scorpion*.

Relief was etched on the faces of the crew as they worked the ship out of Cape Town Bay. Ahead were over 7000 miles of open ocean and at least two months of sailing during which time no one could predict what they might encounter. Yet the crew were happy they were heading home and Oliver Quintrell shared their feelings.

Sailing north-westerly across the Southern Atlantic Ocean, *Royal Standard* was assisted by the north flowing Benguela Current. Although the waters flowing up from the Great Southern Ocean were cold, on deck there were few places to hide from the unbridled sun as they neared the tropics.

Four weeks from the Cape and two large ships crossed their path and *Royal Standard* reduced sail to allow them to pass. Sailing from the coast of Africa and heading west, their colours revealed they were Portuguese – probably slavers heading from the Guinea coast to South or Central America. Having left Africa with a fresh cargo, their passage would have been north-west in search of the trade winds to carry them over the Atlantic in the best possible time. Being stuck, for days or even weeks in the Doldrums, could mean a loss of valuable live cargo necessitating much of it being cast into the sea. The unkempt appearance of the ships, even from a distance, confirmed to both captain and crew what they carried. They posed no danger to the 50-gun ship, and Captain Quintrell had no desire to engage with them in any way.

He always swore he could smell a slave ship before the lookout even saw it.

Chapter 21

Heading home

Rising from the horizon, many miles to the west, was the giant peak of Mount Fogo on one of the Cape Verde Islands. Though it was breathing no smoke at this time, most passing ships were wary of it and chose to steer clear of it.

The thought of explosions, smoke and flame and huge boulders being projected from its vent, prompted the captain to have all hands called to stations for gun practice. The gun crews were pleased to return to their regular stations and the guns they were familiar with. After the exercise, the division captains reported that the new hands performed well and that their times had improved.

Sailing under a billow of canvas, the atmosphere on deck was relaxed. In the forecastle, two of the convicts were patiently showing the three youngsters how to splice two ropes together. A couple of inquisitive young gentlemen quietly looked on. The convict lads were quick to learn. One old salt, whittling a toy boat from a lump of driftwood fished from the sea, drew some attention. And, while knitting was not an unusual pastime, the sailor busy with his wooden needles knitting a hat from the yarn he had spun from the Newfoundland's hair, caused a few sideways glances.

With the captain's permission, Chalmers was permitted to bring Cecil on deck to take some exercise. While a handful of sailors objected to the hound bounding round and round the foredeck and disturbing their games, most of them didn't worry. The dog was a form of entertainment – the sailors rolling an old belaying pin along the deck and watching the dog chase it.

Having been given a scrub with soap in Cape Town Bay, Cecil's appearance and smell was much improved and his hair had already grown an inch since it was shorn. Johnny Kemp volunteered to comb the new tangles out of his coat and Chalmers and the dog had been quite amenable to that. Once brushed, the difference was quite remarkable. Young Johnny, Andrew Kemp's nephew, had taken a liking to the hound and the dog followed the boy around the deck. Having asked his uncle if he could take him home when they arrived in England, Andrew Kemp had explained that when they returned to England, a prison cell would likely be their home for a long time. It was hard for the boy to understand.

With the time the ship had spent in Cork and again on Ascension Island, Oliver had hoped to have mail from England awaiting him in Cape Town. He was anxious for news from Dr Whipple regarding his daughter's removal to Portsmouth and word of Charles Goodridge's progress at the Academy, but there had been no further letters. Despite no news, the captain took time to pen some correspondence knowing full-well they would reach England only at the same time as he did.

With each passing day, the noon sun rose higher and the heat on deck increased till the pitch began to bubble from between the deck beams, making the sailors wary of where they stepped.

For a while, flying fish, porpoises and wandering seabirds picking up scraps from the ship's wake, were the only distractions. The sailors not on watch stayed below deck out of the heat. Lethargy was slowly settling in.

Early one morning, before the sun had chance to melt the deck, the sight of a puff of sail and a broad hull rising from the horizon in the west jolted everyone's attention. Crowding the larboard deck, the sailors watched. Those with their own telescopes related the scene to their mates. She was flying the tricolour. She was a Frog.

As one ship turned into two, and two became three, pulses quickened. All hands were called and the deck boards shook with the pounding feet. Sailors ran to their stations and stood by their guns awaiting further orders. Any evidence of earlier lethargy was quickly cast off.

'What are your thoughts?' Oliver enquired of his first lieutenant, passing the glass to him.

'A large cargo ship, Captain,' Mr Weir said. 'Not a fighting ship – although I don't doubt she is pierced for a good number of guns.'

'And the smaller ships?'

'Looks like a brig and a schooner, to me, sailing as escorts.'

Oliver nodded. 'Any thoughts, Mr Brannagh?'

'I would agree. And reckon she would be worth a tidy penny – heavily laden with holds full of sugar or rum and cocoa. No doubt returning from the French islands in the Caribbean.'

With no intention of antagonising the traders, and not wanting to engage three ships, the captain ordered *Royal Standard* to reef the topsails, slow and allow the French ships to sail by uninterrupted. From the foredeck and in the rigging, the crew watched as the procession slowly swam by. If they had seen the 50-gun British ship on the southern horizon, they were obviously not concerned by it.

But attention was instantly diverted from the French convoy when two ships appeared suddenly out of the brilliant glare of the rising sun.

'Privateers, Captain?' the sailing master queried, seeing the vessels approaching fast from the east and taking the convoy by surprise. They were heading directly towards to the cargo ship.

'Prepare to fire, Mr Weir. Take out the reefs but maintain your course. Let us see what happens here.'

The first lieutenant relayed the message and the call went through the ship. Sailors scurried up the rigging and out on the yards to release the reefs they had only secured a few moments before. Included amongst them were seven convicts now indistinguishable in their recently issued slop clothing.

'Why did the convoy not see them long before now?' the sailing master asked, furrowing his brow.

'Probably, the lookouts were too busy watching a 50-gun British ship appearing on the horizon. They would not have expected the pirates coming out of the sun.'

'Mr Weir, take several of the young gentlemen to the magazine and the three Irish lads. They know what to do.'

'Powder monkeys?'

Oliver nodded again. 'If it is necessary.'

As *Royal Standard*'s deck and rigging was made ready, the two privateers exchanged fire with the leading French escort – a small schooner. Armed with only a pair of swivel gun on her bow and her long guns sitting amidships, she had no defence for a frontal attack and was easily dismasted. As soon as her foremast fell, two cutters were lowered from the privateer and, packed with well armed men, were rowed across the narrow stretch of water between them. Grapples were thrown, shots fired, swords and cutlasses brandished, as a small army of privateers scrambled aboard her. The large cargo ship was ill-positioned to defend itself without firing on its escort.

While Captain Quintrell continued to observe, Mr Brannagh looked anxiously to the ship's captain for instructions.

On the leeside of the action, the second privateers fired its full broadside at the second escort ship, aiming low for the timbers below the gunports. He obviously had no intention of taking this ship, as at such a short distance, it was impossible to miss.

Almost immediately there were cries from the deck of the escort brig indicating she was taking water. Intent of putting boarders on her, the second privateer steered in too close, getting her bowsprit and foreyard tangled in the rigging of the smitten brig. While some of the brig's sailors jumped overboard and swam for the large vessel, those that remained fought with whatever weapons they could grab – staves from the capstans and belaying pins, but they were torn between defending themselves and preventing their ship from going down.

Fully occupied with their own battles, the French crews aboard all three ships paid no attention to the British 50-gunner fast approaching from the south.

Oliver called to the officer on deck: 'Take us around her, Mr Weir. Let us rake her stern then be ready to pour a whole broadside to her larboard side.'

As *Royal Standard* made her turn, the cargo ship's name, *Saint Lucia*, came clearly into view.

The surprise attack from the rear seemed to have little effect on the cargo ship. But the broadside from twenty-two cannon shook the very fabric of *Saint Lucia*. Very slowly, almost gracefully, it heeled to larboard, lying down over on its own escort brig which was still tangled with the privateer.

While the large French ship was intent on detaching itself from the two limpets hanging from it, there was no time for hand-to-hand combat. But no sooner than *Saint Lucia* had righted herself, than the British gun crews were ordered to their stations, to haul in their guns and reload.

By now, *Royal Standard* was ready to deliver another lethal broadside. This time, Captain Quintrell ordered the gun captains to aim for the ship's bowsprit and foremast. He did not want to sink this ship. Nor did he want to flood her dry cargo with sea water. He wanted to take the ship and cargo as a prize.

'Bring us around, helmsman. Show me her starboard side.'

Saint Lucia, though upright, was unable to free itself from the privateer. Attempting to protect itself, the guns set amidships fired at the British 50-gunner. But their aim was set too high and the shots succeeded only in blowing holes in *Royal Standard*'s main and mizzen canvas. Only one shot dropped lower, exploding the belfry to toothpicks and showering splinters over the deck. The noise of battle muffled any orders or cries from the decks, while the gun crews' attention was purely to tending their guns.

Continuing on its path circling the enemy, *Royal Standard* delivered another devastating broadside to the French ship's stern taking out its rudder, and leaving the ship dead in the water. The crew cheered.

That was enough for the French merchant captain who surrendered his ship.

The two privateers, however, had no intention of capitulating. With cutlass blades and axes, the hands hacked through the fallen rigging and, once disentangled, made all sail back to the east.

Without the hull of the privateer supporting it, the escort brig slowly went down.

'Do you want to make chase, Captain,' the sailing master asked.

'I think not. We have one nice prize and have no call for a mob of angry pirates.

As the sun slid down burning in the west, young Lieutenant Weir was given the dubious honour of becoming the captain of the *St Lucia*. The French sailors taken off the cargo carrier were bustled down to *Royal Standard*'s orlop deck and secured in the compound previously occupied by the convicts. For the present, the master and his officers were held in the cage on the deck. With a prize crew put aboard, a cable was attached to the valuable cargo ship and it was in put in tow.

Only when they were under way did Captain Quintrell visit the cockpit to enquire about the butcher's bill.

'Two dead and three injured from splinters, sir. One of the powder monkeys was speared through the chest and I don't think he will survive.'

The captain didn't ask the boy's name. He would discover that later. 'Do what you can, Doctor.'

'I will.'

Returning to the quarterdeck, he was alerted by his steward to a wailing cry coming from the great cabin. 'What is that?' Oliver asked.

'It's one of the convict lads, Capt'n,' Casson replied. 'You'd best come and take a look.'

'Is he injured?' Oliver asked. 'Why had he not been taken below?'

'He's not injured. He's bemoaning the loss of the dog.'

'What? The dog has gone?'

'Seems to be that way, Capt'n. Both the lad and Chalmers went through the ship. They searched from top to bottom but with no success. Take a look and you will see where the gallery rail was smashed. That is where the dog was.'

'Show me,' the captain said, following his steward through the cabin to examine the damage. Squatting in the corner of the open galley was Johnny Kemp.

'Get up boy,' Oliver said. 'Tell me, have you looked everywhere for the animal?'

'Aye, Captain. Me and Chalmers searched, but we couldn't find him.'

'Have you looked in the water?'

'No, Captain, just on the ship.'

'Then I suggest you go around the deck and look over the sides. We are only sailing as fast as a man can walk so, if the dog can swim as well as his breed is reputed to, it's possible he is still swimming.'

The lad didn't give the captain a chance to finish what he was saying before he was on his feet and heading back to the quarterdeck. Leaning over the side and shouting the dog's name, his high-pitched cries quickly attracted several of the sailors to join him, all scanning the sea and hollering the name – *Cecil*.

It didn't take long to spot the hound swimming with the dolphins at the bow. With webbed feet, like those of a duck, the Newfoundland dog was paddling strongly and obviously enjoying the challenge with his new found friends.

Though the ship was only making three knots, the captain called for sail to be reduced. 'Mr Holland. Rig up a hoist and someone climb down to retrieve the hound. The rest of you, go back to your stations.'

Ready to jump over the side to save the dog, Johnny's arm was grabbed by his uncle, while Chalmers clambered out from the head and jumped into the water.

The dog was obviously pleased to see his friend, licking his face, and trying to climb onto his shoulders. With the pair drifting back towards the entry port, a line was thrown over and the hoist was swung out and lowered. Though Cecil wasn't interested in getting in, the sailor pulled the canvas under his belly and held onto the dog while it was hoisted to the deck. Scrambling to jump out before it reached the entry port, the Newfoundland almost slipped back into the sea, but grabbing him by the feet, ears and tail, the sailors hauled him aboard and into the waiting arms of young Johnny.

'Back to work you lot!' Mr Holland ordered. 'You there, get a mop and swab the deck.'

'Well done,' the captain whispered quietly to Chalmers, as a blanket was thrown over his shoulders and one over the dog also.

Chapter 22

Portsmouth

Having clawed its way up the Channel, battling a strong headwind and dragging a fully-laden cargo ship in its wake, the crews of both *Royal Standard* and *Saint Lucia* were relieved to make the Solent before nightfall, and happy to drop anchor when they reached Spithead.

Having sighted his house on the Isle of Wight, Oliver Quintrell reckoned it would be at least four days before he would be free to return home.

The first boats to arrive early next morning were the small powder hoys from Priddy's Hard. After hoisting the barrels of gunpowder from the ship's hold, they were removed to the huge powder store in Gosport, across the water from Portsmouth. Oliver was relieved when the powder had gone.

His next priority was to receive a visit from the prize agent who would examine the ship he had taken, and its cargo, and assess the value. The agent would then decide its fate. If *Saint Lucia* was deemed sound, she would be moved into Portsmouth harbour and unloaded at the jetty. After that she would be repaired then perhaps re-named and put into naval service. In the captain's opinion, it would not be destined for the wreckers' yard as so many prizes were.

With a busy agenda to attend to, Captain Quintrell took a boat to the dockyard and paid a call on the port admiral. Lasting only fifteen minutes, the captain was rowed back to *Royal Standard*, not having addressed all the matters he needed to. At least he was able to collect a large sack of mail for the crew that had been waiting six months for the ship's return to port.

Having met the prize agent at the yard, he arranged for him to visit *Saint Lucia* the same afternoon.

On returning to *Royal Standard*, he was about to sit down in the great cabin when Casson interrupted him.

'Begging you pardon, Capt'n, Chalmers is waiting outside. He asked to speak with you in private.'

Slightly puzzled, the captain asked his steward to show the sailor in. Though he had been in the great cabin many times before, on this occasion, he looked uncomfortable.

'What is it, Chalmers?'

'It's Cecil, Captain,' he blurted. 'What will happen to him, when the ship is paid off?'

'That is something I cannot answer,' Oliver said. 'I was puzzling over that question myself. As you know, Cecil was Captain Chilcott's dog and, as the captain died, he has no master. If no one will volunteer to take him, when the ship is paid off, he will be destined for the Portsmouth alleys along with the other strays.' The captain paused. 'However, as you have been attending to him for two years or more – perhaps you will take him when you leave the ship?'

'Much as I like the animal,' Chalmers said, 'he's no good to me. My wife wouldn't allow him to step inside the house and, what would happen to him when I sign on another ship, he'll have nowhere to go. Perhaps you could keep him on board, Captain? He's used to living on the *Standard*.'

Oliver shook his head. 'I too will be leaving the ship in a few days' time. And who knows what her next cruise will take her.'

'Aye, Captain,' Chalmers said, knuckling his forehead and heading back to the mess.

The dog, having recognised the sailor's voice, stuck his nose into the cabin from the gallery doorway but did not enter.

'Captain,' Casson called, 'You might want to see this.'

Following his steward out onto the quarterdeck, Oliver accepted the telescope handed to him. Although the line of coaches near the foreshore was not hard to see without it, he studied them through the glass. Among them was one stately carriage with seats for four passengers, drawn by six horses. A coat of arms was embellished on the door. Each of the carriages was attended by driver and footmen outfitted in colourful livery. Other conveyanc included a chaise, a barouche and a sporty phaeton.

The spectacle attracted a crowd of urchins from the ragge riffraff who tenanted the back streets.

'They've been arriving since early morning,' Casson said. 'Waiting to collect the young gentlemen, I don't doubt.'

Oliver had no comment. He also had no time to spare to attend to their disembarkation and passed that chore to the purser, advising him that the schoolmaster and first lieutenant could assist him if necessary.

Because none of the young gentlemen volunteers had died and only one had suffered a broken leg in the storm that had subsequently healed, there were no condolences to deliver and Oliver was not inclined to meet with the parents or guardians of the older boys. He had no intention of offering words of praise to inspire them regarding their offspring's future prospects in the Royal Navy.

It took almost three hours and two boats to carry the young gentlemen's personal possessions, packed in wooden chests, to the King's Stairs at the dockyard.

Through the glass, Captain Quintrell observed Dorrington and his cohorts being met on the dock and escorted to their waiting carriages. Shaking his head, he crossed to the starboard rail.

Still awaiting the arrival of the prize agent, the captain's gaze moved to the large East India Company ship anchored a cable's length away. Named, *Bay of Bengal*, it was a four masted ship. It dwarfed the diminutive 50-gunner.

'How long will *Royal Standard* remain on Spithead, Captain?' Dr Hannaford asked.

'At least until the *Saint Lucia* is towed away. I still have a prize crew aboard her. Then we will wait for the men to be paid off. After that, I do not know what plans the Admiralty has for her.'

'Are you going ashore, Doctor, or heading to Whitehall to secure another warrant?'

'I intend to stay in Portsmouth for a few days, Captain – one never knows what might blow in. And you?'

'I shall not leave the harbour until the prize agent has visited *Saint Lucia* and decided what to do with her. She's a sound ship, and will need only minor repairs. With the number of fighting ships lost at Trafalgar, she may well be converted and, with alterations to her gun deck, put into naval service. But first, her cargo must be unloaded and she will need to be taken into the dockyard for that to happen.'

'Did her cargo remain dry?' the sailing master asked.

'I believe it did,' Oliver said. 'And will be worth a small fortune.'

'A tidy prize.'

Oliver did not respond. He had no call for the money, as he was already quite a wealthy man – not from lands and titles, but from prize money he had been awarded in the past. Many naval officers in his position bought country properties to retire to in their dotage, but he had no desire to farm an estate or live inland or buy a seat in the government.

When he had sailed close to Madeira, he had been struck by a desire to return to the island, to climb the hill, balanced on the back of a donkey, and visit the house in which Susanna had lived. Since her demise, he had learned that she had owned the villa and thought, perhaps, if it was tenanted or for sale, he would purchase it. But for what purpose? Perhaps one day his daughter would wish to return to live on the island. But to go there to visit an empty house and mourn Susanna's loss would achieve nothing.

From the quarterdeck, Captain Quintrell surveyed Spithead and observed the large John Company vessel – *Bay of Bengal* – swaying from her cables to the slow ebb of the Solent's main tide. He was joined by the doctor who had come up on deck once again to fill his lungs with fresh air. 'Tell me what you have discovered of that East India Company ship, Doctor,' Oliver asked, 'Is she damaged?'

'Not that I heard,' the doctor replied.

'I see no yellow flag. Is she under quarantine orders?'

'No. I spoke with the port's medical officer yesterday evening and he said the ship was free of disease.'

'That is well.'

'I admit, I was a little surprised.' Dr Hannaford added. 'It is several years since I made a voyage to India, but the Hooghly River, where Calcutta stands, is a disease-ridden place. You see it as you sail in. While many of the dead are burnt on the river bank, some bodies become stuck on the mud flats. Others float out to sea. Some travel for miles.'

'What malignant fever wreaks such a heavy death toll?'

'The plague, leprosy, cholera, malaria, yellow fever —' the doctor replied. 'Take your pick. They all run rampant there. And not a cure for any one of them.'

'I am pleased that you survived,' Oliver said.

Doctor Hannaford nodded. 'I took sick for several weeks but managed to recover.'

'And will that ship be returning to India?'

The doctor was unsure. 'I presume so or to China and the East Indies – when it can find a crew. Word is out that as soon as it arrived in port many of the sailors ran – even foregoing their pay.'

'Indeed.'

'The medical officer said that while away, she had lost a quarter of her crew and struggled to sail home. She was heading for the East India Docks in London but, being short-handed, was unable to sail. The captain was hoping to sign some sailors in Portsmouth before heading up the Channel.'

'Not an easy task. Even without the fear of fever, many sailors run from John Company ships before the impressment gangs grab them and haul them into naval service.'

Oliver Quintrell continued to study the ship. She was considerably bigger than *Royal Standard*, with many guns, but without sufficient crew to man her. It spawned an idea in the captain's mind.

After pondering his thoughts for some time, Oliver approached the group of sailors who had been embarked as convicts and broached his suggestion.

'Since we arrived here, I have spoken briefly with the port admiral at the dockyard about the future of you men. He argued that because he has no jurisdiction over convicts, when the ship is paid off, you should be shipped back to Ireland and returned to the jail whence you came.'

'You promised, Captain,' O'Leary said, to the sighs of bitter disappointment at the thought of *Kilmainham* by some of the other men.

Oliver turned to the prisoner. 'That is something I did not do, nor could I. And since arriving here, I have learned that the quarter sessions do not meet for another two months, so I cannot present your cases until then. Even then, I cannot guarantee your sentences will be commuted.'

The look of acceptance on the men's faces revealed they had already considered this would be their fate.

'However, I have one suggestion,' the captain said. 'But you may not like it.'

The men listened.

'There is a ship on Spithead.'

'A navy ship?' O'Leary asked.

'No, it's the large East India Company vessel you may have seen. She is in dire need of able seamen because she lost many of her hands to illness and desertion. She is heading for the Port of London and from there will be sailing back to the East. She may be away for two years or more. If you are content to remain at sea, I will speak with the captain, explain your situation and ask if he would take you on board.'

The sailors looked questioningly from one to another.

'You must make the choice quickly. There is little time to waste.'

The group hastily discussed the captain's offer between themselves. All agreed they did not want to return to jail – but nor did they want to die of fever in some god-forsaken country they had never heard of. But, the fact the ship would call at other por on the way, meant the possibility of running in a distant port.

'What about Kemp and the two boys?' O'Leary asked. 'We al came aboard together.'

'I commend you for considering your mates,' Oliver said. 'Be assured, I will endeavour to ensure the three are not returned to prison.'

The men huddled together again, then after only a brief discussion, O'Leary, acting as the spokesman for the group, replied: 'We are prepared to serve on the *Bay of Bengal*, if we are allowed to sign.'

'Good,' Oliver said. 'Let me speak with the captain. If he is amenable, I will arrange for a boat to take you to her, as soon as possible. You may be due to receive some wages for your time aboard *Royal Standard*, serving from Cape Town to Portsmouth. I will speak to the purser about that but, be aware, deductions will be made for your slop clothing. In the meantime, return to your quarters and clean yourselves up as best you can.'

The men were surprised at their possible change in fortune and thanked the captain. They all agreed nothing could be as bad as going back to an Irish prison.

It was not until later in the morning Oliver had time to sit at his desk to examine the batch of letters that had been forwarded to the ship.

There was one from Dr Whipple. It was in a pouch enclosing other letters, presumably from the legal firm in Lisbon. Plus, there was a single letter from his wife. He had expected more, but then he had penned only one letter to her and doubted she would have received it.

Her letter had been written in March soon after he had departed from Portsmouth heading to Cork. It had been mailed from Bath. It read:

My dear Oliver,

I trust this letter finds you well.
I am well, but my sister is ailing. I called Dr Wilberforce to attend her soon after you had gone.
Because the house is cold and we are so far from a hospital, the doctor's advice was to remove her to her own home in Bath.
Obviously she could not travel alone, so I offered to accompany her. I am sure the temperature will be more clement in that town than it is on the Isle of Wight.

Bath, Seventeenth of April
My sister resides in a very elegant terraced house on a fashionable avenue.
I have been given a very pleasant room overlooking a park.
I have every comfort I could require and have no desire to return to the cold winds of the Channel.
I intend to stay with her for as long as she needs my company.

It was merely signed – *Victoria.*

Having re-read the letter twice, Oliver shuffled through the other correspondence but, despite the fact it had been written several months earlier, there was no other envelope bearing her handwriting.

After reading through all his mail, Oliver spent a further hour pondering over the fate of the remaining convicts. Sadly, one of the boys had died while running the deck as a powder monkey. Now, only Andrew Kemp, his nephew, Johnny, and one other Irish lad remained.

Late that afternoon, with the sun far from setting, Captain Quintrell was rowed to the East India Company ship. Although his arrival was not expected, he was welcomed aboard and spent an hour speaking with the Dutch captain. His offer to transfer seven young able seamen, of sober habits, to the *Bay of Bengal*, was accepted the ship's master. Having had their backgrounds explained to hire Captain de Graaf stipulated that he would accept the seamen but would confine them below deck during the time they were moored in the Thames. He could not chance losing any more of his crew. Oliver decided not to relate that stipulation to the men.

He was satisfied when he watched the men depart to join the *Bay of Bengal*.

Early next morning, Oliver instructed Mr Holland to bring Andrew Kemp to the great cabin.

Standing before the *Royal Standard*'s captain, the Irishman looked uncomfortable. He knew he had done nothing wrong and wondered what crime he had been summands for.

'Mr Kemp,' Captain Quintrell began, 'you will have noted that the other Irish prisoners have been transferred to the East India Company ship. I did not include you and the two boys in that arrangement.' He paused, and studied the face of the red-haired young man standing before him.

'Tell me, Kemp, you were a smuggler, were you not?'

'That is what the constables charged me with and it was the crime the magistrate sent me down for.'

'And the boy too?'

Kemp nodded. 'We were only scouring the beach, Captain – picking up pieces of flotsam – it's what we did some of the time. You'd be surprised what washes ashore.'

Oliver nodded.

'Other times we fished and sold our catch in the local villages.'

'You said you had your own boat.'

'Aye, Captain, but the British soldiers took it.'

'*Hmm.* And were you a fair sailor?'

'Been sailing all me life, Capt'n.'

'Thank you,' Oliver said. 'Return to your watch. I will call for you later, if I need you.'

Andrew Kemp left the great cabin more confused than when he had entered.

236

Early that evening, with the days lengthening as the year drew towards summer, it was pleasant on deck. The waters of Spithead were calm. The tide was on the ebb.

'Put away *Scorpion*'s jolly boat, Mr Holland. But before you do, have the carpenter scrape the name from its transom. It is not a name I wish to remember.'

'And what to you want to do with the boat, Captain?'

'Load a small barrel of water and a bag of ship's biscuits with a cheese and some onions. And add a few hooks and a fine line. Step the mast, and put a pair of oars on board.'

The lieutenant looked surprised but did not question the captain's order.

An hour later, the captain called Kemp and his nephew to attend him on the quarterdeck. The other Irish boy came along with them. Standing against the rail, the captain glanced down to the boat. It reminded him of a young man who had floated across the Solent in a small hand-crafted boat, some years ago. That same lad – William Ethridge, shipwright – was now helping to repair Nelson's ship, *Victory* at Chatham dockyard.

Captain Quintrell looked across to the sailor. 'I offer you the chance to take these two boys and go free.'

Andrew Kemp was puzzled. 'That's a navy boat, Captain. I can't take that.'

Oliver Quintrell shook his head. 'It is not a navy boat now and never was.'

'But why?'

'As I said earlier, the British justice system is, at times, fickle and unfair. Magistrates are often rich landowners. Most are unqualified, yet they have the power to make decisions over men's lives. In my opinion, their judgements and sentences are inconsistent from one part of Britain to another.'

The Irishman was confused.

'Some months ago, you told me you were committed to jail after the uprising in '98. You spent years in Kilmainham awaiting transportation. Your sentence was five years *beyond the seas*. The year is now 1806 and in my opinion, you have served your time.' Oliver handed the man an envelope sealed with wax. 'I have written these facts in a letter which you will carry with you. I have also enclosed the wages you were due.'

'Wages?' The man was shocked.

'The purser calculated you worked for three months and has classed you as a seaman. For that you have been paid two pounds fourteen shillings and sixpence after deductions were taken out for your slop clothing. You are required to sign your name or make your mark in the ledger.' The purser was waiting at the binnacle with pen and ink.

'There is no money due to the boys but they are permitted to keep their clothing.'

Andrew Kemp did as he was instructed and, after making his mark, returned to the rail and the two anxious youngsters.

'There is one favour you can do for me,' Oliver said.

'What's that, captain?'

'I believe your nephew has a liking for Captain Chilcott's dog.'

The boy looked up, his eyes glinting.

'Too right, he has.'

The captain nodded. 'Then take the boat, and take the dog with you and give it a home. It is a long way to the shores of Ireland from here, but there are many coves and inlets on the Cornish coast where pickings from wrecks are not uncommon. I wandered them myself when I was a lad.'

The Irish convict and his two charges were astounded.

'Chalmers,' the captain called. 'Bring the dog and a length of line, and rig up a hoist to lower the animal into the boat.'

Turning to the trio, the captain added: 'Go now, while the sea is calm and the Solent is running out. Take care and God speed.'

With that matter attended to, Captain Quintrell looked to his lieutenant, nodded to him, turned his back and returned to the great cabin.

Chapter 23

Epilogue

With one final outstanding matter to attend to while at the dockyard, Oliver paid a visit to the Naval Academy and asked the College's head-master, William Bayly, for an audience with Charles Goodridge.

Seated in a comfortable chair in an elegantly furnished drawing room on the building's second floor, Captain Quintrell waited for five minutes until a knock on the door announced the boy's arrival.

'Enter,' the captain called.

Neatly attired in the Academy's uniform, Charles Goodridge entered the room accompanied by a midshipman.

Having grown two inches or more since he had last seen him, Oliver hardly recognised the young man. Wearing a single breasted blue frock-coat with white waistcoat, breeches and shirt with frilled cuffs, his hair was tied back with a black satin ribbon.

After taking two strides forward, the young man stopped and bowed deeply from the waist. With hands clenched behind his back, he waited politely for the captain to speak first.

'Good day to you, young man. How are you?' Oliver enquired, standing to greet him.

'Very well, thank you, Captain.'

'That is good to hear.' Without further ado, he had one pressing question to ask: 'What are your impressions of the Academy, young man?'

'It is a well respected institution, sir.'

'That was not the question I asked, Charles,' Oliver replied.

The boy glanced down to the silver buckles on his shiny black shoes before looking up again. His face and tone lacked the exuberance that had once personified him.

The captain continued: 'How do you find the young gentlemen you are studying with?'

'I do not share many interests with them,' Charles admitted politely.

Oliver could not help but cast his mind to the behaviour of the *young gentlemen* he had suffered on *Royal Standard*. He wondered if the lad carried his own fighting stick with him and if he had had occasion to challenge the other young aristocrats with it. However, he chose not to pose that question and continued: 'I have just retuned from sea, and have not yet spoken with Dr Whipple, but I have another question for you.'

'I will answer it, if I am able,' the young man replied.

'Tell me, Charles, are you still intent on continuing in the navy? Dr Whipple advised me that you had expressed an interest in pursuing a career in medicine. You are at liberty to answer freely.'

Charles Goodridge shuffled from one foot to the other before answering. 'I enjoyed the time I was at sea with you, Captain. It was the best adventure any young man could wish for. More recently, however, I saw the fighting ships return to port after the Battle of Trafalgar and realized how easily men and ships can be broken. I have no desire to fight the enemy from behind the barrel of an 18-pound gun.' He looked the captain straight in the face. 'I hope I do not disappoint you, Captain.'

'Indeed you do not. I appreciate your candour.'

The boy had grown so much in maturity; the change was hard for Oliver to reconcile.

'Dr Whipple says if I work hard, when I am sixteen, I could gain entrance to the University in Edinburgh, and study to become a physician.'

'The doctor is a wise man and I recommend you heed his advice. I will be speaking with him in due course. In the meantime, I presume your studies here are of a nautical nature, whereas the university will require studies in the sciences and proficiency in Latin, I believe.'

Charles nodded in agreement. He had obviously given the matter some prior thought.

Perhaps, one day, like the good doctor, you can combine medicine with some time at sea.'

'I will take heed of Dr Whipple's words. I value his advice on all things.'

Oliver nodded. 'I may not see you again before I sail, but I wish you well.'

'Thank you, Captain,' the boy said. Then he bowed again, turned and departed the room.

Oliver sighed. He felt deflated by how much the happy, ebullient lad had changed in a short time. Was that the price he must pay for naval service? Would his daughter manifest similar changes every time he took up another commission and was absent for several months every year. It saddened him and made him realise he had little permanence anywhere. He was confused. Perhaps, after all, he should settle for a country estate or indeed buy the villa on the hill in Madeira.

Walking through the busy port streets, full of noise and bustle, his thoughts were centred on only one thing. The letters from Dr Whipple and the Lisbon lawyer confirming all was in readiness for Miss Olivia to travel under the care of a nanny on a packet boat to Portsmouth via Falmouth.

The final letter stated that Miss Olivia Vargas had departed from Portugal. The lawyer prayed for a safe journey and wished her well for her new life in England.

Also included with the correspondence was an account for legal services and for the cost of passage for one adult and one child, plus other incidentals. Oliver was not concerned with those matters. Foremost on his mind was the fact that if the arrangements had all gone as planned, his daughter would already be ensconced in the house on the High Street.

Familiar with the location, it took him half an hour to walk to the doctor's house from the dockyard but, as he neared the residence, he decided to continue along the High Street to the George Hotel and partake of something to eat.

Perhaps it was a degree of uncertainty that made him visit the hotel before proceeding further.

After removing his cloak and hat, he was directed to a table the window overlooking the street. A fine meal was served, but i ate without smelling or tasting the food. The glass of win disappeared without him realizing he had drunk it.

With the empty plate removed and the table left bare, Olive sat and gazed at the painting on the opposite wall. It was a portrai of Horatio Nelson in full dress uniform captured by an artist several years earlier. Beneath the picture was a hand-printed note that stated that His Lordship had departed on his final fatal journey to Trafalgar from that very place.

What a life the naval hero had lived and what a legacy he had left – an inspiration to the many young men who would follow him.

Then Oliver compared it to his own humble beginnings, scrubbing the stinking deck of his grandfather's herring boat. He looked at his hand for the fingers he had lost in battle, but there was no comparison to the loss of an arm and an eye that Nelson had suffered.

His mind drifted back to the funeral he had attended in London and wondered how long the British hero would be remembered and his life acknowledged.

He hoped he would not be quickly forgotten.

Rising from the table, Oliver Quintrell donned his cloak and hat and walked the short distance to the house bearing the doctor's name-plaque on the wall.

The housekeeper greeted him politely and ushered him upstairs to the drawing room. It was warm and light and the room had a homely feel.

'Do come in, Oliver,' Jonathon Whipple said enthusiastically, inviting the captain to take a seat. Oliver looked around for anything that appeared different from his previous visit but could find nothing.

'Wait a moment,' the doctor begged. 'Connie,' he called.

Almost instantly, the door opened and Consuela Pilkington, with a radiant look on her face, swept in. Almost hidden within the folds of her skirt, was a small girl, her hair shining like polished jet, her eyes large and enquiring.

Connie Pilkington approached the captain and dropped a polite curtsy. The little girl, holding tightly to her hand, copied her as best she could.

'Captain Quintrell,' Connie said, 'I would like you to meet Miss Olivia Vargas.'

* * * * *

From the Author

Thank you for reading *Nelson's Wake* and if you enjoyed it, I hope you will leave a review on Amazon.
I certainly enjoyed researching and writing it.
A list of the five previous stories in the Oliver Quintrell series appears at the front of this book.

A Facebook page, of the same name, has been set up to support *Nelson's Wake*. It provides additional information about Lord Nelson, his life and death, and HMS *Victory*.

References

THE FUNERAL OF ADMIRAL LORD NELSON 1806 -
Fairburn's second edition -Oxford University digitised May 2007.
AUTHENTIC NARRATIVE OF THE DEATH OF LORD
NELSON – William Beatty (Surgeon) – 1807
TRAFALGAR – An eyewitness History – (Ed) Tom Pocock
THE 50-GUN SHIP – Rif Winfield
TRAFALGAR – John Terraine
THE PURSUIT OF VICTORY – Roger Knight
NELSON'S MEN O'WAR – Peter Goodwin
THE WOODEN WORLD – N.A.M. Rodger
THE BRITISH INVASION OF THE RIVER PLATE 1806-1807 –
Ben Hughes
JACK TAR – Roy and Lesley Adkins
STEERING TO GLORY – Nicholas Blake
Plus the author's personal visits to: The Crypt at St Paul's
Cathedral, HMS *Victory* at Portsmouth Royal Dockyard, and
Gibraltar.

M.C. Muir

Printed in Great Britain
by Amazon